PRAISE FOR
the light we lost

"This love story between Lucy and Gabe spans decades and continents as two star-crossed lovers try to return to each other. . . . Will they ever meet again? This book kept me up at night, turning the pages to find out, and the ending did not disappoint." —Reese Witherspoon

"Your new tearjerker has arrived: Fans of *Me Before You* and *One Day* will love/weep over this elegant novel." —*New York Post*

"Extraordinary."
—Emily Giffin, #1 *New York Times* bestselling author

"[An] engrossing, romantic, and surprisingly sexy story about the power of first love." —*Domino*

"A wonderful and heartbreaking book . . . The kind of heartbreak that's in *The Way We Were*, that you really love to cry over." —NBC New York's *Weekend Today*

"Have your tissues ready. . . . This book will sink its hooks into your heart on page one, and leave you scarred long after you're done." —*Bustle*

"What to say to your friend who always suggests *The Notebook* . . . give her *The Light We Lost*." —The Skimm

"Santopolo explores passion, fate, love, and what it means to truly be a good person. . . . A beautiful and devastating story that will captivate readers."
—*Kirkus Reviews* (starred review)

"Comparisons will be made to David Nicholls's *One Day*, but there is something more romantic here—yet also more grounded—that will draw readers in." —*Booklist*

"A beautiful, thought-provoking exploration of life choices, and how attaining one's dreams can be euphoric and gut-wrenching at the same time." —*Shelf Awareness* (starred review)

"What can be more devastating than love? In her adult debut, Santopolo explores thirteen tumultuous years in the lives of two unique lovers, the difference between what's forever and what's finite, and how what seems fated might not be fact. Gorgeously written and absolutely unforgettable, Santopolo's novel has a beating heart all its own." —Caroline Leavitt, author of *Pictures of You*

"In this intense, deeply moving novel, Jill Santopolo vividly illuminates how our personal lives and loves are changed by the common—and uncommon—events of our troubled world." —Nancy Thayer, author of *Secrets in Summer*

"Jill Santopolo's extraordinary debut novel is a love story—an emotional roller-coaster—that follows the lives of Lucy and Gabe, who meet in New York City on September 11, 2001. The event transforms and shadows their lives. How do they reconcile passion and security, dreams and reality? As *The Light We Lost* enchanted and compelled me, I found myself reconsidering my own choices and wondering at the choices of my friends and the people around me—how did their dreams match their realities? And what if that dream can't include the person you love the most?" —Delia Ephron, author of *Siracusa*

ALSO BY JILL SANTOPOLO

Stars in an Italian Sky
Everything After
More Than Words
The Light We Lost

the love we found

JILL SANTOPOLO

G. P. PUTNAM'S SONS
NEW YORK

PUTNAM
— EST. 1838 —

G. P. PUTNAM'S SONS
Publishers Since 1838
An imprint of Penguin Random House LLC
1745 Broadway, New York, NY 10019
penguinrandomhouse.com

Library of Congress Cataloging-in-Publication Data

Names: Santopolo, Jill, author.
Title: The love we found / Jill Santopolo.
Description: New York : G. P. Putnam's Sons, 2025.
Identifiers: LCCN 2024040378 (print) | LCCN 2024040379 (ebook) |
    ISBN 9780593419205 (hardcover) | ISBN 9780593419212 (ebook)
Subjects: LCGFT: Romance fiction. | Novels.
Classification: LCC PS3619.A586 L68 2025 (print) |
    LCC PS3619.A586 (ebook) | DDC 813/.6—dc23/eng/20240830
LC record available at https://lccn.loc.gov/2024040378
LC ebook record available at https://lccn.loc.gov/2024040379

Internation edition ISBN 9798217046249

Printed in the United States of America
1st Printing

Book design by Ashley Tucker

The authorized representative in the EU for product safety and compliance is Penguin Random House Ireland, Morrison Chambers, 32 Nassau Street, Dublin D02 YH68, Ireland. https://eu-contact.penguin.ie

For my mom, Beth Franklin Santopolo,
with respect, admiration, and, most of all, love

the love
we found

prologue

IT'S BEEN TEN YEARS.

Ten years of missing you, of thinking about you, of seeing you in Samuel's face.

I haven't visited you here before. It was too hard. Too real.

There's so much you don't know. So much you've missed.

I still don't know what I believe about the afterlife—about what happens, where souls go, whether they go anywhere at all.

But in case you're out there somewhere. In case you're listening, I'm here.

And I have so much to tell you.

i

SOMETIMES I WAKE UP AND, FOR A BRIEF MOMENT, you are alive, Gabe. In that blurry place between dreams and reality, you're smiling, your arms are wrapped around me. You're saying, "I love you, Lucy. I will love you until the day I die . . . and then some," just like you whispered to me when we went hiking in Cold Spring two decades ago. We'd climbed to the top of the Bull Hill trail and were taking in the most breathtaking view of the Hudson River. Your whispered words, the reverence with which you said them, made me shiver, made me lean back, turn my head and kiss you, hard and deep, like I needed to show you that I'd love you until the day I died and then some, too.

I forgot about those words for years, but they've come back to me recently. Come back to me in those liminal moments, when I'm not quite asleep, but not quite awake.

And then the sun brightens, or the alarm goes off, and it hits me. You're gone.

I wonder, particularly on those days, about the "and then some." Is there a piece of you somewhere that loves me still? Or is it all in the past? Are we ancient history, and am I the archivist, keeping it alive?

ii

THE DAY YOUR EDITOR ERIC WEISS CALLED ME, nearly nine years after the last time I'd spoken to him, was one of those cold winter days when the wind was so biting it made my skin feel brittle and my eyes tear. I was in my office in Manhattan, reading through the most recent episode of *Tiger & Bunny*, the new TV series I've been producing, when my cell phone rang. I saw Eric's name and couldn't imagine why he was calling.

"Hello?" I answered, making a split-second decision not to let him go to voice mail.

"Lucy!" he said. "It's Eric Weiss from the Associated Press."

"Hi," I said, still not sure why he was calling me.

"So . . . I'm sure I don't need to tell you that the ten-year anniversary of Gabriel's death is approaching." He paused.

"July twenty-fifth," I said. The date you died is tattooed on my heart. At that moment I knew you'd been gone for exactly nine years, six months, and fourteen days. I looked out the window and saw the water in the Hudson River dance in the wind. I wondered if you were dancing with it.

"Yes," he said softly. "Well, the AP would like to do a retrospective of his work and give our readers an update on how the places he photographed are doing now."

"Oh—" I started to say, but Eric continued.

"I took the liberty of calling the publisher of Gabe's book, *Defiant*. They'd like to update the book with some never-before-seen photos and maybe an afterword that I'd write," he said. "But, of course, we wanted to check with you first."

I was surprised. It often felt like I was the only one who still thought about you. But it seemed like Eric did, too. I lifted up the tortoiseshell glasses I had just started wearing so my computer screen wouldn't look so blurry and wiped my eyes with the sleeve of my sweater.

"That would be a beautiful celebration of Gabe's life," I said.

"I'm so glad you think so," Eric replied. "We'll need you to go through his photographs and find the original files for a number of images. I can email you the list. Do you think you can find them?"

I thought about your boxes in my bedroom closet. The ones hidden behind my long dresses. One of them open, the other two still sealed shut.

"Yes," I said. "I can do that. Just let me know what you need."

"Will do," he said. "And Lucy?"

"Yes?" I said.

He paused. "Thank you." But I had the feeling it wasn't what he'd intended to say.

We hung up, and I stared out the window, thinking about the first time Eric had called me, to tell me you'd been hurt and were in a hospital in Jerusalem, that he didn't think you'd recover. Sitting at my desk now, I closed my eyes and climbed into my last memory of you, of your skin against mine, the soft sheets of the hospital bed, the steady whoosh of the machines keeping you alive. I remembered how I rested your hand on my stomach so you could feel Samuel inside me. Your son, our son.

"Lucy?"

I turned my chair away from the window at the sound of Versha's voice.

"I'm here," I said to her. "I was just thinking."

She nodded. As my assistant for the past three years, she knew that staring out the window and thinking was often how I worked through problems or came up with new ideas.

"It's five thirty," she said. "I'm going to head home, unless you need something else from me."

I smiled at her and shook my head. "I'm all good here. Thanks for checking."

"See you tomorrow, then." She turned away, then turned back. "Hope the earmuffs are keeping you warm. Noticed you were wearing them today."

"Very warm," I said. "But are you supposed to be able to hear in them? Everything sounds like I'm underwater."

She nodded solemnly. "It's the trade-off for being trendy."

I laughed and shook my head. "Have a good night," I said as she walked out the door laughing, too.

You'd like Versha, Gabe. She's whip-smart and really funny. And on an endless quest to make me trendy, which is more a running joke now than anything else. I've been lobbying Phil to promote her, because I know if we don't, she'll go somewhere else soon, and I hate the idea of losing her—both professionally and personally. Ever since I lost you, and then Darren and I divorced, ever since we finalized our custody arrangement so I only have the kids with me every other week, the idea of losing more people I care about makes my heart clench.

SINCE THAT FIRST WEEK OF FEBRUARY WASN'T ONE of my weeks with the kids, I stayed late to finish up the script and email my notes to the writers. It was nearly seven when I emerged from my *Tiger & Bunny* zone and started gathering up my cold-weather gear to head home to Brooklyn.

As I did, the conversation with Eric filtered back into my brain. And once it was there, it was all I could think about. I found his email with a list of photographs attached. The whole ride back to Brooklyn, I wondered what it would be like—having a whole world to talk about you with again, instead of just Kate and Eva. What would it mean for me? And what would it mean for Sammy?

iii

ONCE I GOT HOME, I MADE MYSELF A QUICK PB&J
for dinner and then headed upstairs to my bedroom
closet, pushed my long dresses aside, and retrieved your
boxes, which had been waiting there patiently for me.
When the kids are around, I never touch your things.
But sometimes, when they're away, when things feel extra hard, when I'm especially lonely, I open up that first
box and take out your old Columbia sweatshirt. When I
put it on, I give myself permission to live inside our
memories for a moment, an hour, an evening. It's getting
harder to remember some of the details, but there are
certain memories I don't think I'll ever forget. Like the
day we made Samuel.

I close my eyes and build the hotel room around us,
picture the blond curls of your hair, feel the smoothness
of your skin, and when I touch myself, I imagine it's you.
You, stroking me so lightly, so gently. You, sliding inside,

feeling how much I want you. You, moving against me until I orgasm.

I don't do it often, but when I do, I remember joy—until it's over and the ache of loneliness returns.

I was thinking the other day, while reading *Madame Bovary*, about how in French orgasms are called la petite mort—the little death. Could it be that that's what it feels like after death? Do you live in a world filled with that intense beauty, that mind-blowing sensation? Is there a world of even more potent pleasure that awaits us, bright and beautiful? I can't get this question out of my mind, and I wish you could answer it for me. What comes next? Or is there nothing at all?

That night, I pulled all three of your boxes out of my closet. I knew the first box contained the physical items of yours I'd kept—your Columbia sweatshirt, of course, the baseball cap you had on the day we met, your unfinished copy of *All the Light We Cannot See*, an old photograph of you and your mom you'd had framed and displayed in your Jerusalem apartment, another one of you and me at Faces & Names, the scarf I knitted you however many Christmases ago.

I put your sweatshirt on over the wool sweater I'd worn to work and rolled up the sleeves that were far too long on me. Then, with the post of one of my earrings, I pierced the cheap packing tape I'd used to bind up your things. Inside the second box was your laptop—silly of me to save it, I know, but I thought perhaps one day there might be something on it I'd need and wouldn't be able to access otherwise. Your phone was there, too. Your camera. I thought I might give that to Samuel when he was old enough.

With your sweatshirt engulfing my body, surrounded by the things you left behind, looking at the photograph of you and your mother both smiling Samuel's smile, I thought about the secret that Darren and I had kept all these years. The secret that I knew we would have to share at some point. I wanted our son to know about you, about your intelligence, your talent, your eye for beauty and your determination to find it everywhere. But I hadn't told him anything. I hadn't even told him he was yours.

The last box I opened was the one I was looking for: the prints of the photographs you'd had filed in a drawer in your apartment, packed neatly into envelopes by date and location, a flash drive in each one with the original files. I dumped the box upside down to get all the envelopes out and started looking at labels—it pulled at my heart to see your handwriting. When my friend Julia's dad died a few years ago, she got his handwriting tattooed on her wrist, copied from the bottom of the last note he sent her. Now her wrist says *Love, Dad*. Staring at those envelopes I wondered if there was something you'd written I could get tattooed on my wrist, an external symbol of how much you are part of me.

I started putting the envelopes in chronological order, and then a small piece of paper fell from the stack. It was torn off the back of an envelope, not the manila kind you'd kept your prints in, but a light blue mailing envelope. It looked like a return address. In beautiful cursive handwriting it said: *Via Conte Verde, 68 #5A, 00185 Roma, Italia.* Underneath the address, you'd doodled the face of a boy with dark curly hair and wide, dark eyes.

A tumble of questions ran through my brain: When were you in Rome and what were you doing there? Who was writing to you? Who was that boy? And why did you keep this address?

I pulled out my phone and texted Eric Weiss.

Found all Gabe's flash drives. I'll have the images to you by Monday.

Great, he wrote back. *Thank you.*

My thumbs hovered over the keyboard and then I typed: *Did you send Gabe to Rome often?*

The three dots started then stopped then started then stopped again. I stared at my phone until a paragraph appeared: *I'm sure we must have at some point,* he wrote. *Though I don't remember it as an ongoing thing. Gabe did work on a powerful story of the Syrian refugees coming through Lampedusa not long before he died. He got a World Press photo award for one of the images he took there. He may have flown in and out of Rome to get to Lampedusa.*

Thanks, I typed back, pulling the paper out of my pocket and looking again at the beautiful handwriting, the drawing of the boy. *Just curious.*

Was it destiny that made me find that address? I still wonder. Was it you? It's that old question of mine: Fate or free will? How are our lives designed? I'm still wondering, Gabe. And I probably always will be.

Because that address, it led to so much.

iv

THE NEXT MORNING, I TEXTED KATE WHILE I WAS on the subway to work: *Lunch still good today?* *Looking forward,* she wrote back. *Need to discuss!* I knew she was commuting, too, on a Metro-North train from Stamford, Connecticut. We'd made this lunch date because of a new job she'd just had a third-round interview for that she wanted my opinion on.

Looking forward too, I said.

Whenever I was with Kate, just the two of us, a part of me felt like I was twenty-two again, living with her in that amazing apartment her parents rented to us on the Upper East Side. Or sometimes I felt like I was fourteen and we were at the Westport Plaza Shopping Mall, trying to figure out which lip gloss colors looked best with our skin tones. Or sometimes even like we were five, having just met in kindergarten and squealing because we both were wearing the same T-shirt with Rainbow

Brite on it. Kate has known so many versions of me, and I have known so many versions of her.

At noon, I layered on my winter coat and my trendy earmuffs and walked over to Iris, a newish restaurant halfway between our offices.

Before I could even take off my earmuffs, Kate came in, her pink cheeks almost the same blush color as her long cashmere coat.

"Iris is someone," Kate said when we sat down. "From history or Greek myths or something. Not just a flower, right?"

"She's the messenger of the gods in Greek mythology," I answered. "And the personification of the rainbow. I read somewhere that there's a theory Siri, on our phones, is named after her. Iris backward."

"Of course you would know that," Kate said, smiling at me as she opened the menu.

Remember when you called me a Pegasus, Gabe? You said when you were with me, I carried you away from the pain. From the ugliness. I still connect Greek mythology to you, though I don't know if we ever talked about Iris. The thought of you tugged at my heart.

"So tell me about this job," I said to Kate, opening my menu. "Have you made your decision yet?"

"No," Kate said. "And when I called Liz, she said I shouldn't stress, and that the decision will make itself. My sister is so infuriating sometimes. She's basically saying all my hours of thinking and debating and weighing mean nothing." She closed her menu. "We're doing the express lunch, right?" she said, referring to the section that came with mezze platters as an appetizer. "I'm having the ancient grain bowl. With a glass of the house white."

"That sounds good. Me too," I said, closing my menu as well. After the waiter took our order, I could tell she was still irritated by Liz's words. "I think," I said to Kate, "that what Liz meant was that decisions often become clear when they have to. Like, you may have to do all this thinking, but at some point, the decision will make itself known. It's like how Darren and I tried for more than a year to keep our marriage together after Sammy was born, but we got to a point where we knew it just wasn't going to work. It took us all those conversations, all that couples therapy to get to that place, but then the answer presented itself. It wasn't easy, but at some point, the next step became apparent."

"Hmm," Kate said, thinking that over. It gave me a moment to remember that day, eight years ago, when Darren told me he was done. The tangle of emotions I'd felt. The tangle of emotions I still feel when I think about him, about our divorce, about what led to it.

I took a sip of water in an attempt to rinse the memories from my mind, to bring myself back to the present. "How are you on the decision?" I asked Kate.

She took a breath.

"Be honest," I said. "With me. And with yourself."

She took another breath. I waited.

"I want to stay at my firm, but I feel like I should take this opportunity. I like where I am, though. I like who I work with. I like my job. I'm comfortable and happy here."

"There you go," I told her. "The decision just made itself."

She laughed. "I'll have to think about that," she said, and then added, "So what's going on with you? How was your date with what's-his-name, that guy you met in the grocery store in front of the cheddar bunnies last month?"

I made a face. "He was obsessed with mass transit."

"That doesn't necessarily sound bad," Kate said as our mezze plates arrived.

"Believe me, it was," I said, picking up a triangle of pita.

"You have to give these guys a chance, Lu," Kate said as she reached for a triangle, too. "How many first dates have you gone on in the past seven-plus years?"

I shrugged; the answer was probably somewhere around twenty.

"Really the question is," she said, "how many second dates have you been on?"

"Zero," I said, carefully spreading whipped feta on my pita. "But a woman doesn't need a man to be happy."

"I agree," Kate said, "but are you alone because that's what makes you happy, or because your heart is still so filled with Gabriel that there isn't room for anyone else? Because you don't want there to be room for anyone else?"

I didn't answer. I don't know if Kate even expected me to. The truth was, I had been holding myself together so tightly, that I wouldn't—couldn't—let anyone in. If I did, I was afraid I might fall apart. Again. Like I did after Sammy was born, after you died. But I didn't want to get into that, into her telling me I was strong, and me knowing, explaining, insisting, I wasn't. Instead, I said to her, "Eric Weiss called me yesterday. He wants to commemorate the tenth anniversary of Gabe's death. And while I was looking for some image files he needs, I found this."

I pulled the address out of the credit card slot in the back of my phone case. "Why do you think Gabe kept it? Who do you think the boy is?"

Kate took the paper and looked at it, then handed it back to me. "You're going to get mad if I tell you what I think," she said.

"Tell me anyway," I said, wondering what her theory might be.

I wasn't expecting what she said next.

"I don't think it matters, Lucy," she said as kindly as she could. "I think you have to let him go."

But I couldn't, Gabe. I couldn't let you go, not then. Not yet.

V

THAT CONVERSATION WITH KATE SHOOK ME. IT threw me back to the time right after you died, when I felt like I was losing myself, and I didn't think I could go back to the office that way. So I decided to head home early and work from there for the rest of the day. As I sat on the train, a highlights reel—or maybe I should call it a lowlights reel—from that time after your death played through my mind to the rhythm of the wheels whirring on the tracks.

After I came home from Israel, I was broken. Shattered is more like it. Darren was my only true support, the only thing keeping me from falling apart completely, and I couldn't bring myself to tell him about Sam. I couldn't risk losing Darren—not then. So I stayed quiet. It was selfish, I know. But I guess it was selfish in the way that survival is inherently a bit selfish—you take what you need to make it through, to live.

The secrecy made everything worse, though. I see that

now. But then . . . Oh, Gabe, I couldn't see anything then but you in my arms in that hospital bed in Jerusalem.

Samuel's delivery was easier than my first two, but afterward I fell into a deep depression—difficulty sleeping, crying daily. Not even Liam or Violet could make me smile. At my postpartum visit, my OB talked to me about antidepressants, and taking them eventually helped to stabilize me, but for those first few months, Samuel was Darren's baby so much more than mine. Darren brought him to me when he was hungry, and I fed him, but other than that, it was Darren who swaddled Sam when he was tired, played with him on the floor, putting Sam tummy-down on his own stomach when Sam didn't like the mats we used with the older kids. Darren who ate almost all his meals with one hand while he held Sam with the other, brought him to Violet's soccer games, gave him tours of our apartment, introducing him to every single item in every single room on both floors when he was trying to extend a wake window before a nap. *This is the living room. That's our navy blue couch. This is our navy-and-white chevron rug. Chevron is a squiggly pattern that your mommy really likes. These are our bookshelves. Let's look at all the books now . . .*

When I overheard it, the narration reminded me of the ridiculous tour Darren gave me of his neighborhood when he and I first started dating. It reminded me how much I loved him. How much I couldn't keep Sammy's paternity a secret—not from Darren. It wasn't fair to him. I couldn't make him live in my lie. And what if one day Sammy did one of those DNA tests for fun and it came out? Or he needed some kind of medical treatment that exposed everything? I couldn't live that way, always waiting for the world to come falling down around my ears, destroying our family in the process. So I made a plan. I decided that once I hit a string of three days in a row in which I hadn't sobbed for a reason even I realized was absurd, I would be mentally strong enough to have that conversation. When Darren came in that night with Sammy and handed him to me for his pre-bedtime feed, I asked him to sit down.

"How are you feeling?" he asked me.

"Better," I told him. "Not as fragile. Ready to tell you some things."

He cocked an eyebrow at me.

It would have been so easy to keep quiet. You were gone. What did it matter? But it did matter. I couldn't build our son's life on a lie.

"What things?" he asked.

"Do you remember," I said, "about a year ago, before you bought our Hamptons house, when you kept getting mystery phone calls from a woman named Linda?"

Darren nodded. "The real estate agent."

"Right," I told him. "But I didn't know that. And then I realized you'd changed the password on your phone without telling me."

"To keep the house a secret," he replied.

"Right," I said again. "Well, I was convinced you were cheating on me."

"I wasn't," Darren said, his face quizzical, like he was trying to figure out where I was going with this. "I can't believe you would think that." He was still holding Sammy, and I could see his arms tighten around him, almost imperceptibly.

"I know that now," I told him, my voice shaking. I was finding it hard to fill my lungs, to get in a full breath. "But then, I didn't. And I . . . I thought you had . . . I wanted to . . . I slept with someone else."

He looked at me horrified. My heart plummeted.

"Who?" his voice was a painful rasp.

"Gabriel," I whispered. "And—"

"Fuck," Darren said, and then he looked down at Sammy and cringed, as if upset he'd said that word around our baby. "I never trusted that guy. Never trusted you around that guy. I guess I was right."

I looked down, chastened, my eyes starting to fill with tears.

"Is that why he made you his health proxy? Why you traveled to Jerusalem during a goddamn war while you were pregnant with our son?"

"It wasn't a—" I started, but sighed and wiped the tears that had started falling from my eyes. We'd had that conversation so many times. It wasn't a war. But that wasn't the point. "Yes, it's why I went," I said. "But there's more. I'm sorry, Darren. I'm so, so sorry."

At this point, I was whispering so quietly, he had to lean in to hear me. Because I was so ashamed, I couldn't speak any louder. I didn't want to hurt him, but I knew I had to.

"What is it?" he said back, louder, his eyes both angry and anxious at the same time.

"Samuel is Gabe's son."

Darren stared at me, an unreadable look on his face,

then handed me Sammy, got up, and walked out of the room. I heard the front door slam.

Darren went to our Hamptons house and stayed for a week, a week where the kids missed him, Sammy especially. A week where I missed him, too. When he came home, Violet and Liam were in school, and I was on the couch with Sammy. He sat on the edge of the coffee table facing me and said, "I want to stay. I want you to stay. I want us to work through things. For the kids, but also for us."

Sammy turned his head at the sound of Darren's voice. Darren scooped him out of my arms and held him close. "Missed you, buddy," he said. I could see tears in his eyes. I could feel them in my own.

His request wasn't what I'd expected, but knowing Darren, knowing how he felt about family, about love, I wasn't entirely surprised either.

"Okay," I said, tears of gratitude spilling onto my cheeks. "If that's what you want. We'll work it all out." I was willing to do anything to fix my mistake, to repent.

EVEN THOUGH I PUT MY ALL INTO OUR RELATION-ship, into healing our family, I knew pretty quickly that it wouldn't be enough, that we were just prolonging the inevitable. But sometimes you need more time. Sometimes you can't face an ending—and we couldn't, not then. The decision had to make itself.

After six months, we started therapy. The sessions always ended with Darren and me doing our best to hold back tears or harsh words or both—and rarely succeeding. After one of those sessions, nearly a year after I first told him the truth, just after Sammy turned fifteen months old, we were heading back to the subway together when Darren stopped walking.

"What is it?" I asked.

"This isn't going to work, is it?" he said.

It was a thought I'd been having but hadn't voiced, not even to Kate. Barely even to myself.

I couldn't look Darren in the eye. "I don't think so," I whispered.

The decision made itself.

"Lucy," Darren said, his voice thick. "Lucy, look at me."

I looked into his liquid brown eyes and felt the guilt wash over me, as if it were the only feeling I'd ever be able to feel. I knew this was my fault. It was all my fault. Breaking up our family, leaving Darren alone.

"I wish I could trust you again," he said. "I wish . . . I wish . . . I'm sorry. It's just impossible. Every time I see Samuel I remember, and I'm gutted all over again."

"I understand," I whispered, my throat full of tears. "I'm sorry. I wish . . . I wish so many things."

Darren cleared his throat. "I don't want to make this hard. We sell the apartment, split the amount fifty-fifty. Sell the beach house, split that, too. And then the kids can go back and forth—one week with you, one week with me."

I realized he must have been thinking about this arrangement for a while. He'd had a backup plan.

"Okay," I said. "Half the apartment, half the house, and joint custody with Violet and Liam."

"And Sam," Darren added.

"But you just said . . ."

"Sam is mine, too," Darren said. "In all the ways that matter. I love him just as much as I love Violet and Liam. I was there when he was born, I fed him and changed him. I was there when he was sick—when you were sick. Would you rather he have a dead father he can never meet than me? That's not fair. Not to him. And not to me."

His voice broke on the last sentence, and I watched him battle his tears. In that moment, I thought he was right. I thought it was better for Sammy. And I couldn't bear hurting Darren more. He was such a good father, and he loved Samuel so much. I was grateful for that, grateful that Samuel would have that love.

"Okay," I said. "You're right. They're all yours. All three."

Darren let out a breath. "Thank you," he said.

"You love them all," I said. "I don't want to take that away from them—or from you. But we will have to tell Sam the truth one day. I don't want a family built on secrets."

"Eventually," Darren said. "He's only one. We'll find the right time." But we didn't. Every birthday, every Father's Day, every time Sammy made an expression or said something that brought the words *You just reminded me of your dad* to my lips, only to linger there unsaid, I felt caught between Darren's pain and my promise to you.

vi

IT'S AMAZING HOW HUMANS CAN GET LOST IN MEM-
ories. A blessing and a curse. I felt like I was back there
with Darren, overwhelmed by guilt toward him and grief
for you. It was a relief when I was hurtled back into the
present by the subway conductor's voice telling me we
were about to stop at Court Street.

As I was walking down my block, I ran into Eva, who
lives on the third floor of our house—and who had
owned it before I did. "I'm going to get some bread," she
said. "And a new box of Lady Grey tea. Do you need
anything, dear?"

Eva had just turned eighty-nine in November. She
was an artist, a retired children's book illustrator, and had
sold me her house for a song six years before. She was
done taking care of it, she'd said, but wanted to be able to
stay. My friend Julia had put us in touch, and I was so
grateful that she had, that Eva was in my life, and that I

had been able to afford a house to raise my kids in—and then renovate and redecorate until it fit us perfectly.

I shook my head. "We're good—thank you."

She nodded and went on her way. Maybe it's because of her that I thought I might be alone for the rest of my life. Single womanhood looked good on her. But perhaps she and I are different. Or perhaps not. She has told me that deep in her heart there's someone from her past that she still loves, too. But it's a story she's never shared in full. And I've respected her secrets and her reasons for keeping them. I know about keeping secrets.

WHEN I GOT INSIDE, I MADE SOME TEA TO WARM myself up and noticed a missed call from my mom. It was both easy and hard not to tell my parents the truth about Sammy all those years ago. Easy because I didn't have to admit to cheating, but hard because it meant I didn't have my mom or my dad to lean on. I didn't realize the wall it would create, that I wouldn't be able to let them in anymore. At some point, I accepted the shift in our relationship, but my mom never could.

I called her back.

"Hey," I said when she picked up. "What's going on?"

"Your dad and I are in the car. I'll put it on speaker. Say hi, Don."

"Hi, Lulu," my dad said.

"Hey, Dad," I replied. "Where are you off to?"

"Heading over to Jay's," my mom said. "The triplets all have different places they need to be tonight, so we thought we'd help him out—and then keep him company."

It was amazing to me that Jay's kids were seniors in high school now, all planning to head off to different colleges in the fall.

"Where's Vanessa?" I asked.

The distance that grew between me and my parents was small compared to the gulf between me and Jay. My brother and I used to be so close, but it was impossible to have the kinds of conversations we used to have when there was so much I couldn't tell him.

"On a work trip," my mom said. "You should call your brother more."

I poured my boiling water into a teacup. "I'll call him," I said, feeling a pang. "Give him a hug for me. And the kids."

I sat down at our kitchen counter. How had I become so far removed from Jay's life that I had no idea when he was home alone with the kids and needed help? I could've helped him. I was alone this week and could have been there.

I WRAPPED MY HANDS AROUND MY MUG OF TEA AND thought about secrets. About the address in Italy. I wondered if you'd met someone else and started a family you'd kept secret. Another half brother for our Samuel? Even with my mind swirling the way it was, it didn't seem likely, but there was so much about your life I didn't know. I hadn't known you'd won a World Press photo award.

So after a work call, I googled the address. An apartment building in Rome. I looked up the neighborhood,

Esquilino, near Termini Station. It was a neighborhood
of immigrants—mostly from North Africa, the Middle
East, India, Pakistan, Bangladesh, and China. My mind
started whirring: *Was there a story you'd covered there? Is
that how you met her?* Before I went down the rabbit hole
of searching all your photographs for ones in Italy that
included a woman, my phone dinged with a reminder
about my last Zoom meeting of the day. So I closed the
search box but took the address with me.

I knew this wasn't a secret I was going to be able to
leave alone.

vii

SATURDAYS HAVE BEEN ODD DAYS EVER SINCE DAR-
ren and I divorced. I either wait all day for the kids to
come home, or I wait all day to take them to Darren's. I
never feel settled on a Saturday.

When we first created this custody arrangement, I
calculated that out of the 168 hours in each week, the
kids were asleep for an average of 70 hours and at school
for an average of 32 hours, which meant I spent about
66 hours with my kids over the course of two weeks.
That's why those hours are so precious to me. And why
Saturday always feels like a countdown.

While I waited for the kids that Saturday, I cleaned
the house, went grocery shopping, and looked at the
schedule for the week: Valentine's Day was coming up.
Sammy had already made Valentines for his third-grade
class, but I realized I hadn't gotten any cards or treats for
the kids. So I went out again to the local Duane Reade.

I've read that when you become a mother, your brain

chemistry is altered completely. And it never goes back to the way it was. Your body does this thing called synaptic pruning, where the brain kind of clears away the gray matter it doesn't need so it has space to grow new synaptic connections in areas like protection and empathy. Your brain chemistry is literally changed so that you center on your children. It's fascinating.

In the last few years, I've come to visualize my life like a puzzle. There are so many pieces that fit together—my relationships with each of my kids; my relationships with Darren and his new wife, Courtney; with my parents, my brother, my friends, my job. Some pieces are bigger, and some are smaller, but they all fit together to make my life. And Violet, Liam, and Sammy are at the center.

Some people might have looked at my life and said I was missing a piece—the romance piece—but for a long time that piece was still you, the memory of you, the dream of you. And I was so afraid to lose that, Gabe, so afraid that if I removed you from the puzzle, it wouldn't fit together anymore, that it would fall apart. But now I realize I'll never lose you. There are more pieces now, and others have shifted; they create a richer picture. But we're not there yet, are we? There's still so much more story to tell.

viii

VALENTINE'S DAY WAS ONE OF THOSE DAYS OUR
souls found each other in the liminal dream space, one of
those days that began with tears when I awoke fully and
realized that your arms around me were only in my mind.
It was a Wednesday morning when I had the kids, so I
tried my best to pull myself together before I left my
room. We all met in the kitchen for breakfast, the way we do
every day before school and work. Violet, looking impos-
sibly mature in jeans and a red cashmere sweater she'd
stolen from my closet, was pouring cereal for herself and
both her brothers. Liam, his AirPods already in his ears,
was grabbing a carton of milk from the refrigerator. And
Sam was setting the table. They're really close, all three
of them. Fifteen, thirteen, and eight. It's incredible to see.

"Morning, Mom," Sammy said, giving me his mega-
watt smile, the one that shows your dimple. He looks so

much like you that sometimes I think you're there with me. "Happy Valentine's Day!" he added.

He handed me a homemade card with a drawing he'd made of me and him sitting in a movie theater, along with a box of Sno-Caps—our favorite candy.

Violet gave Samuel an indulgent eye roll. "Liam and I have something for you, too, Mom," she said. "Sammy went his own way."

"I wanted to make it myself," Sam said with a shrug. "It's more fun. Plus I know you like my drawings and I wanted to make one for you."

The parents in the neighborhood call him "The Muralist." He'll often show up at the park and find an empty part of sidewalk or a brick wall and start drawing the outline of something with chalk. A tree, a sun, and some flowers. A big bus with faces looking out the window. A school of fish. And whenever any kid comes by to see what he's doing, he offers them a piece of chalk and a job. By the end of the afternoon, most of the kids at the park have joined him.

Liam grabbed an envelope from the sideboard. "Happy Valentine's Day, Mom," he said, handing it to me.

I opened the card and laughed. They'd found a *Rocket Through Time*–licensed Valentine's Day card. I still think of it as our show, Gabe. Remember when you helped me work out storylines in our studio apartment in Hell's Kitchen?

"I love these gifts," I told all three of them. "They're wonderful. There's something from me in your lunchboxes today. Don't peek!"

I've always thought of packing their lunches as a little hug from me to each of them during the school day, a way for them to know that they're loved and always will be. Violet sometimes replaces her lunch with food from the Brooklyn Tech cafeteria, but I like knowing she has a meal waiting for her, just in case she wants it.

I poured myself a bowl of cereal and sat with them.

"Everyone has their homework packed?" I asked.

They all nodded.

"Sam, you have your Valentine's Day cards for the class?" He nodded.

"Vi, you have yours for Ji-ho?" She nodded. She started dating Ji-ho in the fall, and they were pretty inseparable.

"What about you, Liam?" I asked. "Are there any cards you need to remember to bring?"

He turned pink but shook his head, which made me wonder. He's the least communicative of my three kids. I've joked with Darren that it's why he plays the drums. He needs to be loud somehow.

"What about you, Mom?" Violet asked softly. "Any Valentines for you this year?"

I smiled at my daughter. "Not this year, sweetie," I told her. "Maybe one day." Maybe one day when I felt stronger, when I wasn't afraid that entrusting my heart to someone else could lead me into darkness. I'd made it out once, but I lived in fear I wouldn't be able to again.

I looked up at the clock. "Okay, everyone, time to go."

While we walked to the Court Street subway stop, each lost in thought, my mind turned to you, as it often does, to the way I'd seen you that morning before I'd fully woken up. You'd seemed so real. I wondered if that was the universe's way of having the two of us spend Valentine's Day together. Or maybe it was yours. Are you out there, making things happen? Pushing us together? Keeping us connected? Don't worry, Gabe. No matter what, a part of my heart will always belong to you.

ON MY WAY BACK HOME, I PULLED OUT THE ADDRESS
in Rome again and imagined the woman who might have
such elegant handwriting. Was she a photographer like
you? An artist? Was the address her studio? The boy her
son? Was the apartment one you knew well? One that
felt like home?

I remembered the night a few months after we first
moved in together, when your friend Justin sent you the
listing for the apartment he'd just rented, and it was one
of those fancy buildings with a gym and a pool and a roof
deck in Long Island City. It was after dinner, and we'd
both opened up our computers to check our email or
whatever, and when I looked up at you, your face was
contemplative.

"What?" I'd asked. "What happened?"

You turned the computer my way. "Am I supposed to
want this?" you asked, showing me the apartment and
the building.

It was interesting because it wasn't something I ever actively wished for, but also if someone handed it to me, I would've been happy to have the luxuries.

"You don't want it?" I asked.

You shook your head.

"What if you had all the money in the world?" I asked. "And it didn't matter what you spent on anything. What would you want then?"

You thought for a long time, such a long time that I thought you weren't going to answer. But then you said, "Cozy little apartments like this one, but all over the world. One here, one in London, one in Shanghai, in Rome, in Sydney, in Johannesburg, in Mexico City, in Delhi, Jerusalem, São Paulo, Lagos, Istanbul . . . as many as I could buy."

"You haven't been to those places," I said. "At least not most of them. How do you know you'd want apartments there?"

"I know I haven't," you answered. "But wouldn't it be amazing to call all of them home? To know that we have places to welcome us all over the world?"

I thought about it then. It isn't what I would do with unlimited funds, but there was something appealing about it. I wasn't sure, though, if it was an apartment that would make a city feel like home, or a person—you. If I were with you anywhere, I'm pretty sure it would feel like home.

That's what I said to you then. "You're my home, Gabe."

And you smiled that slow smile of yours, that seductive one. And all of a sudden, we were somehow naked on the couch, and when you slid inside me, with your eyes closed, your face blissed out and beautiful, you said, "I've come home."

And those words made me orgasm. I was your home. I was your safe space. I was yours.

I used to think about that. I used to wonder if you felt like that with the other women you dated. Did they feel like coming home?

Was there a Roman woman with beautiful handwriting who'd made Italy your home?

X

THAT NIGHT, AFTER THE KIDS WERE IN THEIR rooms, I climbed into bed with my laptop and a flash drive of your photos from an envelope that said *Spring 2009*. The first photos I saw were of the Sri Lankan cricket team in Lahore after the terrorist attack on their way to the stadium. Then there were photos of the destruction after an earthquake in L'Aquila. Then photos of Baghdad, all labeled with clear file names.

Even now, I find it mind-blowing to think about what you've seen. The devastation you bore witness to. No wonder you were done. No wonder you wanted to come home. After a decade of that, even you, with your face pointed toward the light and your eye for beauty, started to become subsumed by the darkness.

I scrolled through the photos. None of them were the ones Eric wanted. And none of them showed me what I'd been waiting to find—the Colosseum, the Pantheon,

St. Peter's Basilica. The contours of the Roman skyline. A woman, smiling at your camera lens.

I went to Rome once, years ago, with Darren. We were trying to repair our marriage, but everything kept reminding me of you. Every sculpted angel was the angel Gabriel; every blond man with a camera, your ghost.

I looked at another one of your photos and then opened a browser window and, without giving myself a chance to second-guess it, typed in *flights from NYC to Rome*.

The next week was February break and Darren was taking the kids to Florida. His mom was turning seventy-five, and she wanted her whole family together to celebrate. I know it shouldn't be a big deal when Darren takes the kids away, but something about knowing that my children aren't just around the corner puts me on edge the whole time. The few times I arranged my own travel—a girls' trip with Julia or Kate, a retreat with the *Tiger & Bunny* writers' room—it was better. But work had been so busy, I hadn't planned anything this time around. Maybe this was my chance to change that.

A handful of options popped up on my browser, one flight leaving late Sunday night that was much cheaper than the others. I clicked on it. Direct flight from New York City to Rome on ITA Airways. Eight hours and twenty minutes. I stared at my screen for a moment, thought about the way I'd started my day in tears over you, about the way this address had been haunting me, about the long, lonely week missing my kids that stretched out before me—and then I pulled out my credit card and bought the ticket. Leave on Sunday, home on Friday. More than enough time to be back for the kids. When it was done, I felt a rush of adrenaline, and then I felt calm. Calmer than I had since I'd gotten that call from Eric Weiss the week before. It felt like I was doing something, pointing myself in a direction instead of spinning in circles.

xi

I MEASURE YEARS DIFFERENTLY NOW. I MEASURE them in school breaks, in custody handoffs, in family dinners. The weekend after Valentine's Day, the weekend of my trip to Rome, I brought the kids back to Darren's with all the things they needed from my place for their trip to Key West.

"Does everyone have sunglasses, hats, bathing suits?" I asked as we stood with their backpacks on our front stoop, mentally thinking about what I would need to pack once they were safely with Darren and Courtney.

They all nodded.

"Stuffies? Devices? Chargers?"

"Floppy Bunny!" Sammy yelled, and then raced back inside the house.

"Phone charger?" I asked Violet again. I'm always extra worried that she'll forget a charger and I won't be able to reach her.

"Two," she said. "I promise I'll keep my phone charged."

"She always does," Liam added.

I smiled. "I know," I said. "I'll stop momming now."

Sammy came back and we headed down the street, the kids carrying their backpacks.

We stopped at the Häagen-Dazs on Montague, following our every-other-week routine of getting ice cream along the way—and buying two chocolate chip cookies for Darren and Courtney's twin girls. The walk was always slightly melancholy, and years ago, when Violet suggested ice cream on the way, it became a tradition, something exciting to look forward to. Of course, Darren's girls saw the ice cream and wanted a treat, too, so the cookies became part of the routine.

When we got to Darren's brownstone, Courtney was waiting outside on the stoop with Ivy and Sage.

When the girls were born, I wondered if my three would be jealous. I even asked Violet, who was about ten at the time, if she wished she lived in one place and didn't have to move back and forth every weekend. She shrugged. Then shook her head. "Maybe sometimes," she said. "But also sometimes it's cool to have two families." I'm still not sure whether that was how she truly felt, or whether she was trying to please me. She's such an empathetic kid and is really good at reading emotions, at saying what she knows people want to hear. Sometimes to her detriment.

"Violet!" Ivy said, racing down the steps for a hug.

"Liam!" Sage trilled, running behind her.

Then "Sammyyyyy!" they both shouted, nearly bowling him over with a double hug.

I'm not sure how this tradition started, but it's the same every week. After Ivy and Sage double-hugged Sam, they swapped, Sage giving Violet a hug, and Ivy wrapping her arms around Liam.

I walked over to say hi to the girls, and gave them each a cookie, and then all five kids walked up the stairs in an amoeba of arms and legs and sweets, heading into the house.

"Good week?" Courtney asked me. "Anything we should know about?"

"Nothing too exciting to report," I told her. "The kids had a good Valentine's Day. I made sure they have all their important items for the Key West trip. But if they forgot anything they want to take with them, just text me and I can bring it by before you head to the airport tomorrow morning. They have suitcases and summer clothes here, right?"

"They do," Courtney said. "And thank you in advance. There's always something, isn't there?"

I smiled. "Always. And the kids already know, but I'm taking a quick trip to Italy this week. I'll have my cell phone if you need me."

Courtney raised an eyebrow at me. "Sounds fun," she said.

"I hope so," I answered.

Before I first met Courtney nearly seven years ago, Darren had told me about her in a way that reminded me of when his friends called me a paper doll. "She's a special education lawyer," he said. "Grew up in the suburbs of Philly. Went to Bryn Mawr undergrad. NYU law school. A couple years younger than you. Never married."

"Mm-hmm," I said. "And you're serious about her? Serious enough that you want her to meet our kids?"

We were standing outside my old apartment—the kids had run inside to check on their toys after being away from them for a week. He'd said he needed to talk to me about something important, so I'd stayed in the hallway. We hadn't quite fallen into a rhythm yet, but we were getting there. Our divorce had been finalized a few months before, and one of the things we'd agreed on was that if either of us wanted to introduce someone to the kids, the other parent would meet them first.

Darren looked down at his feet and then up at me. "I am," he said. "She's sweet and smart and funny and loves kids. She wants more, and I do too. It's been moving quickly."

The look on his face, the words he said—I felt them physically. I knew I'd given him up, I knew he'd loved me first and a part of him loved me still—but all of that was intellectual. Emotionally, even if he was ready for someone new, I wasn't, and it felt wrong somehow to have him moving forward when I knew I couldn't. But it wasn't about me. So I nodded.

A WEEK LATER, COURTNEY AND I GOT COFFEE AT Gregorys and walked around Cadman Plaza Park together. Before I met her, I wondered if we would look similar, if Darren had a type, but other than being about the same height, there weren't many outward similarities. She had auburn hair in a pixie cut that brought attention to her bright blue eyes. The day we met she had on a pair of tight jeans and a gray V-neck T-shirt with a pair of ballet flats and small silver hoops in her ears. Her arms were toned in a way that made me wonder if she played tennis, and she had a big, open smile that reminded me a tiny bit of yours. She really was lovely—friendly and easygoing and warm. I could see why Darren liked her. And I could tell right away that she would be great with our kids. She knew their names, their ages, had memorized their likes and dislikes. She cared.

"My parents divorced when I was eight," she told me on that walk. "And I had wonderful stepparents. I really lucked out. My stepmom is a special education teacher and was the reason I went into special education law. I want to be a positive force in your kids' lives, the way she was in mine."

I nodded. "I believe you," I said.

"And I know you'll always be their mom," she continued. "I'm not vying for the spot. From experience, I know there's space for both of us in their lives."

I know it might sound ridiculous, but I started to cry then. It was such a relief to know that this woman who understood the situation so intimately, who thought about it so sensitively, would be the one whom Darren brought into their lives—but also I felt guilty that my choices had put my kids in this complicated place. That they would have to learn to navigate it like Courtney did. That they would have to find that space in their heart for everyone.

In that moment, while tears dripped from my eyes, we

stopped walking in the middle of the park and Courtney put her arms around me. "It'll be okay," she said. "I promise you they'll be okay."

And although we never became good friends—I didn't really expect us to—we're a solid team. Me, Darren, and Courtney, all working together, all giving each other the benefit of the doubt, all trying to make sure that this is as easy on Violet, Liam, and Sammy as it can be.

I still feel guilty. But I also feel grateful that this is how the story of Darren's and my divorce ended, with him married to a woman who loves my kids and who understands their experiences in ways I may not. I'm grateful for her. And grateful to the universe that Darren found her.

xii

THE SUNDAY MORNING AFTER DROPPING MY KIDS off at Darren's always feels empty. And the first Sunday morning after I moved into my house, it felt even emptier—me, all alone in that huge space. It was a few days after the anniversary of your death, which always hits me hard. And without the need to hold myself together for anyone, I'd let my emotions take over; I rode the waves of grief and sorrow like a tiny boat in a storm-tossed sea. In the midst of my sobbing, Eva knocked on my door. I'm not sure why I opened it.

"Hello," I said, my voice thick with tears.

"I came to see if you needed anything from the grocery store," she started. Then her eyes widened at my appearance. "But perhaps instead you might prefer a walk and a pastry?"

I appreciated the offer but couldn't imagine leaving my house. "I don't think I'm ready for public consumption right now," I told her, sniffling.

She smiled kindly and said, "I don't think you're ready to be home alone either. Do you have a big pair of sunglasses?"

I realized she was right, so I grabbed my purse, put on my sunglasses, and followed her out into the July heat. We talked a lot that day and solidified our friendship. Now we have a standing date, every other Sunday morning. We've learned so much about each other over the years, and I treasure my relationship with her. Kate jokes sometimes that she's been usurped by an octogenarian.

The Sunday after I dropped the kids off at Darren's for their trip to Key West, Eva rang my doorbell at ten A.M., as usual. When I bought the house from her, we created a separate entrance for her to go to her apartment, so we're neighbors instead of roommates.

It was a warm day for February, but still chilly, and she looked old-school elegant in her long, robin's-egg-blue coat, gray faux-fur hat, gray leather gloves, and a blue, gray, and white scarf she'd knitted herself. I've always tried to dress up slightly for our Sundays together—it feels respectful, somehow. So that day I'd put on my black wool coat, red leather gloves, and a knit hat and scarf that Julia had gotten me for Christmas. I'd brushed my hair out so it hung down to the middle of my back. I didn't hold a candle to her, but at least I wasn't in a puffer jacket and a ponytail.

I offered Eva my arm and she held me on one side and the railing on the other to walk down our steps.

"How's your tapestry coming?" I asked her as we walked toward Montague.

Eva was an extraordinarily talented painter who had

illustrated children's books for decades and found moderate success as a fine artist. But these days painting was difficult due to a slight tremor in her hands, so she'd taken up knitting and weaving. She said it was just for fun, but if the small tapestry she was weaving was any indication, she'd be able to sell these, too.

"Much faster now that I can see better," she said, tapping her new glasses.

I smiled. "Good, I'm glad."

On that first walk together I'd told her our story—about you and me, and even about Sammy. She was one of three people I'd told the truth to—Darren, Kate, and Eva. I hadn't meant to say anything about Sam, but without that piece of information, our story wasn't our story. And it seemed important, once I'd starting telling her about us, that she know the truth, know what you truly meant to me—what you and I truly meant to each other.

"How has your week been, darling?" she asked me as we waited to cross the street.

I smiled. Eva feels like a surrogate grandmother, though she'd hate to hear it.

"It's been . . . surprising," I told her. "Emotional."

"Oh?" she asked, turning her face toward mine as we walked. "A new gentleman?"

I laughed. She knew there hadn't been any new gentlemen worth speaking about in all the time I'd known her. She kept asking, though.

"I found an address mixed in with Gabriel's things. It's an apartment in Rome. And I can't stop thinking about it. I actually . . . bought a plane ticket. I think . . . I think I'm going to Italy for a few days."

"Well!" she said. "That's one way to get to the bottom of things."

I told her about the retrospective, about the reissuing of your book with new photos. About how I kept wondering if you had another family in Italy.

"A brother or sister for your Sammy?" Eva asked softly.

I nodded. She has an incredible way of knowing what's in my heart.

"Do you think it's possible?" I asked her, almost not wanting to hear her answer.

"Possible? Yes," she said. "Probable? No."

"But possible," I echoed.

"Almost anything's possible," she said.

"Almost anything?" I asked.

She smiled sadly. "Well, my parents aren't coming back from the dead. My sister either. I can't change the past. I can't breathe underwater. I can't grow a striped banana."

She had moved into quoting from a children's book she'd written, I realized. That last sentence, *I can't grow a striped banana*, was from a story that Sammy and Liam both loved about everything the narrator can't do: *I can't grow a striped banana, I can't stretch like a giraffe. I can't hear an earthworm's whisper or make a spider laugh.* But then the last line of the book is: *But, my darling, here is something that always will be true: No matter what, I'll find a way to show my love for you.*

"Is that where you got the idea for *Striped Banana*?" I said. "I can't believe I never asked before."

"I don't know if I could have survived without turning my pain into art," she answered me, her hand tight on my arm.

Eva was the only one of her immediate family to survive the Holocaust. After the German occupation of Hungary in 1944, when she was nine years old, her parents sent her to a convent that was hiding Jewish children. When the war ended a year later, she found out her parents and younger sister had been murdered on the banks of the Danube that October. One of her cousins, a woman I'd once met named Zsuzsanna, had seen it happen and had managed to escape. She was ten at the time and ended up being raised by her teacher. She later converted to Christianity and then became a teacher herself, married and raised a family, but was haunted forever by what she'd witnessed.

"So you think I should go?" I asked Eva. "That it's the right choice?"

She nodded. "If you need answers, you should look for them," Eva said. "And maybe that will help."

"Help with what?" I asked.

"One day," she said, "when I ask you about a new gentleman, I hope your heart will be free enough to say yes."

I nodded, realizing she and Kate were trying to give me the same advice, but in different ways. I liked Eva's way better.

Honestly, I'm not entirely sure if I would have followed through with it all if she hadn't encouraged me. And then where would I be now?

xiii

LATER THAT AFTERNOON, MY PHONE PINGED WITH a text from Violet—a photo of all the kids together in the pool from earlier that day—and I called her.

"Are your brothers with you?" I asked.

"Mm-hmm," she said. "The Airbnb we're staying in had a room with a bunk bed and a single, so we're all together."

"Liam's on the top bunk?" I asked, knowing that Violet would have claimed the single bed for herself, and the boys would have let her.

"The bottom," she said. "Sammy wanted the top, and Liam didn't care."

"Is there a bar on the side of the bed?" I asked her before I could stop myself.

I could almost hear her roll her eyes at me. "He's almost nine, Mom, he doesn't fall out of bed."

"Right," I said. "Anyway, I wanted to hear your voices before I leave for Italy tonight."

"You never said why you were going," Violet answered. "Are you doing an Italian *Tiger & Bunny*?"

"That would be awesome," I replied, evading my daughter's question. "Anyway, I'll be back Friday night, so you won't miss me at all."

On the other end of the phone, somewhere beyond Vi, I heard a voice calling: "Movie time!"

"Gotta go, Mom," she said. "Uncle Charles figured out how to make the projector work, so we're watching Nana's favorite movie: *The Parent Trap*. The original one, not the Lindsay Lohan one."

"I had no idea that was Nana's favorite movie."

"Violet! Do you want popcorn?" came through the phone.

"Love you, Mom," she said. "Have fun in Italy. I'll tell Liam and Sam. Call us when you land, even if it's super late or early or whatever over here."

"Will do," I said. "Love you too. Love you all."

She clicked off, and I felt a hole open up in my heart. We've been doing this for eight years, but it still hurts, being away from them, knowing that they're making core memories, having new experiences, and I'm not part of it.

I wiped my eyes and put on my cold-weather running gear for a quick run before I finished packing. There was no better cure for loneliness than running on the streets of New York City.

xiv

AFTER DINNER, I ZIPPED UP MY DUFFEL AND SHOULDER bag and called a car to take me to JFK. Whenever I travel internationally now, I think of you. I think of boarding that flight to Israel, of how sick I felt. And then I think of boarding the flight home. I was a zombie, barely functioning, my body wrung dry from so many tears, holding on to my sanity by a fraying string.

For a while, I didn't want to travel at all, and now, when I do, I always think of that trip.

Before I'd left my house that evening, I'd gone into your boxes again. I took your copy of *All the Light We Cannot See*. I'd promised you that I would read the book for you, finish what you started. And on the flight to Italy, I finally did. Maybe that was the first step, Gabe— the first step of finishing what *we* started, of making space for more.

XV

THE SMELL OF ESPRESSO GREETED ME AS I GOT OFF
the plane in the Rome international airport. I spotted
Caffè Lavazza and instantly felt the adrenaline rush of
being somewhere different. Signs I couldn't understand.
The buzz of so many languages being spoken at once,
lilting Italian making its way over the din.

Instead of going straight to the taxi stand, I stopped at
the Caffè Lavazza and had my first Italian coffee of the
trip. It was rich and smooth with undertones of something dark and chocolatey. The last time I'd landed in
Italy with Darren for what we'd called our second honeymoon, we'd stopped for coffee in the airport, too, and
he'd laughed at my description of the flavors. He said I
sounded like a coffee sommelier. Maybe it's true. I like
wine, but I appreciate a good cup of coffee more.

As I finished my coffee, I felt shaken out of the loop of
sameness I'd been in at home. The predictability, the cy-
cle of work and kids and work and kids. I felt invigorated.

After my taxi ride from the airport, I got out at my hotel in Rome's city center, and I heard the tolling of the church bells. I stood still on the sidewalk, listening. I'd forgotten how beautiful the church bells in Rome were. More than beauty, the bells gave the city an air of holiness, of spiritual continuity.

"Benvenuta a Roma, signora," the doorman said as he took my duffel bag.

"Grazie," I said, remembering the handful of words I'd picked up on my last trip. But my American accent must have betrayed me, because he switched to English.

"Will you be staying with us long, ma'am?" he said.

"Not long," I told him. But I hoped long enough.

As I checked in, I kept thinking about the church bells. The first night Darren and I were in Rome, we went to the bar on the roof of our hotel. It was enclosed with hip-high glass, the whole city unfolding before us in a panorama. And while the sun was starting to set, the church bells rang at vespers and Darren put his arm around me. The whole world seemed to pause. My senses were heightened, and the moment seared itself into my mind.

Sometimes I have those memories of Darren—the wonderful ones, the loving ones—and I think about the different paths I might have traveled. Do you remember when we saw each other at Faces & Names on my twenty-third birthday and you quoted Robert Frost to me? *Two roads diverged*, you said. Now I think of it more like three roads, or maybe four, or five, or six. At every choice there are different directions to take. We always have to choose—even not making a choice ends up being a choice. We were wrong that night, Gabe. We never get to travel the same road twice, because we are not the same people from day to day, year to year.

I was in Rome again, but I was a different version of myself. And it made me think that if you and I hadn't slept together, if we hadn't made Samuel, I would be living a different version of my life—maybe you would be living a different version of yours. Maybe you would be living.

"THANK YOU," I SAID TO THE RECEPTIONIST WHO handed me my key, and I took the elevator up to my room alone, wishing for the first time in a long time that I wasn't, that I had someone to share this adventure with. I crushed the feeling as soon as it appeared—I'd been telling myself for years that I didn't deserve love, that I was horrible at relationships, that I'd failed at the two defining romantic relationships of my life. I never gave the first dates I went on a chance. I didn't want a third strike against me, a third opportunity to ruin my life— and someone else's. But even though I squashed it down, that little spark of desire was there.

xvi

I HADN'T REALIZED IT CONSCIOUSLY THEN, GABE, but finding this address, going on this journey, it was a step to making space in my life for more, for changing the shape of the "Gabe" puzzle piece so I could add in another one.

Last year, in school, Liam learned about the butterfly effect. His class was doing a unit about World War II, and Liam's teacher, Mr. Garcia, had them research a group of people he called simply "the heroes," the people who continuously risked their own lives to save others: people like Oskar Schindler, of course, and Nicholas Winton and Corrie ten Boom and Aristides de Sousa Mendes . . . Liam was even quieter than usual at dinner the day Mr. Garcia assigned this project. I'd asked all the kids how school was, and after Violet and Samuel chattered on about their teachers and classes and friends, Liam's response was: "Did you know that if Nicholas Winton hadn't canceled his ski trip and then visited a friend in Prague who was helping refugees, six hundred sixty-nine children probably would have died?"

I was surprised by his answer but tried not to show it. "Tell me more," I said, hoping for some context.

Liam took a deep breath, put down the fork he'd just loaded up. "He was a British stockbroker who was alive during World War II, and he was supposed to go skiing for a vacation. But he decided not to—Mr. Garcia didn't know why, I asked—and instead this guy, Nicholas Winton, he decided to go to Prague to visit his friend. And his friend was helping refugees, and when Mr. Winton saw that, he decided he wanted to help, too. And he saved the lives of six hundred sixty-nine kids. Brought them to England and found foster families for them to live with. I just . . . I can't stop thinking: What if he decided he wanted to go skiing?"

I nodded. Sometimes my kids say things and I don't know how to respond. When I heard what Liam had been contemplating, I wanted to figure out why he was sharing that particular piece of information, what exactly it meant to him, what it was making him worry about or feel inspired by. Even with the additional context, I had no idea how best to respond to Liam that night. But then Vi said, "It kind of makes me think we shouldn't ever go skiing." And it clicked. In his own way, Liam was asking my question: How meaningful—how powerful—are our choices? Are our lives fated, or are we guiding our own journeys? Or is it a little of each, taking the current where it serves?

"You know what I like to think?" I told all three of them. "I like to think that even if Mr. Nicholas Winton

went skiing, he still would have ended up saving those
six hundred sixty-nine children. That maybe his friend
would have sent him a letter, or he would have seen
something else that caused him to make the same decisions. Follow the same path. And that the effect he had
on the world would be the same."

I'm telling you this now, Gabe, because of what I
found out in Rome. Because sometimes I think you were
destined to make certain choices, too, choices that af-
fected people and changed the trajectory of their lives.

After I got to my hotel room, I watched couples, families, tour groups walking in and out of a church across
the street, and I decided not to put off traveling to that
address on the torn envelope any longer. As I got ready,
washing my face, putting on makeup, braiding my hair, I
started to backpedal. Should I find a translator? Someone
to go with me? Was I ready to face whatever I found
there? I took a breath. This was a chance to have a new
conversation with you, to learn something more about
who you were, how you lived your life. What if what I
learned changed everything?

But I hadn't come so far to turn away now. So I got in
a cab in front of the hotel and showed the driver the address. We pulled up in front of a concrete apartment
building painted in stripes of different shades of beige.
The door was metal and glass, done in an interesting pattern. There were names written next to the buzzer for
each apartment—many of them Italian, with a smatter-
ing of other nationalities. The one next to apartment 5A
said *Hassan*. I swallowed hard. Who was I going to meet?
What was I going to learn? My mind started spinning

with new possibilities—another journalist you'd worked with, a translator you knew—and then back to my fear— a woman you'd loved more than you'd loved me. I rang the buzzer for apartment 5A and heard a female voice speaking Italian come through the tinny speaker.

I fumbled with my phone, trying to bring up the Google Translate app, but realized I was taking too long. I *should* have brought a translator with me. Or at least prepared something to say in Italian in advance.

"Um," I said uncertainly, as I kept typing in the translation app. "I'm so sorry. Do you speak English?"

I heard the woman saying something in what sounded like Arabic to someone else in the house. Then the static stopped.

The moments stretched out and my heart plummeted. It seemed like my first attempt to learn why you were connected to this place was a failure. I turned to leave, to find someone who could translate for me, when the door to the apartment building opened up and a tall young man stepped out.

"Can I help you?" he asked me in accented English.

My heart rose in my chest again. I gave him a smile. "I hope so," I said.

I pulled out the small square of torn light blue envelope and held it out to him. "I'm looking for someone who was living at this address approximately ten years ago," I said.

He held out his hand for the piece of paper, and I gave it to him.

When he looked back at me, I was surprised to see tears in his eyes.

"That's a drawing of me," he said, "from when I was a child. And this blue envelope . . . this is my mother's handwriting. I remember sending it. Do you . . . do you know Mr. Gabriel?" His words were tentative.

I nodded, and the tears in my eyes matched his. "I do," I told him. "I did," I corrected.

"Yes, did," he said. "Past tense. I saw it on the computer."

There was a little café not far down the street with tables outside, and he pointed toward it. "Do you want coffee?" he asked.

I nodded and then he sent a message on his phone, and we talked as we walked to the café.

"My name is Lucy," I told him. "I'm—" And then I didn't know how to describe myself. What words could I use that would convey our relationship, Gabe? What we meant to each other? "I'm the mother of his son," I finally settled on, realizing this man was now the fourth person whom I had told the truth to: that you were Samuel's biological father.

"I'm Bashir," he said. "Bashir Hassan. I met Mr. Gabriel when I was eleven."

Bashir nodded at a man in the café, and we sat down at one of the outdoor tables.

"You like coffee?" he asked me.

"I do," I told him with a laugh. It's so strange how tiny preferences, small pieces of who we are can lead to so much. I met Darren because I loved coffee.

He motioned to the same person inside the café again, and two coffees appeared on our table, brought by a dark-haired waitress.

"My uncle, Farid, is one of the baristas here," Bashir said.

I turned and gave the tall man inside a small wave. He inclined his head in return.

"So tell me," I said, too eager for answers to spend time on pleasantries, "how did you meet Gabriel? Why did he give you his mailing address?"

I was pretty sure, since he called you Mr. Gabriel—and because of his age—that Bashir was not your son. Samuel didn't have another half brother.

Bashir smiled ruefully. "Probably I was the most persistent," he said. "My family came here to Italy from Syria," he added.

I remembered the photographs you had taken of Syrian refugees. The articles they accompanied were about journeys to safety, what they risked to leave. I looked closely at Bashir's face. Was he in one of those photos?

"It was a rough journey, especially for a child," he added.

I nodded, trying to remember those photos. "I can't even imagine," I said, and took a sip of my coffee.

"Good, eh?" he asked.

"Very good," I answered, as I felt this second cup of coffee work its way into my system, the caffeine fighting against my jet lag.

"So my family, we traveled from northern Syria to Libya when the war came to our town and our house was shelled. My aunt and baby cousin died in the attack. My mother, my father, my grandfather, my uncle, my little sister, and I all left after that. My parents paid a smuggler to take us through Jordan and Egypt to Libya. From

Tripoli, we took a boat to Lampedusa. My grandfather"—
he shook his head—"he didn't make it to the end of our
journey."

I could see the pain in Bashir's face when he talked
about his grandfather, his aunt, his cousin. Even though
he must have recounted the story numerous times, the
wound was still there. It made me want to ask what had
happened, and also not want to ask at all.

"I'm sorry," I said.

"Thank you." He took a sip of his coffee. "When we got
to the reception center, we were there for longer than we
should have been because my family had been deemed
witnesses in a case against our boat driver, who was being
tried for smuggling. The judge kept us on the island until
the case was resolved. While we were waiting, a ship capsized offshore. It was horrific. Many, many people died,
and many journalists came, including Mr. Gabriel. He
was taking photographs for a reporter who was writing a
series on us, on Syrian refugees, on our journeys and what
happened when we arrived—here, in Turkey, in Greece,
wherever we traveled to find safety. And Mr. Gabriel, he
played with us, this group of kids—some who had just
arrived, some who had come without adults so had to stay
until there was placement for them, and some, like me,
who had been marked as witnesses. We followed him
around like a pack of puppies. He sat down and showed us
how to use his camera, and then gave us each a turn. He
told us, first in broken Arabic, and then through a translator, how important it was to notice what was around you,
to share the world as you saw it, to tell people your stories."

I wish you'd told me about this, Gabe. I wish I knew

what you thought of these kids, of this experience. What moved you to let them take photographs, to use your camera, to share your wisdom?

"He promised us that when he got home, he would print our photos and find a place to display them on the island. Some of the kids didn't believe he would keep his word, but I did."

I smiled at Bashir, at the grin on his face. "And did he keep his word?" I asked.

Bashir nodded. "A woman from Rome was working with people on the island to start a children's library," he said. "Mr. Gabriel spoke to the group working on it, and they told him that when the building was finished, he could hang our photographs there. He had all of us write a statement about our photos before he left and said those would hang next to our images."

"Have you seen them in the library?" I asked him.

Bashir smiled. "I have," he said. "I went back to Lampedusa after I graduated from high school. The photographs were even more powerful than I remembered. Mr. Gabriel's were there, too."

He glowed when he talked about that memory, when he talked about you.

"Back when I was eleven, I told him I wanted to be a photographer like him when I grew up. I wanted to help give people hope, share their stories. And he gave me his mailing address. He said to keep in touch. And so I wrote to him to give him our address here in Rome. And he wrote back. I wrote again, and then nothing. I was mad for a long time, until I searched for his name one day at school. That's when I saw he had died. And I knew why he never wrote back. I wasn't . . . well, of course, I wasn't mad anymore. I was just . . . sad I hadn't been able to tell him how much he meant to me." Bashir looked down at his hands, then back up at me. "I'm sorry, that was a lot of talking."

"I appreciate the talking," I said. "I wanted to do the listening." I took a last sip of coffee and then he lifted his cup to his mouth, too. "And, for what it's worth, I bet he knew. How much he meant to you, I mean." We were both quiet for a moment. Then Bashir looked at me.

"So why are you here?" he asked.

I gave a rueful laugh and adjusted my position in my chair. "Well," I said, "I can't let a mystery go unsolved, I guess. When I saw your address in Gabriel's box, I had to know who meant so much to him that he kept it. I had to know whose image he thought was important enough to draw."

Bashir blinked back tears again. "I'm in journalism school now," he said. "Because of him."

I so wish he had been able to tell you that, Gabe. It would've meant a lot to him. And I know it would've meant a lot to you, too.

"I'm also working with his editor to commemorate the anniversary of his death, to commemorate his life," I told Bashir. "And we're looking at all his photographs. I would love to see the ones you just mentioned."

"I imagine they're still at the library," he said. "You should go; it's a beautiful island. In the summer it's a tourist spot."

"Really?" I asked.

He nodded. "Yes, though Lampedusa was in the news

a lot this past autumn, when tourist season ended. The ocean was calm and there were so many migrants arriving. Seven thousand people arrived this past September in just one week. More than the population of the island. And those are just the people who make it across the sea."

I shuddered involuntarily.

"'No one leaves home unless home is the mouth of a shark,'" Bashir said. "That's a quote from—"

"Warsan Shire," I finished for him. "'No one puts their children in a boat / unless the water is safer than the land.'"

"Right," he said. "That poem says a lot of how I felt. How I feel."

I nodded and reached my hand across the table to squeeze his. Sometimes there are no words. Sometimes there is only human connection. Human touch.

I first learned about Warsan Shire's poetry in 2017 when I saw lines from it written on signs protesting the ban on people entering the United States from Muslim-majority countries. The lines made me want to read more. You would be so moved by her words, Gabe. They brought me to tears the first time I read her poems.

My mind was racing now—there were photos of yours I'd never seen before. I wanted, needed, to know what they looked like. Why you chose the ones you did. Why you hadn't said anything about them.

"Bashir," I said, "is it far from here? The island?"

Bashir drained his coffee cup and put it back on the tiny saucer. "It's south of Sicily," he said. "Actually, closer to North Africa than to Sicily. But you've already come all this way. It would be a shame not to complete your assignment. Or is it your mission?" He smiled shyly at me.

I smiled back. "You're right," I told him. "I've come all this way. Might as well take the next step."

"Before you go," he asked hesitantly, "will you come meet my family?"

It made me feel like your ambassador to the world of the living. It made me feel closer to you, but at the same time further away. There were things about your life I didn't know. That I will never know.

I nodded. "I would be honored," I told him. And truly, I was. "I'd also love to see your photographs."

Bashir looked at me, a bit bashful. "Really?" he asked.

"Absolutely," I told him.

He opened up his phone and then showed me his screen. It was a beautiful photo of his uncle Farid, standing behind the counter, serving coffee to an unseen patron, his eyes alight, a grin on his face, as he made some kind of joke or laughed at what the patron was saying. The way Bashir captured that moment of connection looked like something you would do. Then he swiped to show me his cousin, on a rocking chair with a baby in her arms, her eyes closed as she rocked. Then he swiped again and the edge of the Tiber came into focus, the moonlight and city lights reflecting off the water, a small silhouette standing at the edge.

"These are wonderful," I said. "Gabe would have loved them. He would have been proud of the photographer you've become, the eye you have for light, for composition, for emotion."

"Thank you," Bashir said quietly. "Thank you for saying that."

I nodded.

I wish you could have been there with me, Gabe. It should have been you seeing how you made a difference in this one young man's life. It should have been you, taking me to Lampedusa to show me your photographs. It should have been you introducing me to Bashir and his family. But I guess, in some ways, it *was* you. I never would have been there without you.

You're still altering my path, orienting my future, opening me up to new and exciting possibilities.

It's always you, isn't it.

xvii

BASHIR AND I WALKED BACK TO HIS FRONT DOOR.
His mother, Sahar, was waiting downstairs for him and
took both of my hands in hers. She said, in halting English, "I'm sorry for you. He was a good man."

"Thank you," I told her.

I love that there are probably other Bashirs in this
world whom you touched, whom I still may meet. It's
like getting you back for a moment, seeing you through
their eyes, hearing your story in their words.

Bashir's mother conversed with him in Arabic, and
then Bashir turned to me and said, "My mother would
like to see a photograph of Mr. Gabriel's son."

I smiled at her. It was a touching request. But in that
moment, I realized that telling Bashir the truth about
Samuel meant Bashir's whole family would know, that
maybe the secret wouldn't be mine and Darren's to control anymore. It felt uncomfortable, them knowing when
Sammy didn't. Still, I pulled out my iPhone and showed

her the first picture of Sammy in my recent photos, of him standing next to a huge Lego castle he built. He'd been so proud of it and asked me to take a picture. In the shot, he's grinning broadly, his blond curls are a little wild, and he has his hands on his hips. A power pose, Julia would call it.

"Jamil, mash'Allah," Sahar said.

"She said he's beautiful, and then that Allah wills it. That second part, it's to protect him, to ward off evil," Bashir explained.

"Mash'Allah?" I tried saying it slowly and carefully.

"Yes," Bashir answered. "You say 'mash'Allah' after you give a compliment, for protection."

I turned to Sahar. "Your son is beautiful, too," I told her. "Mash'Allah."

Bashir started to translate, but she waved him away, smiling. She'd understood.

"He looks just like Mr. Gabriel," Bashir said, looking more closely at the photo.

"He does," I said. "It takes me by surprise sometimes."

"I can imagine," Bashir said. He was quiet for a moment, then added, "Are you going to Lampedusa?"

"Yes," I told him. "I think I am."

He nodded. "There was a hole in the fence then," he said, "and the polizia turned the other way when we kids wanted to get out. There was a woman there with a bake shop on Via Roma, Signora Paola. She would give us a treat if we could share a new word we'd learned in Italian. If you happen to run into her, would you tell her I say hello?"

I nodded. "Of course," I told him.

Bashir translated for his mother, who nodded.

"Good luck," she said to me slowly. We clasped hands once more, and I walked down the street in the direction of my hotel.

It had been a wild imagining, that the address would lead me to another family you'd had tucked away in a Roman apartment. But while it wasn't your family, it was a family who held a piece of you I was able to retrieve.

ON MY WAY BACK TO MY HOTEL, I SAW SIGNS TO THE Trevi Fountain and decided to take a detour. I'd gone with Darren on our second honeymoon, the one where I couldn't stop thinking about you, and remembered the wishing rules: You had to turn around so your back was to the fountain, and then throw coins over your left shoulder using your right hand. If you threw in one coin, it meant you'd return to Rome one day. Two coins meant you'd return to Rome and fall in love. And three coins meant you'd return to Rome, fall in love, and have a happy marriage. Darren and I both tossed three coins into the fountain, wishing we'd fall back in love with each other and that the rest of our marriage would be happy. Later, when he met Courtney and married her, I wondered if that was his coin toss coming true. And if mine ever would.

As I walked toward the fountain, I paused. It was as stunning as I'd remembered, with far fewer people thanks to the February cold. The fountain was a gorgeous baroque sculpture—Oceanus surrounded by horses and mermen, all so much larger than life it made me feel tiny. Seeing artwork like that, so grand, so beautiful, so awe-inspiring, made me wonder where talent comes from. As I stood there, admiring the statues, I thought about Sammy. I wondered where his talent would take him. Whether, with enough study, enough discipline, enough passion, his talent might create artwork on this scale of wonder.

"Thank you," I whispered to the universe, "for this feeling, for this beauty."

I wondered then if you'd ever visited the Trevi Fountain, maybe stood on the exact same spot and admired the scene. If you'd ever turned your back to Oceanus and thrown three coins, wishing you'd fall in love, get married. If you did, did you wish that one day you'd get married to me?

I moved closer to the fountain and zipped my coat up higher as a winter wind blew through the piazza. I had just two coins in my pocket: a return trip and love. No marriage this time. That seemed better, somehow.

I stepped forward, turned my back to the fountain, and tossed, listening for them to plink into the water.

When I turned back around there was a woman standing next to me. She smiled.

"English?" she asked me.

"American," I said.

She laughed. "I meant, do you speak English. But nice to know where you're from as well."

From her accent, I could tell that she herself was English.

"How many coins did you throw in the fountain?" she asked.

"Two," I told her. "That's how many I had in my pocket."

"You know a secret I've heard?" she asked.

I shook my head.

"If you whisper your heart's desire to Oceanus, he'll deliver."

"Oceanus the statue?" I answered. "Did that happen to you?"

She nodded. "I'm living here now. That was my dream. So now, whenever I pass by, I stop to say thank you." Then she looked at her watch. "Oh! I've got to run. Enjoy your time in the Eternal City."

I looked up at Oceanus. He was so much larger than life. He looked like he might be able to grant a wish. I checked on either side of me—no one was close enough to hear.

Then I leaned over the side of the fountain and whispered. "Oceanus, on the chance that what the woman said was true, I wish for"—I paused—"freedom."

It wasn't what I'd planned to say, but as I began speaking, my body filled with a deep longing for freedom. My heart wanted to grow wings.

"Heal me," I said softly, perhaps to Oceanus, perhaps to the universe, perhaps to myself. "Heal me, please."

I'd had a wound, Gabe, for a decade. You had been my wound. And I needed to be healed, to be free, to live my life without your ghost beside me. It was time.

xviii

WHEN I GOT BACK TO MY HOTEL, I HAD A MISSED call and a voice mail from Kate. I listened: *Hi Lu, just wanted to make sure you're okay. Give a call when you can.*

She picked up after one ring.

"Lucy!" she said. "I'm so glad you called back. How was the flight over? How are you?"

"I'm good," I said. "Flight was fine. I'm a little tired, but pushing through."

I could feel Kate nodding on the other end of the phone.

"So," she said. "When are you going to the address?" She said "address" as if it had a capital *A*.

"I went already," I told her.

"You did?" she said, surprise in her voice. I heard her kids in the background, then her voice, muffled: "I'm talking to Aunt Lucy. Give me a minute."

"Everything okay over there?" I asked.

"Fine, fine," she said. "They wanted me to adjudicate a dispute. But it can wait. So you went to the address?"

"Mm-hmm," I said. "And I found a young man and his family."

"And . . . ?" Kate said. I'd told her my initial idea about you having another family in Italy.

"Not his kid," I said. "But a kid he meant a lot to. A kid who's in college to be a photojournalist because he was inspired by Gabe. And he told me there are more photos Gabe had taken, in a library on an island called Lampedusa, photos I've never seen before. So I think I'm going to go."

There was a pause, and then Kate said, "Call the editor. The one who wants you to gather the photos. Maybe there's someone from the AP who's in the area who could go with you. Or at least he can make some phone calls for you. Find you a driver or something, someone who can translate for you. Journalists know people."

She was right. I should have thought about calling Eric myself. But I wasn't thinking straight just then, my mind and body muddled by the time change and jet lag, and my heart overwhelmed by the realization that someday soon I needed to let you go.

"Thanks, Kate," I said. "I'll call him after I get off the phone with you. What would I do without you?"

"Get into a lot more trouble," Kate said.

I laughed and heard her kids again in the background.

"I think I have to go," she said. "But let me know what happens."

Kate looks out for me and has the kind of mind I don't—the one that calculates risks and ameliorates them as quickly as possible. I'm so thankful for her.

I called Eric Weiss, and when I told him why I wanted

to go to Lampedusa, he said he could absolutely set something up for me, to give him the day, and he'd call me back tomorrow.

It was late by then, so I sat down on my hotel bed and ordered a room service pizza. Then I picked up your copy of *All the Light We Cannot See* and started to read it again, but I couldn't stay focused on the book. I was tired and wired at the same time.

I closed my eyes. Here I was, in Italy, alone, following your long-gone footsteps. My emotions were so close to the surface. I didn't have the strength to bury them. The sadness, the loneliness felt like a tide coursing through me, rising and rushing through my body. And I began to sob, to sob like I did when I was holding you in your hospital bed, to sob like I did after Samuel was born, like I hadn't let myself do in years. I wanted someone to hold me, to help keep me together. I wasn't sure I could do it myself anymore.

Lying on my bed, with my hand on my diaphragm, I breathed in and out, focusing only on that. In and out. In and out. In and out. And then I remembered the Sunday when I was twenty-four years old, and you and I were living together. My mom called to say that my grandfather had died.

I hung up the phone, and you looked at me and instantly knew something was wrong.

"What?" you'd said. "Luce, tell me. What happened? You look so pale."

I reached my hand up to my cheek, as if I could feel the paleness with my fingers.

"My grandfather's dead," I said. "I'll never see him

again. I'll never hear his voice, or hug him. Or feel his sandpapery chin against my forehead. He'll never send me another newspaper clipping that made him think of me. I'm going to lose so much."

You held me as I wept.

"All those things you just said," you whispered to me, "all those things you are afraid of losing, you won't ever lose. They'll always be a part of you. *He* will always be a part of you. He helped grow your beautiful brain, your generous soul, your wonderful self. And one day, you will pass those parts of yourself on, but it won't just be you you're passing on, it'll be him. He won't ever die."

You wiped your fingers under my eyes and dried my tears on your T-shirt.

"I never met my grandparents," you said, "and that's what my mother told me. That they were a part of her, and because of that they're a part of me."

I loved that notion. And it's true. My grandfather is a part of me. Everyone I've loved and lost is a part of me. But just then, alone and weeping on that too-big bed in Rome, I wanted someone to be there, to be with me, in person.

I took a deep, shaky breath and closed my eyes.

And for a moment, it felt like you were there, your arms holding me tight.

Who knows? Maybe you were.

xix

YOU KNOW WHEN YOU'RE IN SUCH A DEEP SLEEP that when you wake up, you actually don't know where you are? That was what happened to me the next morning when I awoke to Eric Weiss calling. I had passed out in my hotel room, a dark and dreamless sleep, and when my phone rang, it was like swimming from the depths of the ocean to the fresh air on top.

"Hello?" I finally mumbled after a few rings, worried I wouldn't catch it in time.

"Are you okay?" he asked.

"Fine," I said, "fine. The time change got me. You're up early." I looked at the bedside clock. My eleven A.M., his five A.M.

"Always," he said.

I'd only met Eric in person once before we started planning this retrospective. He was part of so many important times in my life, but he'd always been a voice on a telephone.

He was always kind, though. Incredibly kind.

"Anyway," he said on the phone, calling me back to myself, "I have someone who can meet you this afternoon on the island of Lampedusa and show you around. A local guide, fluent in English, who helped some of my reporters out a few months ago. Her name is Rachele—I figured you might be most comfortable with a woman. And I just emailed you the name of one of the agents in our bookings department—she'll help you with your flights and hotel."

The sleep had shaken itself from my brain at this point. "Oh no," I said. "Please, you don't have to put yourself out that much for me. I can book my flights and hotel."

"I do," he said. "And before you protest again, it's not just you. I'm doing it for Gabe. I want to see those photographs, too."

"Okay," I said, swallowing any further protestations, "got it. Thank you."

"Of course," he said. "Let me know what you find."

"I will," I told him.

The booking agent, Elaine, who worked the early shift, was kind and funny and put me on the next plane to Lampedusa. Then she booked me a hotel for two nights, and a flight back to Rome so I could make my flight from there home to New York.

"Easy as toast," she said when she was done and sent my confirmations through.

"Toast?" I echoed. I'd never heard anyone say that before.

"I know it's supposed to be pie," she responded, "but

have you ever tried to make a pie? Not actually so easy. Toast, on the other hand? Super easy."

I laughed and remembered the time we burned our toast after getting caught up watching *Jaws*, which you couldn't believe I'd never seen before. "I've messed that up, too," I told her.

"So, easy as what?" she asked.

I thought about what was easy . . . "Does it have to be cooking?" I asked.

She laughed. "I guess not."

"Then . . . easy as telling a story."

"People are different, aren't we?" Elaine said.

"Different," I said, "but also the same. We all have some things that are easy and other things that are hard; they're just not the same things."

That's something I've been thinking about a lot, Gabe, with everything going on in the world. The shared humanity in all of us. The way when you look at details, we can be so incredibly different, but when you take a step back, we're all essentially the same. You just need that larger view.

"I like that," Elaine said. "Nice to meet you, Lucy Carter Maxwell."

"Nice to meet you, too," I answered. "Thanks for your help."

"My pleasure," she said before hanging up the phone.

After I hung up, I got off the bed and stretched. I wondered if Elaine might have booked your travel, too. I should have asked.

XX

THE SUN SEEMED BRIGHTER IN LAMPEDUSA, AND IT was really windy.

"Do you want to drop your bag at the hotel?" Rachele asked when she picked me up at the small island airport that afternoon. The main section of the airport was decorated with paintings of fluorescent turtles and, incongruously, had a shining black grand piano in the middle of the entrance hall. I wondered if they had airport concerts there, and if they did, what kind of music was played.

I shook my head. "It's okay," I said. I hadn't packed much, just a small duffel bag I was wearing cross-body.

"Okay," she said. "Then to the library we go."

On the way there, she explained the history of the island to me. "There's been a reception center for migrants on this island for the past thirty years," she said. "And typically, the people who come through are political refugees or economic migrants. There were a lot of arrivals from Tunisia in the '90s, then Libyans and Syrians who crossed through Libya to travel here, and now there are many migrants from Tunisia again."

"When my friend was here to report on Lampedusa," I told her, "there was a big shipwreck."

"There are many shipwrecks," she said. "But perhaps he was here in 2013? That was the worst one. We have memorials to the victims on the island—and we honor the survivors every year."

"Yes," I said. "It would have been 2013."

Rachele nodded as she drove. "The boat sank off the coast. When they saw land, someone set a blanket on fire to attract attention. The fire scared the people on the ship, who rushed to the opposite side. The ship couldn't balance with so many people on one side, and it capsized. The coast guard here were able to save more than a hundred and fifty people, but an estimated three hundred and sixty-eight drowned. It was awful. A lot of journalists came to the island to cover it."

"And now?" I asked.

"This past September we had the highest number of arrivals since that time. Fewer people attempt the trip in winter, when the ocean is rough, but when it calms in the summer and autumn, many more boats arrive. With the state some of those boats are in, it's amazing they get here at all. My father and brother are fishermen; they have found boats while they were out fishing and called the coast guard. They once caught a body in their net."

I shivered. "It's a problem, then, so many people at once, and so little space."

"A big problem," Rachele said. "The Red Cross has

taken over the center, but they can only process people so quickly. And then the sea has to cooperate so that the ferries can cross, taking the migrants to Porto Empedocle in Sicily. In September many islanders did what they could, bringing food and clothing—and toys for the children. This is only a first-response center, so migrants aren't meant to be here for more than one to two days, maximum. That's not always the case, though, in reality."

"Wow," I said, my words failing me as I tried to wrap my mind around everything she had just said.

"Do you want to drive by the hotspot?" she asked.

"The hotspot?" I echoed.

"The Italian Red Cross calls this place the Lampedusa Hotspot," she explained, "but most people here just say hotspot."

"Okay," I said. "Let's go to the hotspot." Maybe seeing it would help my mind make more sense of her words.

She turned to the right, and we drove for a while. She pointed to the right and said, "We called that the collina della vergogna, the Hill of Shame. People slept there on plastic sheets, lived there for weeks, when the reception center was too full and the processing too slow."

"My god," I said, immediately imagining Bashir and Sahar there, then myself and my children. "Do you take people to the reception center often?"

Rachele shook her head. "Not so often right now. But I'm usually the one called when an English- or French-speaking journalist or documentarian comes to Lampedusa. Otherwise, I give nature tours of the island to tourists."

"I'm not a journalist," I told her.

"I know," she said. "But you are trying to follow one. That's what my contact at the Associated Press said."

I laughed. "I wouldn't have put it that way, but I guess you're right. I'm walking in his footsteps, trying to uncover his past."

"Ah! So an archaeologist!" she said.

I laughed again. "An archaeologist of stories, I guess."

I liked Rachele. She was open, easy to talk to, quick to smile—and she knew so much.

"You never met Gabriel, did you?" I asked, wondering if she might have been around then. She seemed like she was in her thirties, and had clearly grown up on the island.

She shook her head. "I only started working with journalists from the Associated Press a few years ago."

She stopped the car. "Here we are," she said.

We were in front of a gate that was patrolled by uniformed guards and had a mobile medical trailer in the front, along with a Red Cross tent. One of the guards came over to us to ask what we were doing there, and Rachele introduced me as a curious American archaeologist. The guard nodded at me, and I nodded back.

"Is there anyone here now?" I asked.

Rachele shook her head. "We had two boats arrive on Thursday and Friday of last week, but I think everyone who came then has been processed by now. I saw the ferries leaving for Sicily this weekend."

There was something so incongruous about this beautiful tourist destination being the gateway to Europe for so many desperate families.

Rachele and I sat in silence, both reflecting.

"You need a coffee?" she asked finally. "A moment?"

I was thinking about Bashir, about the thousands and thousands of Bashirs. And about you, absorbing and documenting pain along with beauty. I was so overwhelmed, Gabe. I needed more than a coffee, more than a moment. But I shook my head.

"Let's go to the library," I said.

I had no idea what I would find there.

Did you know, Gabe? Did you know what I was really looking for?

xxi

RACHELE PARKED HER CAR, AND WE WALKED DOWN
Via Roma—a kind of pedestrian zone filled with shops
and restaurants—to a square building on a corner that
had yellow and green turtles painted on it like a wrap-
around mural. There was a small window that looked almost like it could be used to serve ice cream to people on
the street, and beside it were a few steps that led up to a
door.

As we got closer, I could hear someone reading a story
in lilting Italian.

"The library is only open a few hours a week," Rachele
said. "And run entirely by volunteers—including my
friend Michela, who is reading that story about a mouse
looking for his underpants." That explained why the kids
were laughing.

"Do they have lots of activities there?" I asked.

"It's a bit impromptu," Rachele said. "Sometimes the
volunteers will read with the kids or do art projects. And

they have the largest collection of wordless picture books in the world—a collection sent here by the International Board on Books for Young People. Michela said the books have come from eighty different countries."

We walked up the steps.

"There's an American doctor who volunteers here sometimes," Rachele said. "He's working with a non-profit, going out on their search-and-rescue ship to patrol the area around the island."

I nodded, listening but focused on the fact that I'd see your photographs soon.

"Do you know where the photos are?" I asked in a quiet voice as she opened the door. Libraries always make me want to talk softly.

Rachele nodded. "You'll see them pretty much immediately. The library's not that big."

I looked around and saw tall shelves of books, children and adults sitting together at tables. The walls had quotes on them—one attributed to Malala and another attributed to Francis de Croisset. And then my eyes landed on a wall of photographs and my breath caught. It was your work, unmistakably, and I couldn't believe I was getting to see it for the first time—nearly ten years after you'd left this earth.

I walked closer. The first one was a cropped-in photo of a beautiful little girl in a bright green dress, looking down, so her face was hidden. She was hugging a doll that looked a little worse for wear—one of the doll's painted-on eyes was nearly rubbed off, there was dirt smudged on its face, and its foot looked like it had been chewed, perhaps by a family pet. The girl clearly was not letting go of that doll, no matter what. Next to that photo was another of two young boys in silhouette. They were holding hands, racing toward a sunset. Then a girl, her hair braided down her back, kicking a scuffed soccer ball. A boy walking upside-down on his hands. Underneath them all was a caption that you'd written. It was in English and had also been translated into Italian. It said: *I spent two weeks with children at the Lampedusa first-response center. Together we explored every inch of their surroundings. I took photographs, and they did too. We chose the ones to hang here, a record of their time in this place, a record of the life they've all led, a record of the beauty that is all around, everywhere we look for it.* —*Gabriel Samson, 2013*

Next to those photographs was one of bright purple flowers growing against the fence. It looked like the caption was in Arabic and Italian.

I turned to Rachele. "What does it say?" I asked her. She translated: "'I was so surprised when I saw these flowers. They were growing all by themselves. I thought they were beautiful.' Hala Khaled, age nine."

Then there was a photograph of an old woman's hands. A pile of books. A Coca-Cola, the glass bottle dripping with condensation. A man and a little boy hugging. A neatly made bed. A table with what looked like bread and soup on it. And you, Gabe. There was a picture of you.

"What does that one say?" I asked, pointing to the caption next to your photo.

Rachele took a step closer. "It says: 'Mr. Gabriel is beautiful. Not because of how he looks, but because of how he sees all of us. He makes us feel special, and that is beautiful.' Bashir Hassan, age eleven."

It was Bashir's!

I walked closer to the photograph. I hadn't looked at your face in so long, Gabe. Bashir said your beauty wasn't in how you looked, but to me, it was there, too—how you looked and how you saw the world, both were beautiful. And, Gabe, in that photo you were luminous. I reached my fingers out to touch your face through the glass, your lips, your nose.

Behind us, someone cleared his throat and said something in careful, accented Italian.

I turned around.

"Dr. Armstrong," Rachele said. "Hello. This woman is here from America. She wanted to see the photographs."

I looked up at Dr. Armstrong then, and his eyes connected with mine. They were a golden hazel. There was a sadness there, but also a spark of something—hope? Curiosity? I found myself unable to look away. The American doctor Rachele had mentioned, the one working on the nonprofit's search-and-rescue ship. He cleared his throat again.

"Dax Armstrong," he said, stretching out his hand to shake mine. "Welcome to Lampedusa."

I felt myself blush, though I didn't know why. "I'm Lucy," I said, sliding my hand into his. "Lucy Carter Maxwell."

"I've been wondering about these photographs," he said. "I look at them every time I volunteer at the library. Do you know the story? Why they're here?"

I didn't know what to say. I've had so much trouble explaining to people who you are to me. I know it shouldn't matter, but I want them to know what you mean to me.

"I didn't know anything about them until recently," I said.

He looked at me, and I could see him notice how close I was standing to the photograph of you. Maybe he had seen my fingertips on the glass.

"The photographer was someone special to you?" he asked.

"Yes," I answered. "He died a little less than a year after these photos were taken. I didn't know they existed. And now . . . well, there's a retrospective. Ten years after his death, and . . . we might include some of these photos. I'm supposed to send images back home."

I didn't know if I was making sense, but Dr. Armstrong seemed to be following me.

"Home is . . . ?" he asked.

"Brooklyn," I said. "And you?"

"Manhattan," he said with a small smile. "I guess we're neighbors."

The pull toward him was so strong that I'd forgotten Rachele was standing next to us.

"My kids think Manhattan is practically another country," I said.

He smiled, but I saw pain in his eyes. Real, raw.

"I should leave you to take your pictures," he said. "To send back home."

"Thanks," I said. "It was nice to meet you."

My hair had fallen into my face, and I tucked it behind my ear. It was still hard to look away from his eyes.

"Um, listen," he said. "I don't usually happen upon

many New Yorkers on Lampedusa. If you want, I could show you around after I finish up here? Or we could grab something to eat? Maybe you could tell me more about your photographer."

I didn't even have to think about it. "I'd . . . I'd like that, Dr. Armstrong," I said.

"Dax, please," he answered. "Lucy?"

I can't explain why, but when he said my name, it felt familiar, like he had been saying it for years.

"Lucy," I confirmed.

"Lucy," he said again. "The girl with kaleidoscope eyes."

"Lucy in the Sky with Diamonds." The song that had defined my high school years, the song people sang to me in the hallways and at parties. I used to roll my eyes, but really I loved it. Loved the attention, loved the song.

"I'll make you cellophane flowers," I said. "Yellow and green."

He laughed. "I'll find you some rocking horse people, some marshmallow pies."

"Sounds great," I said. "Where can I find you for these rocking horse people and marshmallow pies?"

He handed me his phone and I put in my contact info.

"I'll find you on WhatsApp," he said.

Then a little boy pulled at his sweater, and Dax turned toward him speaking, again, in careful Italian.

"I'll just take some quick photographs," I said to Rachele. "And then maybe you can show me some more of the island."

"Of course," Rachele said.

As we turned to leave, Dax was sitting with the little boy, an open book in front of them. The two of them were pointing to different items on the page, and the boy was identifying them in Italian, while Dax was identifying them in English.

"They're giving each other language lessons," Rachele said with a laugh.

Dax must've heard her, because he looked up and smiled at us one last time before I walked out the door.

I have to admit, my mind was drifting during Rachele's tour. While she talked about the geology, vegetation, and history of the island, I found myself wondering what Dax's story was, where that sadness in his eyes had come from. As she brought me back to my hotel, I asked Rachele if it might be possible to buy cellophane somewhere nearby. I had promised flowers, and I wanted to deliver.

xxii

THERE ARE SOME PEOPLE YOU MEET AND FOR WHAT-
ever reason it feels like your bodies vibrate on the same
frequency—or maybe it's your souls. After I freshened up
a bit at my hotel, I headed back to Via Roma on foot to
sightsee a bit. I stopped to take a photograph of a farmacia to send to my brother, who is still working as a chem-
ist at a pharmaceutical company. Which reminded me
I'd never spoken to Jay about Vanessa being away for
work. And actually hadn't told my parents I was away.
The distance between me and my family was so huge,
sometimes it shocked me. I never would have predicted
this was how our relationships would turn out.

I snapped a photograph of the view of the beach and
sent it to my parents. *Hi Mom and Dad*, I wrote, *I'm on a
small island in Italy. Here for work. It was a last-minute
thing, and I took advantage while the kids were away. Be
back in a couple of days. Thinking about you!*

A message came back from my mom immediately.

Looks like a beautiful place.

Even though that's all she wrote, I know what she was thinking. I could read the unwritten: *I can't believe you're on another continent and we didn't know.* It's what I'd think if one of my kids sent that note.

Then I sent the photo of the farmacia to Jay. *I'm in Italy and look what I found! Maybe some of your compounds are here! Talk when I'm back?*

He sent a thumbs-up; it was all I got.

I sighed and went to put my phone away, but then it vibrated. I pulled it out again and looked at the screen. It was Dax Armstrong.

I felt an electric charge when I saw his name there.

Hey Lucy. Just left the library. Looks like I'll have to work tonight, but I have a few hours free. Any chance you like gelato?

I found myself smiling as I wrote back: *"Like gelato" would be putting it mildly.*

His reply was instantaneous. *Meet me at Gelateria Voscenza in ten minutes then? It's the best gelato I've ever tasted.*

I quickly Google Mapped the gelateria and found I could walk there in five. *Perfect*, I said.

I turned around on Via Roma and took my time walking over but still arrived first, so I stood outside the shop, my face raised to the sun. It felt heavenly in the midst of the frigid New York winter—as did the fizzy feeling of anticipation coursing through my body.

"Hey," I heard Dax say, and snapped my head toward him. "You look like a flower, soaking in the sun like that."

"Maybe I'm just vitamin D deficient," I said.

He laughed. "I can always order a blood workup . . ."

"I'd prefer a gelato," I deadpanned.

"Me too," he said as he opened the door for me, still laughing.

As I walked through the open door in front of him, I thought: *Darren would approve of the gentlemanly gesture.* Then I shook him from my head and looked around. There were small tables with brightly colored chairs scattered throughout the space, and twelve gelato flavors were set out in a freezer display. We were the only people in the shop, other than the man behind the counter.

"Which is your favorite?" I asked Dax.

"Nocciola," he said to me. "Hazelnut."

I looked them over. Some were easy to figure out, like cioccolato and caffè. There was a pink one, too.

"Fragola is?" I asked.

"Strawberry," he said.

"And bacio?" It was a light brownish color.

His cheeks turned slightly pink. "It means kiss," he said. "It's a mix of chocolate and hazelnut. Like those hazelnut truffle candies covered in chocolate. Baci."

"Wait," I said. "Are Baci where Mr. Hershey got the name for his chocolate kisses? Or did Hershey's Kisses come first?"

He smiled at me. "I have absolutely no idea," he said. "And have literally never thought about that. Let's find out." He pulled out his phone and after a few pokes with his thumbs said, "And the winner is: Hershey's Kisses. Made in 1907. Baci were invented in 1922 by a woman named Luisa Spagnoli. Though no indication if she had ever eaten a Hershey's Kiss."

"Huh," I said and smiled at him. "Well, I guess I'll try a kiss." I was surprised by how easily the flirtation fell from my lips.

His eyes twinkled at me as he ordered for us both in his careful Italian, and when he went to pay with his credit card, I stopped him.

"My treat," I said. "Please."

He looked at me for a moment, then put his card away. "Well, thank you, as long as I can return the favor by taking you out to dinner tomorrow night. Will you still be here?"

"I will," I said. "I got a note back from Gabe's old editor that he wants us to take the photos down and scan them properly, just in case we can't find the original files. So I'll be here one more day, and then back to Rome, and from Rome to New York."

"So, tomorrow night?" Dax asked.

"Tomorrow night," I said, trading my credit card for a cone of gelato al bacio.

WE SAT OUTSIDE ON A BENCH, MY GAZE LOOKING down the road to the shimmering sea, drinking it in.

"This place is beautiful," I said, looking at the expansive pink sky, the sun starting to set over the ocean. I wondered if we would see boats of migrants arriving in the distance, like Rachele had said, searching for safe harbor.

"Isn't it?" he answered. "Just a bizarre juxtaposition—so much beauty, and so much suffering all in one place."

Then he pointed to a spot on the darkened horizon.

"There was a ship last week that ran out of fuel right over there. The NGO I work for brought the passengers on board and got them to shore, while I started treating the worst cases of dehydration and hypothermia. It was a lucky group. Sometimes . . ." His voice drifted off.

He reminded me of you in that moment, Gabe, not able to find the words for what he'd witnessed. But still here, facing it.

"I'm sorry," I said. "Sorry that it happens. Sorry that there are people you can't help."

He sighed and I watched his gelato melt a little down the side of his hand.

"The nocciola," I said, pointing.

He licked it off quickly. "When I think about it too long, the unfairness of the world really bowls me over."

"I know what you mean," I said. "How did we get to be the two people sitting here, eating gelato, and not, instead, two people risking our lives to come to this island."

"Luck of the draw," he said, looking at me as if he were trying to engrave the moment in his memory.

"Fate," I answered.

"Maybe," he said, with a small smile. He licked some more of his cone. "Sorry," he said, "I get a bit philosophical sometimes."

"I don't mind," I answered, licking my own gelato, reveling in the sensation of the cold sweetness on my tongue, in the heat radiating off his body next to mine. The casual intimacy of the moment, the comfort I felt with him here, so far from home, surprised me.

We were both quiet for a moment, and then at the same time, both started to talk.

We laughed, and he said, "You first."

"I was just going to ask how long you've been working here."

He smiled. "Well, I was a Doctor Without Borders here way back when. Last year a friend of mine from those days started an NGO that has boats patrolling the waters around Lampedusa and the Greek islands of Crete, Gavdos, and Lesbos, looking for boats so we can get the people to shore quicker and more safely. Each boat has a doctor on it, and I volunteered for a six-month rotation starting in September. I'll be back in New York in a month." He said the last part emphatically, his hazel eyes on mine.

"So you'll have borders again soon?" I asked.

He nodded. "Borders again."

His cell phone went off and I saw his face tighten. "Gotta get this," he said, and picked up. "Okay," he said into the phone. "Okay. Yup. On my way."

"Is everything okay?" I asked.

"That was our ship's captain. We just got a report that there might be a boat a few miles offshore and they want to leave now. I've got to go. But I'll see you tomorrow night?"

I nodded. "Tomorrow night."

"Thank you for the gelato," he said as he got up. "Sitting with you has been the best part of my week."

I stood up and gave him a hug. He wrapped his arms around me, extending the moment. My head fit into the crook between his broad shoulder and his neck; he smelled like citrus shampoo. I could feel his muscles, strong underneath his T-shirt, and the strength and warmth of him made me shiver.

"See you soon, Lucy in the sky with diamonds," he said against my ear.

I watched him go, then sat on the bench to finish my gelato. There was something in the air that made me feel like change was coming. And the feeling excited me.

xxiii

THE NEXT DAY I WENT BACK TO RETRIEVE YOUR photographs with Rachele. The library was closed, but Rachele had gotten the key from her friend Michela. There was something so lovely about the community on the island. Everyone seemed to know everyone else, and I was touched by how out of their way people went to help me, too.

Thanks to Rachele's connections, we'd found a flatbed scanner at the local newspaper office that was big enough to fit your prints. Once the photographs were all off the walls, Rachele and I headed over.

The *Lampedusa Oggi* offices were small, with a few people inside laying out the next week's edition on large computer screens.

Rachele spoke to a man at one of the computers and he led us to the scanner at the back of the room.

"Posso farlo io," he said, looking pointedly at the framed photographs in my arms.

"He's saying he can do it," Rachele said.

I looked at her, and she inclined her head, which I figured meant it was okay to accept the help—or that I was supposed to. Maybe he didn't want us using his scanner.

"Okay," I said to him. "Thank you. I'll just take them out of the frames." I mimed the action while Rachele translated my words.

He nodded and walked back to his computer.

"That's Giacomo," Rachele said. "We went to school together. He was a year behind my brother."

I imagined that Rachele would be able to find a first- or second-degree connection to anyone we met.

She and I worked together to undo the backs of the frames as carefully as possible. We used letter openers to pry up the small nails. Once the photographs were free, we handed them over to Giacomo.

"Alta risoluzione?" he said.

"High resolution?" translated Rachele.

"As high as he can," I answered, following Eric's instructions.

Once Giacomo had finished, I gave him my email address, and he sent over a link to an FTP site where he'd stored the large files. I forwarded it to Eric immediately, and then Rachele and I reframed the prints.

"I have plans to meet Michela later," she told me when we finished, "so I can drop these off at the library when I do."

"Sounds good," I said. "Thank you so much."

I went back to my hotel, checked in with the kids, with my office, with my parents, with Kate. Read a bit more about Lampedusa and its history until it was time to get ready to meet Dax.

I wasn't thinking of my dinner with Dax as a date per se, but I couldn't deny that there was something pulling me to him. My body physically responded to him in a way it hadn't to anyone since you. Judging from our hug goodbye, I thought he might feel the same way about me. I looked through my duffel bag. There were very limited wardrobe choices. After going through all my options twice, and contemplating going shopping in town, I decided on a pair of black jeans, a white button-down with the sleeves rolled up and the top two buttons undone, and black ballet flats.

For my fortieth birthday, Darren and Courtney gave me a beautiful gift—a necklace with each of the kids' birthstones on it. Topaz for Violet, garnet for Liam, and aquamarine for Sammy, who was born in March, his birthday five days before mine. I wore it all the time and had it around my neck when I left for Italy, so it was there, completing the outfit. I brushed my hair out, put on a little bit of lip gloss and an extra coat of mascara, and decided that would do. The more I stared at myself in the mirror, the more the butterflies took over.

Rachele and I hadn't been able to find cellophane, but we did find plastic straws and tissue paper, so I'd made two tissue-paper flowers to bring with me—yellow and green.

Dax had WhatsApp'd me the name and address of a restaurant in the center of town. The restaurant was within walking distance of my hotel, and I got there one minute past the hour. Dax was already waiting, and when he saw me holding the tissue paper flowers, his face lit up in a way that made me wonder if that was what he'd always looked like before whatever it was happened that made his eyes so sad.

"Not quite cellophane," I told him, "but the best I could do."

"They're lovely," he said. "I'm impressed you knew how to make flowers out of tissue paper."

"It's remarkable what you can find a tutorial for on YouTube," I answered, and he laughed, that light filling his face again.

"I have some ideas about rocking horse people," he said. "But I'm a bit stumped as to where to find marshmallow pies."

"Not a baker?" I asked.

"Not a baker," he affirmed, as he opened the restaurant door and then stepped back to let me through first. "Though also not sure if they have marshmallows here. Do you know how hard it is to find peanut butter?"

The restaurant was small but nicely decorated, and the aroma of tomato and spice filled the place.

"That smells spectacular," I said as the waiter pointed us to a table.

"I eat here often," Dax said, pulling out my chair for me. "But it's usually just me and a book for dinner. I prefer being out, though, to being home alone."

I felt like this man was dropping crumbs, and I was trying to figure out what the whole meal looked like. "What book are you reading?" I asked.

"*Wild* by Cheryl Strayed," he answered.

It said something nice about him that he was reading

a memoir by a woman. "I haven't read it," I said, "but heard it's fascinating."

"It is," he replied, picking up the menu. "I find human beings so fascinating. The way we think, the way we act. It's why I became a doctor."

I laughed. "I could say the same, but then end with: It's why I became a storyteller."

He looked at me for a moment, then said: "Let's put a pin in that and order. I recommend the fish couscous, if you like fish. Everything is caught fresh daily."

I looked at the menu and said, "What about the first pasta dish? Pasta con le sarde?"

"Also delicious," Dax said.

A waiter came over and took our order, and then Dax said to me, "Would you want to split a bottle of wine? Red?"

"Works for me," I answered, mentally telling myself not to drink more than a glass or two.

"My favorite is this Barolo," Dax said, pointing to one on the menu that said it was made in Alba. The vineyard was called Villa Della Rosa. "The man who runs the vineyard came here on vacation once and struck up a friendship with the owner, so now he imports the Barolo from the north."

After the wine was ordered and the waiter left, Dax asked about you.

"So I've been staring at the photos your friend Gabriel took for the last five months," he said. "I'd love to know more about him."

I nodded. Over time, it's gotten easier to talk about you, but there are still moments—many moments—that thinking of you, talking about you, brings tears to my eyes. I didn't want to cry in front of Dax.

"He . . . he was a photojournalist who always wanted to find the beauty in any situation," I said, playing with the gems on my necklace, sliding them back and forth on the chain. "He died on assignment almost ten years ago."

He seemed to absorb that as the waiter brought over two red wine glasses and gave us each a generous pour of Barolo before leaving the bottle on the table.

"This goes down easy," Dax warned me as we lifted up our glasses and clinked them together.

"To Lampedusa," I said.

"To New Yorkers in Lampedusa," he answered.

We drank and he was right. The wine was delicious.

"I see how this could be dangerous," I said as I took a second small sip.

"And Gabriel was your friend?" Dax asked.

"Sometimes," I answered. "Sometimes more than that."

"But not your husband," he said.

I shook my head. "No, that was someone else."

We were both slowly drinking the wine, and I could feel my body loosening up.

"I'm divorced, too," he said. "Three years last week."

"Seven years for me," I said.

The food came, and the waiter refilled our wineglasses.

"Any kids?" I asked him, remembering his eyes when I mentioned my kids. Was it because he had left his behind?

There was a long pause.

"I never know how to answer this," he said, "other than to say that I had a son, but he died."

I felt the blood drain from my face. "Oh my god," I said. "I'm . . . I'm so, so sorry."

He closed his eyes for a moment and then opened them again. "Thank you."

And then he didn't say anything. I didn't say anything either. I wasn't sure where to go from there, what to say next.

Dax cleared his throat. "How about we talk about something else?"

"Of course," I said, taking another sip of wine.

So we talked about my trip to Italy, I told him about meeting Bashir, that I'd been to Rome once before, though this was my first time on Lampedusa. He told me about how terrible his cooking is, how he burns eggs pretty much every morning, how he can never quite get toast done properly.

The wine bottle and both of our wineglasses were empty when I stood up to use the restroom and stumbled slightly. "Whoa," I said. "I think I'm switching to water when I get back."

I was tipsier than I'd planned to be, but not so much that I was drunk. More like a really strong buzz.

When I sat down again, Dax looked at me and said, "My son died of COVID in the early days of the pandemic. He was being treated for leukemia, and the chemo was working, but then he got COVID and . . . I . . . I do want to talk about him, but it's always so hard."

His eyes were glassy, but he'd managed not to cry.

"What's his name?" I asked.

"Zachariah," he answered. "He preferred Zac. He was eleven when he died. I think every day about what it would be like if he'd lived. He'd be turning sixteen this year."

"Just like Violet," I said softly, more to myself than to him.

"Violet's your daughter?" he asked.

I nodded. "What did Zac like to do?"

Dax smiled in a way that told me he appreciated the question, appreciated that I'd asked about Zac's life and not his death. "He loved math—facts and statistics. He loved sports, too, but more watching than playing. He started his own fantasy baseball league in fourth grade. It was the perfect marriage of sports and statistics for him. His dream was to become the general manager of the Yankees."

"My son Liam would have loved a fantasy baseball league in fourth grade," I said. "I wish they'd known each other." Sammy, on the other hand, is not at all into watching sports, as much as Darren tries to entice him. He's like you, Gabe.

"You have a daughter and a son?" Dax asked.

I nodded. "Two sons. Liam and Samuel," I added. I felt guilty for having three healthy, living children.

"How old are they?" He took a piece of bread from the plate in the center of the table.

"Violet turned fifteen last November. Liam just turned thirteen in January. And Sam will be nine next month."

"You must have your hands full," he said.

I smiled. "A bit," I said.

"Are they with their dad a lot?" he asked.

"Half the time. Every other week. But Sam . . . he's actually Gabriel's son." I hadn't intended to tell more people, to tell Dax in particular, but it was like once I told Bashir, I couldn't stop. The truth will out, people say, and this truth kept popping out of my mouth.

I saw Dax's eyebrows rise for a split second, and then his face went back to neutral. Maybe a skill he'd perfected for talking with patients?

"Is that why—" he started.

"My marriage ended?" I finished for him. "Essentially, yes."

"I was going to say is that why you're here," Dax replied, lifting his glass to see if he could find a last drop of wine there.

I laughed, slightly embarrassed. "Oh. No. I'm here because I can never leave well enough alone," I said, stopping there. We were both quiet for a moment.

The waiter came by with another bottle of wine and refilled Dax's glass. He went to refill mine, but I put my hand over the top.

"Have you heard of Aviva Landsman?" he asked, taking another sip of wine.

I squinted. Her name sounded familiar, but I couldn't place her. I knew there was a story, though.

"Broadway singer who . . ." he started.

"Got COVID in March of 2020, at the very beginning of the pandemic, and gave concerts during lockdown out her window to build her breath support back!" I said, remembering the articles in the *New York Times*.

He nodded. I knew there was more to the story, and I

was searching around in the recesses of my brain to find it. It was a while ago, but I remembered talking about it with Julia.

"Her . . . her husband was an ER doctor, and her son had—oh," I said, realizing. "Your ex-wife?"

"My ex-wife," he said.

"I remember those stories. She's starring in . . . in . . ."

"In *Into the Woods* now on Broadway. As the Baker's Wife."

I nodded. "I'm not so into Broadway," I told him, "but that's a good part, right? Sara Bareilles played the role, too."

He smiled. "Want to know a secret?"

"Sure," I said.

"I prefer TV to live shows, particularly the ability to pause them after a long day of work. But I couldn't admit to that the whole time I was with Aviva."

Now it was my turn to smile. "I work in TV," I told him. "Children's television."

"As an actress?" he asked.

I shook my head, "A producer. *Rocket Through Time* was mine—not sure if you ever watched that with your son. And now I'm working on *Tiger & Bunny*."

"*Rocket Through Time?*" he said. "No way! Zac loved that show."

"I'm glad," I said. "It means a lot to me when people like that show in particular. I based one of the characters on Gabriel."

"You know," Dax said, after a moment, staring into my eyes. "I think we may have messed up here. I don't think you're supposed to talk about previous relationships ' on a first date."

I raised my eyebrows. "Is this a date?" I answered, flirtation curling around my words. The wine was making its way through my system.

"Do you want it to be?" he answered back, resting his hands on the table in front of him. They were beautiful hands, long fingers, perfectly trimmed nails. "And, I guess, actually, yesterday was our first date. This is our second." He gave me a small smile that felt like it thawed my heart.

"I haven't gone on a second date in a decade," I told him, wondering, too late, if admitting that was a bad move.

"So then this can be your first," he said, not acting shocked or surprised. Just accepting that that's where I was and meeting me there. "Your first second date. That's a big deal. Let's make it count."

His response made me smile—and then made those butterflies come back, because he wanted this to be something that counted. He wanted to be someone who counted. "How about you?" I asked, tucking a piece of errant hair behind my ear.

"Do I date?" He answered my question with one of his own.

I nodded.

"I've been on a few in the last couple of years," he said. "Nothing serious, no one now." He looked at me, as if he was making sure I understood what he was saying.

I nodded again.

He motioned to the waiter to bring the check.

"I think I owe you some rocking horse people, right?"

"That's the rumor," I said.

"Then let's go." He stood and held my hand, helping me up from the table. When our fingers touched, I caught my breath and looked up at him. He was already looking at me, and our eyes locked. My body seemed to melt a little more.

I truly hadn't felt that way since you. And I couldn't believe I was feeling it there, with him, for the first time in forever.

xxiv

SOMETIMES THINGS FEEL PREDESTINED. LIKE THAT
old "take the current when it serves" line from Shakespeare that I think about all the time. These preordained
moments are there, waiting for us, and we can grab hold
of them when we want to, do with them what we will.
Kate and I talked a while ago about that text meme going
around the internet that says: *Life isn't about what happens
to you, but about what you do with what happens to you.*
And that feels so true to me these days. What did I do
with the life I was given, with the choices presented?
What did you? What did any of us?

That night, after dinner, Dax walked me to an over-
look with a view of the harbor. There were sculptures
there—a three-dimensional mural of sorts made from
objects that had washed up on the island. An installation
piece that looked like a chalkboard with the English
words *Before I die . . .* printed on it. People had filled in
the sentence below it, an array of different handwritings

and languages. I wonder what you would have written, Gabe. And whether it was something you'd ended up accomplishing.

Past that art piece was a bench facing the sea, with two rocking chairs next to it.

"I've asked around about these," he told me. "And the story I got is that years ago a man named Teodoro left a rocking chair here to sit in while he watched the sunset each night. And then a friend of his brought one to join him. Both of them are gone now, but the rocking chairs remain."

"Can we sit in them?" I asked him.

He smiled. "Nothing stopping us."

Dax held my hand as we walked to the rocking chairs, the island wind whipping through my hair and the touch of his fingers warming me all over. I stopped at the chair that had a moon and stars carved into the back. It was calling out to me.

"Okay if I take this one?" I asked.

He nodded and sat in the chair next to mine, a simple spindle-back with armrests.

We both started rocking slowly, then gradually picked up speed, like my kids used to do on the swings in the park, pumping their legs as quickly as they could until their feet sailed over my head.

"I feel like I'm flying!" I said.

I thought about how much Sam and Liam would love this.

"I feel like a cowboy!" Dax said, swinging his hand like he was holding an imaginary lasso.

We both laughed as we rocked. And then the laughing slowed and so did the rocking until we eventually stopped doing both.

"I'm glad you let your adventure take you to Lampedusa," he said. "And I'm glad I could share this time with you."

"Thank you," I said. I reached my hand out and he reached back, so we were holding hands across the chairs. Being with Dax felt like finding the key to a locked box in my heart and opening it a crack, letting out the feelings I was afraid to experience again.

I tilted my head back to see the stars. They were so visible here, with hardly any ambient light. "I'm glad you're here," I said, "though I'm sorry about the reason why. I'm sorry so many people have to take this journey to begin with."

Dax nodded. "I . . . I have more to say about that, but let's save the conversation for when we know each other better," he said. I could feel the weight of the promise in his words. "Are you looking for Lucy in the sky with diamonds?"

"Just admiring the stars," I said, and then I tipped my chin back down and found him looking straight at me. "Hi," I said softly.

"Just admiring you," he replied, letting go of my hand and pushing himself off the chair. "I think all we have left on our agenda this evening is marshmallow pies. Do you want to teach me to bake?"

We were standing now, facing each other, only a few inches apart. He reached for my hand and caught my gaze with his. The moonlight held us, sparking in Dax's eyes.

"Sure," I answered.

"Good," he said, coming closer.

And then he bent his head and touched his lips to mine, and I melted into him.

I brought my hand to his chest and felt his heart beating, steady beneath my fingers. He was so real, so solid, after years of kisses only being in my imagination.

Our lips broke apart and he rested his forehead against mine, his fingertips soft on my waist, our breaths mingling as he said, "Lucy, Lucy. You're so lovely. Can we . . . can we keep each other company tonight?"

"I didn't expect this," I whispered. I basked in his warmth, in the feel of his forehead resting on mine, the echo of our lips meeting. And for the first time in years, I wanted more. "Come to my hotel."

"Yes," he said, pulling me closer, laying his cheek against my hair. "You are so, so lovely."

It wasn't something I was used to being called, but I liked it. I took his hand, and we walked the four blocks back to my hotel, our fingers intertwined, holding each other tight.

WE WERE QUIET ON THE WALK BACK, AND I WAS worried that things would feel strange once we made this decision, once we knew where the evening was going, but it didn't. Everything felt easy between us, natural, and electric. I could feel the current where our hands touched and did all I could to contain the anticipation that was verging on panic. Was I actually going to sleep with someone else for the first time in more than seven and a half years?

"How did you choose this hotel?" he asked as we walked through the lobby.

"The Associated Press travel department," I said. "Gabe's editor asked them to help me out."

Dax nodded. "He really meant a lot to you."

"Still does," I said. "Always will." I wasn't sure if that was something I should admit to the man who was coming up to my hotel room, but I've realized over the years that it doesn't make sense to pretend. I am who I am, I feel what I feel. And there's no reason to hide myself anymore. I'm forty-four years old, and at this point, people can take me as I am, or not at all.

"Feelings that strong are beautiful," Dax said, and squeezed my hand with his.

I smiled at him. He was taking me as I was. The only response I could think of was "Thank you."

ONCE WE WERE IN THE HOTEL ROOM, DAX WALKED to the window. I followed.

"I always like being able to see the sky," he said. "Maybe it comes from working for so many hours in interior rooms in hospital ERs, but I can breathe better when I can see the sky."

I tucked myself against him so I could see what he was seeing, and he slid his arm around my back. "It's beautiful," I said, marveling at the fact that there was a man here whom I could touch, who could touch me, whom I wanted to touch me.

"Lovely," he agreed, and I leaned my head against his shoulder, breathing in his scent of citrus and spice.

"You like that word," I noted.

He laughed. "I guess I do. You are lovely, just like the sky, just like the stars."

And then we kissed again, and it felt like relief, like my body was exhaling for the first time in a long time. Our kissing moved slowly toward the bed, our bodies pressed so close that when one of us took a step, we both did. There was no air between us, just heat. When we got to the bed, he sat down and pulled me onto his lap.

"Is this okay?" he whispered softly.

"Yes," I answered.

And then his lips were back on mine, and his hands were on the nape of my neck, his fingers caressing my hair. It felt so good. It had been far too long since I'd been kissed like that, touched like that, with tenderness, with reverence.

Dax bent his head to brush a soft kiss against my collarbone and then looked up at me. "Thank you for inviting me over," he said.

I laughed, my head tilted back slightly, and he caught my neck with another kiss, sliding his lips down to where my shirt was unbuttoned.

"I can take that off," I whispered.

"That would be—"

"Lovely?" I finished for him.

He laughed against my skin, his breath trailing goose bumps across my body. "How about 'great'?"

I pulled my shirt over my head, revealing the black bra I had on underneath.

"God," he said, his eyes on my chest and then my lips and then my eyes. "You are spectacular."

"*You*," I said. "*You* are spectacular."

We started kissing again, and then he fumbled at the buttons on his shirt.

"Let me," I said softly, undoing them one by one. My hands were on the top button of his jeans. "Yes?" I asked.

"Please," he answered.

So I unbuttoned and unzipped his jeans, and he reached toward me to unbutton and unzip mine. We separated a moment to kick our pants off, and I looked over at him. He had on gray boxer briefs, patterned with tiny black diamonds.

"Cute," I said.

"I play poker," he answered. And then he took those off, too.

I slid my black underwear off, and the two of us paused for a moment, standing at the side of the bed, staring at each other. I felt the heat of his gaze, bathing me in desire, his and mine.

"Lucy in the sky with diamonds," he said. "You are something else."

I pulled the quilt off the bed and sat down on the soft hotel sheets. "Come here," I said.

Dax complied. I was at just the right height to stroke my fingers down his erection and bring it to my lips. I ran my tongue down the length of him and then took all of him in my mouth.

He was breathing hard, and I could feel his thigh muscles clenching under my hands. I took my mouth off his erection.

"You okay?" I asked.

He looked down at me and cupped my face in his hands, his thumb stroking across my lips. "Oh god, yes." Then he slid down to his knees and gently pushed me back against the mattress. "My turn," he said as he braced my legs on either side of his broad shoulders.

I closed my eyes and felt his tongue dragging against the most sensitive part of me. My every nerve ending seemed to pulse with light. *I* pulsed with light. Like I truly was Lucy, in the sky, sparkling with the glow of a thousand diamonds.

A sound escaped my mouth that was part sigh and part moan. I was out of my mind with the beauty of how I felt. The majesty of it.

He stopped and looked at me. "Lucy," he said, his voice husky with desire, "I have a condom, if you want . . ."

I liked that he didn't assume. And I did want this. I hadn't wanted anyone inside me for so long. But Dax felt right. More than right, he felt like a reawakening. A gift.

"I do want," I told him.

He bent down and found his jeans on the floor, and then pulled three condom wrappers out of the billfold of his wallet.

As he unrolled one of the condoms, I could see him pulse even harder.

"Come here," he said, climbing onto the bed.

I came closer and his mouth was back on mine. I could feel my nipples stiffen, my body go molten.

"Now you," I said, lying down and opening my legs. "You come here."

Dax hovered above me for a moment, then slowly slid inside, leaning down to kiss me as he did.

"Yes," I breathed out, when I felt him fill me. "Oh my god, yes."

It felt like bounty after years of deprivation, luxury after years of scarcity.

He started rocking his body and I moved against him, matching his rhythm.

Pressure built between my legs. It felt divine. It felt miraculous. "Dax, I'm gonna—" I said, but couldn't even finish the sentence before a glittering orgasm started rippling through me and I was bucking against him.

"Wow," he said when I was trying to catch my breath. "That was intense."

"I meant to wait," I said, my breath slowing down again.

Still inside me, he stroked my hair off my forehead. "It's okay," he said. "You never have to wait. But let's see if you can do that again."

He moved inside me, and I shivered. "God, you feel perfect," I told him.

"You too," he whispered as he thrust harder.

We changed rhythms, changed positions a few times, until finally he peeled off the condom, wiped off the lubricant. I laid my cheek on his lap and ran my tongue along the rim of him, hearing him moan. I closed my lips around him, stroking with my tongue.

"Lucy, Lucy, yes, oh god, Lucy," he said, the words crashing into each other.

He rolled away for a moment, gasping, and then put a new condom on.

I climbed onto his lap, pulling him back inside me, wrapping my legs around his back, bringing his mouth to mine.

"I'm so far in," he said into my lips. "You're so wet."

"I know," I whispered back.

I could feel him hitting that spot deep inside me that would make me orgasm, not like I had initially, the glittery kind that happened when someone rubbed against my clit, but the deeper kind, the kind that echoed throughout my whole self.

I pulled him in even farther with my legs.

He thrust hard, again and again and again. I was so close, couldn't believe I was going to orgasm again. I felt his breath on my face, his hands in my hair.

"I'm gonna—" he said.

"Me too," I answered, using my last bit of focus to form the words.

And then we both lost ourselves in the shudder and the breath and the power of it all. It was bliss, it was ecstasy, it was both of us dancing together in oblivion.

After a moment, we lay back, our breath still coming heavy and fast. Dax rolled over so I was on the bottom and he was on top, our bodies still together.

"My god," he said, his breath slowing down. "My god. I've never . . ."

"I know," I answered. "That was . . . transcendent."

How could I have found him? There? On Lampedusa? Another man who made me feel like you did, Gabe?

I didn't know how much I needed that. I needed sex. I needed sex with Dax.

We called down to the front desk for a toothbrush, and he put on his boxer briefs and his button-down, open like a robe. I put on my underwear, too, and grabbed a

T-shirt from my duffel. It was an old one from a race I'd once run, and it had gotten soft and threadbare with age. It was one of my favorite sleep shirts.

Dax ran his fingers along the fabric. "It's as soft as it looks," he said.

"Mm-hmm," I answered, pulling my hair into a ponytail.

"Glad I get to cuddle with that T-shirt all night," he said, a small smile on his face, before he went to the door to greet the toothbrush deliverer.

When he left the bed, the enormity of what had just happened hit me. Another man had been inside me. Another man had made me orgasm. And now another man would be sleeping in my bed. I'd be sharing my bed for the first time in nearly eight years. The kids crawled in with me sometimes, but usually it was just me, sleeping alone. My mind was telling me to panic, but my body was saying no. I turned off my mind and listened to my body. A Mary Oliver poem came to mind about letting the soft animal of my body love what it loved. And my body, sure as anything, loved Dax.

After we brushed our teeth and washed our faces, we climbed into bed and Dax turned out the light. I was aware of him, of his heat, his breath, the spicy scent of sex and sweat and his citrus shampoo. I wondered how I'd ever fall asleep with him there, with my body wanting so much more.

But then Dax curved himself around me, like you used to do, and I closed my eyes. "Want to hear a bedtime story?" he asked.

"Sure," I answered sleepily, pulling his hand so his arm wrapped around my torso and our fingers were intertwined.

"Once upon a time," he said, "there was a queen . . ."

But I didn't hear what came after that, because I was already asleep.

XXV

THAT NIGHT, WHEN DAX WAS IN MY HOTEL BED, I awoke to him gently shaking me.

"Your phone, Lucy," he said. "Your phone's been ringing."

He gave it to me. "It says Violet," he said. "I think she's called a number of times."

My heart started racing. Violet? A number of times? In the middle of the night? I went to swipe the phone call open when it stopped ringing. Before I could call her back, my room phone rang. I grabbed it instantaneously.

"Hello?" I breathed.

"Mom!" Violet was on the other line. "We're going to the hospital. With Samuel. He cut his foot on a huge shell at the beach, and it was bleeding everywhere. He wants to talk to you."

She was talking loudly enough that Dax heard and moved closer to me. I grabbed onto him.

"Is he—?" I started, but Violet had already passed her phone to Sammy.

"Mo-om," he wailed on the other line. "I'm bleeding so much. It really hurts. Mom, what if they can't fix me? Mom, what if, what if—" And he dissolved into sobs.

"It's gonna be okay, Sammy," I said, saying what I hoped was true. "I know it's really scary, I know it hurts, but it's just a cut. It's just a really big cut. And they're going to fix it right up and stop the bleeding, I promise."

I could hear his breath slowing a little bit. "Liam says they're going to stick needles in me and sew me up. Will I . . . will I have a Frankenstein's monster foot? Forever?"

I never knew whether Liam was trying to help or trying to mess with Sam, but these kinds of things happened all the time, Liam telling Sam something and freaking him out. Darren was always certain Liam was messing with Sam.

"The way they put medicine in your foot to make it stop hurting is with needles, and you might need stitches, but once the cut heals heal up, your foot will be fine. Just maybe a little scar that will fade with time as your foot grows. Is Daddy there?"

"Yes," Sam said. "He's driving."

I heard Darren's voice. "He's going to be fine!" he shouted from the front seat. "I'm not even sure it'll need stitches! Maybe just glue or something!"

"Okay," I said. "You heard Daddy. You're going to be fine. But I'll stay on the phone with you for as long as you need me."

Sam was calmer now, and told me the story about

what had happened, how it was dinnertime and they'd been eating on the beach and then he was finished, so he was trying to race the waves to shore and wasn't looking where he was going and then stepped on something really hard. It was a shell and it was stuck in his foot and when he pulled it out the whole sand turned red.

I had the phone on speaker at that point, and Dax whispered to me, "When was his last tetanus shot?"

"Right before kindergarten," I whispered back.

Dax nodded. "Should still be good," he said.

"That must've been really scary," I said louder, to Sam.

"It was," he said, then his voice brightened a little. "I bet Abe will think it's really cool I saw so much blood and am going to go to a hospital."

Abe is Sam's best friend who is really into medical stuff. His parents are both surgeons and fully support his obsession.

"I bet he will," I said. "Maybe you can call to tell him about it after you get all fixed up."

"Oh, I will! Maybe I'll call him now. Bye, Mommy. Love you."

He clicked off and I shook my head. Then I turned to Dax. "I guess he's fine," I said.

"Mommy medicine is pretty powerful," he replied. "It even works over the phone from five thousand miles away."

I looked at the clock. "Two thirty," I said. "I guess we should go back to sleep?"

Dax lay back on the pillows. "It may take me a while to get back to sleep after that. My adrenaline always kicks into gear when I hear a phone go off while I'm sleeping. Probably something my body learned from being on call at the hospital."

I lay next to him and pulled the blanket up over us both.

He grabbed my hand under the sheets. It felt so nice to have him there, for support, for reassurance. I'd learned to be strong on my own when my kids needed me, but it was nice to lean on someone, too.

"I can tell you're a great mom," he said.

I smiled at him in the dim light. "I try."

He squeezed my hand. "So when do you leave Italy?" he said.

"I fly back to Rome . . . later today, and then home tomorrow morning."

"I'll be home in five weeks. Maybe we can FaceTime or WhatsApp until then?"

I looked over and saw how earnest his face was. How open, how vulnerable.

"I'm . . . I'm not good at relationships," I said, a feeling of panic fluttering in my heart. "I'll mess you up. I'll mess me up. I'm bad news."

Dax cocked his head at me. "You're bad news?"

"I was in two really great relationships in my life, and I fucked them both up royally. I hurt people I love. I hurt myself. I hurt my kids."

"So . . . your plan is to be alone forever?" Dax answered.

I was silent.

"Is that what you want?" he asked again softly.

"No," I said, equally softly. "But it's what I deserve." I

was afraid of having more, of screwing it up, of losing myself.

He opened his mouth, as if to protest, but then closed it again and moved closer to me, brushing his lips against my temple.

"I'm not banished," he whispered, "right? That was a warning, but I can proceed at my own risk?"

His hand wandered across my stomach, slid under my T-shirt. I shivered.

"You're not banished yet," I breathed, my fear replaced by desire.

He dragged the side of his hand over my clit and I sucked in my breath.

"Good," he said. "Let's start with fingers this time."

Fingers turned to tongues and then into more orgasms.

I lay beside him again, breathing hard. "Ready to go back to sleep now?" I teased.

"I think so," he said, wrapping his arms back around me.

We nodded off. Until a few hours later, when my phone started to ring, waking us again. This time I grabbed it before Dax did. It was a FaceTime call from Violet. I ran my fingers through my hair, glad I hadn't decided to sleep in the nude, and answered the call.

Samuel's smiling face was on the other side. "Mom!" he said. "Mom! Look! They fixed me all up. They did it with disintegrating stitches! And then with cream and a bandage and I'm supposed to try to mostly stay off it for a few days, but then I'll be okay again! I sent Abe pictures, and he thought it was so cool."

"I'm so glad, Sammy," I said, still sleepy but feigning alertness. "And I can't wait to see you in three days."

"Me too, Mom. And guess what. Dad says I can have as much screen time as I want tomorrow. That it counts as being sick."

I laughed. Darren and I had made a rule with the kids that, as long as they follow doctor's orders, when they're sick, they get as much screen time as they want.

"Well, make the most of it," I said. "You can marathon *Rocket Through Time*."

He smiled. "Maybe I will."

Violet popped on the screen. "We've gotta get back into the car," she said to him. "Hi, Mom. It's super late, but don't worry, I'll make sure Sammy goes to bed right when we get home, and I'll trade beds with him 'cause of his foot."

I waved and smiled at her. "Hi, Vi. Thanks for going to the hospital with Sammy and Dad and for looking out for Sam tonight—and always."

She shrugged. "It was getting kind of boring at the house anyway. Love you, Mom."

She clicked off the phone, and I found myself still smiling at the darkened screen. I don't know if it was the divorce or if it's just who she is, but when I'm not around, Violet has always been Sammy's protector.

Dax opened the bathroom door, dressed in his clothes from the night before. I hadn't realized he'd gotten out of bed.

"I should probably go home," he said. "Get some new clothes, burn myself some eggs."

I laughed, then wondered if I should offer to go out to

breakfast with him, or to scramble him some eggs. But before I could say anything, he spoke again.

"Will you be back at the library this afternoon?" he asked.

"I'm afraid not," I said. "I have to catch my flight to Rome." I got up from the bed and walked over to him. He looked a little unsure of what to do next, but then we wrapped our arms around each other and held each other close. I rested my cheek against his chest, and he pressed his lips against my forehead.

"Thank you for last night," I said, half wanting to tell him just how momentous this was for me, how much this night would mean even if we never saw each other again. But I didn't. I just pulled myself a little closer, held him a little tighter.

"You still didn't teach me to bake marshmallow pies," he answered. "Maybe when I get back to New York, I'll text to see if the offer still stands."

I pressed my lips gently against his. "Sounds good," I said.

I was so afraid, Gabe, so afraid of the power that I would have over Dax, that he would have over me, if anything more were to happen between us. That power scared me. It still does.

XXVi

I HAD NOTHING SPECIAL TO DO IN ROME, SO I DE-
cided to visit the Colosseum and look for gifts for my
kids. I ended up finding a graphic novel about Italian
artists for Sam, an Italia soccer jersey for Violet, and a
vinyl record of an Italian band called 883, which the man
at the record shop swore was fantastic, for Liam.

I treated myself to pasta at the hotel bar and fought
my desire to text Dax. I messaged Jay instead, since he
still hadn't replied with anything more than a thumbs-up
to my last text.

*I'll be home tomorrow, maybe we could find time to
catch up?*

I saw that he read it, and then a few minutes later he
wrote back: *Sure, once you're back, let me know when you're
free.*

I sighed; I knew that was code for *Let's see if you follow
through. How much do you actually want to see me?* I knew
this code, because I often employed it myself with people

I didn't want to outright reject but didn't really want to get together with either. When had I become one of those people for Jay? I knew I had to fix what was broken between us. I thought I might know how, but it wasn't only my choice to make.

xxvii

SOMETIMES THERE'S TOO MUCH ON MY MIND FOR
me to function well—it feels like all the thoughts are
fighting for attention, and it turns my mind into one big
discombobulated mess.

When I landed in New York, that was what my mind
was like, swirling with thoughts of Dax, and you, and
Bashir, and your photographs. I ended up meandering
through JFK, not quite sure which direction the signs
wanted me to go. After finally making it through pass-
port control and customs, I ended up at the bench that
you and I sat on with Violet the day you told me your
mom had died. What are the odds, right? This is why I
can't believe that life is random.

Not even in people's choice of television shows. For
years I've been watching *NCIS*. I discovered it after my
divorce, though it's been on since just after we graduated from college. I think you'd enjoy it. It's kind of like
Law & Order for the Navy, and you know how much I

love *Law & Order*. Anyway, there's this character in the first twenty seasons or so named Gibbs. And he has this list of rules that he lives by. There are a lot of them, but rule #39 is that there is no such thing as coincidence. He meant in criminal investigations, but it struck me when I heard it. Could that be possible? Could nothing at all be coincidental? Is there meaning in everything?

That day when I returned from Rome, when I saw the bench where you'd mourned your mom, it made me wonder: *Is it finally time to tell Samuel the truth?* I'd been living my life, moving forward, but always with this secret at the core, always with this piece of you I was keeping silent about. And as long as that secret was there, it seemed impossible to mourn you, mourn us, mourn what we could have been. Maybe that's why it felt so natural to tell people in Italy who you were to me. Maybe that's what my wish for freedom had meant at the Trevi Fountain. I realized that might be what I needed to share to heal my relationship with Jay, and with my parents, too.

All of that might not be enough to warrant shaking up our family again, except that as I'd spent time looking through Gabriel's photographs, hearing from Bashir how you'd changed his life, and seeing those photos in the library on Lampedusa, I couldn't help thinking that Sammy deserved to know you, too. To help him figure out who he is, where his talent came from, why he's tall and blond and the rest of us aren't. I thought of the feelings Dax had stirred up, the ways they'd felt joyous but also terrifying. Unburdening myself of this secret felt that way, too—the idea of freedom from the hold it had on my life was both joyful and terrifying. And it was the step I'd have to take to create a family based on truth, to let Sammy live a life based on truth. I hoped it would set us all free.

WHEN I GOT TO THE TAXI LINE, I MESSAGED DAR-ren: *Just wanted to let you know I've landed. See you tomor-row. Also: I was wondering if you might have a moment this week to talk?*

xxviii

WHEN DARREN BRINGS THE KIDS BACK TO MY HOUSE
on Saturday nights, there's less of a set tradition than
when I bring the kids to his. I know they'll arrive around
seven P.M., right after they finish dinner at his place.
Sometimes they walk over with Courtney and the twins
in tow. Sometimes they come with bags of treats, other
times not. Sometimes, if they're running late, Darren or
Courtney drives them the few blocks, the kids tumbling
over each other like puppies when they pull up in front of
my stoop. That night Darren drove them over, and Liam
jumped out of the car first to get a set of kid-sized
crutches from the trunk to hand to Sammy.

"Oh!" I said. "Hadn't heard about those." I was thinking about our house, the stairs, the narrow hallway the
bedrooms all spun off of.

"Only a couple more days," Sammy said. "And Liam
figured out how I can go up and down stairs on my butt,
so it's not a big deal." Darren's house had a lot of stairs, too.

Violet pulled everyone's backpacks out of the trunk, gave Liam his, and held on to hers and Sam's.

Then Darren drove away, and I hugged all three of my kids at once.

"How was Key West?" I asked, taking Sam's backpack from Violet.

"Fun minus the foot problem," Sammy said. "Lots of other stuff happened, too."

"Oh?" I asked. "Nice," Liam said at the same time.

"It was cool to see everyone and celebrate Nana's birthday," Violet added, "but we missed you."

I've wondered for years if Violet says things like that because she doesn't want me to feel bad when they have fun without me. Or if she truly means it. It's been so hard for me to know how much she's anticipating my feelings and how much she's sharing her own.

When we got to the stoop, Liam took Sam's crutches, and Sammy sat on his butt and bumped himself up the stairs backward.

"Easy peasy," he said.

"As easy as telling a story," I answered.

He smiled at me. "Speaking of stories," he said. "You won't believe what Harry did!" Harry was Darren's youngest sister's youngest son, who had just turned two.

"He's a real pain in the butt," Liam added. "I know he's little and whatever, but a real pain."

"He's not that bad," Violet added. "He's just a little kid."

"Little kids can be pains in the butt," Liam said.

"He's just kind of bananas," Sam said as he crutched

himself over to the living room couch and sat down. "He, like, literally ran around with a pull-up on his head for probably ten minutes, and then peed on the floor. Dude, the pull-up was on your head!"

Violet laughed and I did too.

"I know some two-year-olds who were equally bananas," I said.

"Not us," Liam said. "No way."

"Way," I said, ruffling his hair. "Now, I know you had dinner at your dad's, but what about dessert?"

"Well," said Sam, "we each got one cookie, but that doesn't seem like a whole dessert."

"Agree," said Liam. "How about we finish dessert here?"

I just love those kids, Gabe. They are my whole heart.

"Sounds like a perfect plan," I said. "I picked up some ice cream this afternoon."

Liam headed to the freezer, and Violet helped Sammy up so he could crutch his way to the table.

Italy seemed like a distant memory.

LATER THAT NIGHT, I WENT THROUGH YOUR BOXES again, looking for the right envelope that might have the Lampedusa photos in it. I knew what dates to look for, approximately, but there were so many envelopes, so many photographs.

I picked up the photo of you and your mom again and put it up on my dresser while I searched. I found what seemed like it might be the right envelope and opened it up. Inside was a flash drive that, when I opened it on my computer, had photos that looked like the ones from the library.

I opened up a new email to Eric Weiss: *Jackpot,* I typed, then attached one of the photos. The file size was so big that I uploaded the rest to my Google Drive and sent him the link. *Anything else you need?* I added at the bottom.

I put the flash drive back into the envelope and started getting ready for bed.

As I climbed under the covers, exhausted, my Whats-App pinged. It was Dax.

Hope you got home safely. Thanks again for such a great night. We brought 200 people to shore just after you left yesterday, so it's been incredibly busy. And now a case of strep throat seems to have broken out among the crew of the Maspero.

I wasn't sure what to write. I'd told him I was bad news, but being with him, eating dinner with him, sleeping next to him, walking hand-in-hand—it had felt wonderful, so much better than I was willing to admit to myself. But had it felt good enough to quell the fear of letting someone new into my heart?

Thanks, I wrote. *Home safe and sound. Thank you again for a great night too. And glad you were there to help the people who arrived. Good luck with all the strep. Hope you don't get it—*

His response came back quickly: *Even if I do, I have friends here with prescription pads, so should be okay.*

I gave him a thumbs-up, and our conversation seemed to end there.

Now that I was back in my house, back to reality, the whole trip to Italy seemed like a fever dream that somehow had real-life consequences. A fantasy with a serious realization at its core . . . I closed my eyes and wondered what I would dream about that night.

The answer, Gabe, was you.

XXIX

DARREN AND I DECIDED I WOULD COME OVER WITH the kids on Tuesday night so they could watch a movie with the twins, and we'd talk while they watched. Whenever I anticipate having a difficult conversation with someone, I run through the different possible responses in my mind so I have an expectation of where the conversation might go and know what to say in any eventuality. But I didn't anticipate how badly Darren would react to what I said. Since our divorce, we hadn't argued much. We both wanted to put what was best for the kids first; the trouble, of course, came when we didn't agree on what that was.

I thought it was better for Sammy to know the truth. Darren did not.

WHEN WE GOT TO HIS PLACE THAT NIGHT, COURT-ney had set up the living room with pizza, cut-up strawberries, popcorn, chocolate-covered blueberries, water thermoses for each kid, and two huge fleece blankets.

The kids sat around the coffee table, and Sage climbed into Violet's lap while Ivy sat as close to Sam as possible without actually being on his lap.

Darren and Courtney's house was beautiful, and fancier than mine. All Miele appliances, mahogany floors, and designer-brand furniture. They'd had a decorator come in and do it all for them, and on the rare occasions I went inside, I felt like I was in a magazine or at a photo shoot or something.

"So you wanted to talk," Darren said. "How about the study?"

I nodded.

Darren had a room on the first floor filled floor-to-ceiling with books that they called the study. There was a table in the center and a reading nook with two cushy chairs, a small table, and floor lamps. There was even a child-sized nook with a shelf of picture books for the girls, and a beanbag area with slightly older books for Sammy and Liam. I guess they figured Violet was old enough for the adult books now.

Darren sat down in one of the big chairs, and I sat down across from him.

"I want to talk about Samuel," I said.

"I swear I was watching him when he cut himself," Darren said. "It was a freak accident."

I smiled briefly. "I wasn't worried about that, Darren. I know you take great care of the kids."

He let out a breath. "Okay," he said. "I just . . . I've been living that moment over and over, wondering if there's anything I could've done to stop him from getting hurt. He was my responsibility, and I failed him."

When Darren says things like this, it reminds me why I loved him, why I married him, why I feel so bad for hurting him.

"You're a wonderful dad," I said. "I doubt there was anything you could have done differently." I cleared my throat and then looked up at Darren. "I think . . . I think it's time to tell him the truth."

"The truth?" Darren asked, his brow furrowing.

"The truth about Gabe," I said. Darren's whole demeanor changed; his face went cold and his back straightened—his body bracing for a fight. He started to protest, but I put up my hand. "Please. Just give me a second to explain."

He nodded, but I could tell he wanted to walk out of the room. He was fidgeting, looking anywhere but at me.

"So the tenth anniversary of Gabe's death is coming up. I'm working with his editor on a retrospective of his life, and they're going to relaunch his book with updates, and put a new show up of his photographs at the Joseph Landis gallery. As the person who owns the copyright to all his work, I'll have a say in what they show, but . . . regardless of whether I'm in it or not, with all the conversations coming up about Gabe, with all the time I'll be working on this and thinking about this, I just think it'll be better if Sam and the other kids know the truth. If I don't have to keep more active secrets from them."

Darren was quiet for a moment. Then he said, "So since this editor and publisher and gallery owner want to honor Gabe, you think we should tell Sam. You're letting strangers make decisions for our family. That's ridiculous."

"Is it, though? The outside world forces people's hands all the time. There are conversations we had with our kids about social justice, about racism, about antisemitism because of the outside world."

I could feel my heart racing. You know how much I hate confrontation.

"That's different," Darren said. "Those conversations are about the world and our place in it. This is really personal."

I tried another tack. "The longer we hide it, the longer we keep this secret, the bigger of a shock it will be when we tell it, and the more upset the kids will be that we lied to them," I said. This was the main reason I hadn't wanted to go down this road of secrets initially, the main reason I'd assumed that once I told Darren the truth, our whole family would know, the whole world, if we wanted to share.

"That's operating under the expectation that we're going to tell them at some point. What if we never do? Would it be so terrible for Sam to think I'm his biological dad for his whole life?" Darren responded, playing with a cuticle on his thumb.

I clenched my fists, though I couldn't say I was surprised he'd brought up this option. "We always said we'd tell him," I reminded him, doing my best to keep my voice steady, not to shout. "And what happens if he does a DNA thing for Ancestry.com or heaven forbid has a medical problem. That would force our hand, too."

"So let it," Darren said.

"Hmm?" I asked.

"Goddamn it, Lucy," he said. "If there's a medical crisis, and it would save his life, of course we'd tell him. But the likelihood of that happening is so small. You're grasping at straws here."

"Think about how that would feel: to have a medical crisis and then find out his life is a lie on top of that? I know this is right," I said. "I know in my heart this will be better for him, for all our kids, in the long run. Secrets fester. They push people away. They've made me push people I love away. They've put a wall up between us and our kids."

"So this is about you now?" Darren said. "You want to tell him because it'll be better for you? Because it sure as hell won't be better for me."

"Are you even listening to anything I've been saying to you? A piece of this is about me, sure, but mostly it's about Sammy. He should know where his talent comes from, his height, his blond hair. He shouldn't be building his identity on a lie. This really is about him. You're making it about you!" I was so angry I was shaking. I hated his hypocrisy, his self-righteousness, the way he completely glossed over the deal we'd made when we divorced—that we would tell Sammy one day. That we would find the right time. Now it seemed like Darren thought it would never be the right time.

"Of course I listened." He was one step away from shouting. "Goddamn it, Lucy. Why do you always think I don't listen to you?"

"Because you don't!" I said. "You never think my thoughts or feelings are as important as yours." I took a breath and looked him straight in the eyes, willing to draw a line, to take a stand for my happiness and for Sammy's. Because it was, in part, about my own survival, but more than that, it was about the survival of our family in the future. I'd seen how this secret had degraded my relationship with my parents and brother; I couldn't imagine what it would do to my relationships with my kids if I continued to keep it buried. "This was a courtesy," I said, my voice filled with as much steel as I could muster. "I don't need your permission to say anything I choose to my son."

Darren's face turned white. "You wouldn't dare," he said.

I shrugged, my heart pumping so hard, I could feel it in my neck.

"Just give me some time. You can't spring something like this on me. It's not right," Darren said. "There's no urgency here. We can talk again next week? We should do this together. We should make this choice together. We agreed when we separated—he is both of ours."

I decided to quit while I had the upper hand. And before I said something I truly regretted. "I'll call you after the kids are in bed next Tuesday," I told him.

He nodded. "I need a minute," he said. I could see his hands shaking now. "But feel free to go catch the end of the movie with the kids."

I clearly had been dismissed, so I headed into the living room, grabbed a slice of cold pizza, and sat down on the edge of the couch.

I looked at Sam, cuddled up with Ivy, and it struck me that he actually wasn't biologically related to the twins at all. Once we told Sam, there would be a huge ripple effect, not just in what he knew about himself, but in the contours of our entire family unit. He would still be their brother, of course, but his understanding about what they shared would shift.

I could understand why Darren wanted time, wanted to delay, but I knew that sooner or later, the truth would have to come out. It wasn't fair to Sammy otherwise.

XXX

WEEKS WITH THE KIDS ALWAYS FEEL FASTER THAN the ones without them.

That Friday, while the kids were in school and still staying at my place, I saw Darren's name pop up on my caller ID. Worried that something had happened and the school had called him before me, I picked up quickly.

"Hey," I said. "Is everything okay?"

"I didn't want to wait until Tuesday," he said. "To tell you that my answer is absolutely not. I don't want to tell Sam. Now or ever. If something medical forces our hand in the future, so be it, but I'm his father and that's all he has to know. And if you tell him anything without me, I'm going to our lawyer to fight for sole custody."

I was in my home office and got up to shut the door, my phone against my cheek, even though there wasn't a chance anyone was there to hear. I was so angry I could barely contain myself.

"Darren," I said. "You would never win that fight.

We'd be in court for years and you'd bleed us all dry, emotionally and financially. Are you insane? You are his father. You will always be his father. It would be the same if we'd used a sperm donor to conceive, or we'd adopted Sammy. You'd still be his dad. But he should know his whole story. It's only fair."

"Not to me," Darren said. "The last thing I need is him turning into you, comparing me to Gabriel Samson for the rest of my life. And how will it look to all our friends when they find out you cheated on me? When they realize I've been raising the child of that affair?"

I could feel a headache coming on and massaged my temple. My computer pinged, telling me I had a meeting in fifteen minutes. "Darren, I can't have this conversation right now. I'm working. That's why we'd agreed on a time to talk. And as far as what our friends think: First of all, they might not even find out. And if they do, they'll probably think you're an amazing guy for raising Samuel as your own, and I'll be the awful wife who cheated. You'll be the hero, and I'll be the one with a scarlet letter painted on my chest."

"As you should be," Darren said.

I felt a charge of rage surge through my body. He's rarely cruel, but once in a while, he'll say something that cuts so deep I don't know what else to call it.

"Darren, you're a fucking asshole. I've got to go. We can talk more about this on Tuesday night."

The line was silent for a moment.

"I said no," he said.

"And I said yes," I replied. "You don't have veto power.

I'm willing to keep talking until we come to a conclusion we can both live with. But don't you ever threaten to fight for sole custody again or I will go nuclear on you."

"Go," he said. "If you have something new to tell me on Tuesday, call. Otherwise, my refusal still stands."

I didn't even bother saying goodbye. How could he make that kind of threat? How could he be so cruel? There were many moments with Darren that made me remember why I married him, but this one made me remember why I divorced him.

I navigated to the Teams chat with my assistant. *Versha*, I typed, *I need to take a walk. I'll be back for the meeting.*

I headed out into the early March chill. It was Sammy's birthday month. Mine, too. Sammy had told me he wanted to celebrate his birthday by doing a scavenger hunt at the Met he'd learned about from Abe. Would Darren and I be speaking by March 15? Were we speaking now?

I looked at my phone, wanting to call someone, but the problem with secrets is that when you keep them well, you box yourself into a corner when you really need someone to talk to. Kate was arguing a case in court this week. Eva turned her phone off when she worked in the studio. Dax's name flashed in my mind. I could call Dax. But that wouldn't be fair to him. As amazing as our connection had been, I wasn't sure I was ready for things to get serious, and calling him when I was in crisis would send a different message.

I put my phone in my coat pocket and concentrated on breathing in the winter air, the feel of the cold clearing my airways, the steady rhythm of my feet on the pavement clearing my mind. If I could refocus, I'd know what I had to say in this meeting.

But what could I say to Darren that would change his mind? And what would I do if he didn't?

xxxi

THAT NIGHT AT DINNER, THE KIDS AND I DID OUR usual "best, worst, and wished" list around the table. I knew I couldn't say my real worst and wished. And wondered if the kids ever hold back their answers from me. I hadn't contemplated it before, but I realized it was probably true. I was certain that there were things Violet didn't want me knowing about, or her brothers knowing about. And probably the same with the boys.

"Best," I said, "dinner with you three."

"Mom, you always say that!" Sammy replied. He was doodling on his plate with his index finger, using ketchup as paint. I couldn't quite see what he was making.

"It's always true," I answered. "Worst: I tried to put milk in my coffee today at lunch, and it had curdled."

"Good thing we had muffins for breakfast today instead of cereal," Liam added.

"Very good thing," I said. "That milk smelled vile."

"And wished?" Violet asked.

"Wished life were simpler," I said.

She nodded solemnly. "Me too."

I had to hide a smile. Fifteen is pretty grown-up, but sometimes I look at her and she seems like a little kid in my borrowed dress and high heels, pretending to be an adult.

"What about your other two?" I asked.

"Best: I finally got my robot through the maze in Robotics Engineering," Violet said. "Worst: I tripped over the bottom of my jeans and really bashed my knee on the ground when I was walking to the subway after school. I think it's black and blue."

"Oh no!" I said. "I'll get your jeans shortened—give them to me when you take them off tonight."

"It's not a big deal," Violet said.

"It's avoidable," I said, "so we might as well avoid it."

"My turn," Sammy said. "Best: One of my drawings got chosen for the school art show! Worst: Abe's drawing, which I thought was the best thing he's drawn all year, didn't. Wished: It did, so that we could both be in the show together and our families could all go out for ice cream after."

"Hey, congratulations!" Violet said. "Sorry 'bout Abe, though."

"You're a better artist than he is anyway," Liam said. "You're probably a better artist than any kid in your grade."

I could see Sammy's cheeks turning pink. "Thanks, Liam," he said.

Liam shrugged. "Whatever, it's true," he said. "I wouldn't say it otherwise."

I laughed. "I'm excited for the art show. Do you know when it is yet?"

Sammy nodded. "It's on a paper in my backpack, but I think it's in two weeks. Or maybe three."

"We'll make sure we're all there," I said, speaking for the whole family.

I knew Darren, Courtney, and the girls would want to go. Though I didn't know if they'd want to go with me. Or if Darren would, at least. I wasn't sure if Courtney knew who Sammy's biological dad was. Or where he got his artistic talent or his curly blond hair or his dimple. It was times like these that I wished you and your mom both had had a chance to meet Sam. It would've been so cool for her to see her talent passed down to her grandson, to give him lessons, to let him look at her work, to be someone he could look up to and learn from. I keep thinking I should talk to Eva about mentoring him.

"What about you, Liam?" I asked. I always feel for Liam, my quiet, thoughtful, introverted boy stuck between two talkative extroverts.

"Best," he said, "you gave me a salami sandwich for lunch. Worst: My teacher made me read Shakespeare out loud in class today. Wished: We could read nonfiction quietly to ourselves in English class instead."

"Which play are you reading?" I asked him.

"*Romeo and Juliet*," he said. "And I had to be Mercutio. The real worst part is the teacher said I did a good job, so she's going to choose me again."

Violet laughed. "That's cool that you're good at reading Shakespeare."

Liam sighed. "I think it's because it's all so rhythmic. I can kind of feel the meter when I read it."

"That's actually pretty impressive, Liam," I said. "Most people probably don't pick up on that so quickly—or at all."

He sighed again. "I guess. I just prefer not to read out loud."

"Could you ask your teacher not to choose you to read again?" Violet asked him.

He shrugged. "I think it's part of my participation grade. So probably I should just do it."

"Did I ever tell you about my favorite Shakespeare play?" I asked.

The kids shook their heads.

"Well, it's not quite my favorite," I said, "but it means a lot to me. It's one I was studying in college on September eleventh, in 2001, when the planes hit the Twin Towers."

"I can't believe you lived through history like that, Mom," Violet said.

"Sometimes I can't either," I told her.

"So what was the play?" Sammy asked.

"*Julius Caesar*," I said. "And there are some lines that will be stuck in my head forever. They go: 'There is a tide in the affairs of men / Which, taken at the flood, leads on to fortune; / Omitted, all the voyage of their life / Is bound in shallows and in miseries. / On such a full sea are we now afloat, / And we must take the current when it serves, / Or lose our ventures.'"

"Ms. Shah would like your Shakespeare reading, too, Mom," Liam said. "You got the rhythm down."

I smiled. "Thanks, Liam. I appreciate it."

"What does it mean, Mom?" Sammy asked.

"Well," I said, "to me it means that we get to decide what we do with things we're handed in our lives. Daddy and I got divorced, right, and that could have gone a lot of different ways. We could've each fought to have you guys with us all the time. We could have decided we never wanted to talk to each other again. But we both made a choice to make decisions we thought were best for you all. We decided to give each other grace and try to be good parents to you three, even if we couldn't be a good husband and wife to each other. Things will happen in your lives, and it's up to you to decide how to move forward."

I saw Liam nodding. "Maybe reading Shakespeare's not that bad," he said. "I guess he's kind of a smart guy."

"Can dinner be done?" Sammy asked.

I nodded. "If you're done, just bring your plate to the sink."

Sammy popped off his chair. I saw his plate and it looked like the ketchup was an attempted duplication of the design of the stained-glass window above the front door.

Violet got up, too.

Liam lingered a moment longer. "Mom?" he said.

"Liam?" I asked back.

He smiled, but then his face was serious again. "Did you and Dad both want us all the time?"

I nodded. "Of course. But we thought it would be

better for you three and for our family if you were raised by both your mom and your dad equally. Do you think we made the right choice?"

Liam was quiet for a moment. "Yeah, I guess so. Sometimes I wish we just had one place to stay, you know? But if we lived with you, I'd miss Dad a lot. And if we lived with Dad, I'd miss you a lot. So I guess this is the best choice given the situation. That's what you were talking about, right? There's a situation, and you have to choose the best option after that."

I gave Liam a hug. "That's exactly right," I said. "I love how thoughtful and insightful you are, my sweet boy."

I waited for Liam to duck out of the hug, but he stayed. And I stayed. And we hugged for a minute, maybe two.

"Are you okay?" I asked him.

"Yeah," he said. "Just, some things are a lot to think about."

"I agree," I told him, resting my cheek against the top of his head. He'd be taller than me soon, no question.

THAT NIGHT I GOT A MESSAGE FROM DAX. SEEING his name in my phone while sitting in my house in Brooklyn felt surreal—and made my stomach flip. I clicked it open, my body humming. *Just wanted to see how you were doing*, he wrote. *I rewatched your TV show. Brought back some bittersweet memories of watching with Zac. But I really enjoyed the show itself.*

I looked at his words. I thought about the conversation the kids and I just had over dinner. I had a situation. I had a choice. Over and over, I had a choice: to pursue my feelings for Dax and his for me, or to pull away before I got too attached. Would I change the one I'd been making?

I took a deep breath, put on pajamas, and closed the app. I'd decide tomorrow.

XXXii

THE NEXT NIGHT WHEN I DROPPED THE KIDS OFF AT Darren and Courtney's, I tried to figure out what Courtney knew, but her face didn't give anything away.

"See you next week!" I waved to the kids as they walked inside.

"Bye!" they chorused.

As I walked back home, feeling their absence in the quiet that surrounded me, my phone buzzed in my pocket. I pulled it out, and there was another message from Dax: *I was thinking: Was the Rio character inspired by your photographer friend?*

I smiled involuntarily. I loved that Dax put that together. So few people knew I had based that character on Gabe. There was never a reason to talk about it, to tell anyone. But it was true. I thought again about the conversation I'd had with the kids about making choices. And I decided to make a different one.

You might be the only person who's ever figured that out, I wrote back.

Do I get a gold star? came back quickly.

Sure, I answered, adding a gold star emoji to my message. *There you go!*

I'll treasure it, he replied.

The conversation ended, but I realized I didn't really want it to. That as much as my head was terrified of letting Dax in, my heart wanted to. I decided to dive into uncharted waters, hoping against hope I wouldn't drown— or take anyone else down with me.

It's late over there, I said, opening up the conversation again.

Having trouble sleeping, Dax responded.

I took a deep breath. *Want to talk about it?* I typed.

He didn't respond for a moment. Then I saw the dots starting and stopping and starting and stopping. I put my phone back in my pocket and continued the walk home. Just as I was heading up the steps of my front stoop, my phone vibrated again.

Actually, that would be really nice was all it said.

I wondered what he had typed and deleted, what he had almost said but didn't.

I'll give you a call in a minute, I typed from my stoop.

Butterflies fluttered in my stomach. I took a deep breath, unlocked my door, and, after hanging up my coat, sat down on the couch and called Dax.

"Lucy?" His voice was deeper than I remembered, but maybe it was just because he was tired.

"Hey," I said, trying to calm down the butterflies. "Are you okay?"

"It's just been a rough day," he said. "I took a kid off one of the migrant boats yesterday, and he a fever and a nosebleed. I could tell from the dried blood on his clothing and under his nails that this was far from his first. And he was pale and tired. I asked his parents how long this had been happening, and they said it had started while they were in Tunisia. They thought maybe it was something in his diet while they were traveling. I looked at him more closely, and something in my gut said he had leukemia, just like Zachariah. I sent them to the island hospital for a rush CBC test. The results came back this morning, and I was right. I had hoped I wasn't, but . . . deep down I knew. So this morning I went to the hospital and, along with the island pediatrician, told his parents that their seven-year-old had cancer and that the Red Cross would process them quickly and helicopter them to the hospital in Palermo. I was as upbeat as possible, but after they left for the Red Cross center, I was so sick about it. And I just keep thinking about Zac, about the treatment he had to go through that Nasser will have to go through, how sick it had made him, how sick Nasser will be. The images keep flashing through my mind and it's just . . . it's hard to sleep," he said.

My heart ached for him, ached for Nasser and his family. All I wanted was to put my arms around Dax. I knew that would mean more than any words I could find. But we were thousands of miles apart. "I'm so sorry," I told him. "I wish I could hold you right now."

"I wish you could, too," he said, his voice gravelly.

I scrolled through my mind for phrases, for stories, for anything I could think of that might offer a small bit of comfort.

"I think a lot about destiny," I said to him. "About the idea of fate. And I wonder if you were meant to be there for Nasser. If another doctor might have missed the signs, might have ordered a different test or tried antibiotics first, might have delayed his diagnosis. Maybe it was meant to be you, there, to give Nasser the best chance possible."

I heard Dax take in a breath, then let it out. "I like that perspective."

"It might not make it any easier," I said, "but maybe at least the pain might be purposeful."

"I can take the pain if it's purposeful," Dax said. "If me being here gave Nasser a better chance at life, then I'm glad I was."

My heart squeezed for him, Gabe. He seemed so broken, but so brave; so sad, but so smart. And, I knew, so alone.

"You are a good man, Dax Armstrong," I said to him.

I heard him laugh. "You are a good woman, Lucy Carter Maxwell. Thank you for that." Then he yawned.

"You ready to go to sleep now?" I asked.

"Mm," he said. "I think so. I think now I'll be able to. Good night, Lucy."

"Good night, Dax," I said.

We both clicked off our phones. I sat on my couch a little longer, thinking about him, thinking about our night together. And then I closed my eyes and relived that night in my mind. His kisses, his fingers, the warmth of his body, the softness of his lips, that heat of him inside me. For the first time in a long time there was another man in my heart, Gabe, another man who had found the way into my soul.

XXXiii

AT EXACTLY TEN A.M. ON SUNDAY MORNING, EVA
rang my doorbell for our biweekly walking date.

I look forward to our Sunday morning walks the way
I looked forward to library day each week in elemen-
tary school. Then, I never knew which story we would
hear, which book I'd take home with me. Now, I never
know where Eva's and my meandering conversations will
go, which stories will imprint themselves on my heart.
Eva has a lot to say. She's experienced so much, and it's
given her a fascinating perspective on the world.

"Good morning," I said when I answered the door.

"You look chipper today," she replied. "Perhaps a little
happier than usual?"

"Perhaps," I said. She and I hadn't spoken since before
I'd left for Italy, and I knew she'd love hearing the details
about my trip and about meeting Dax. But what I really
wanted her opinion on was Darren and Samuel and what

I should do. "You look happy, too," I told her. "Anything new going on in your world?"

"Well, darling," she said, "it's been a busy two weeks."

I linked my arm in hers, and the two of us started walking to our coffee shop. Eva told me about running into someone she knew from her fine art days, about his invitation to take her to the opera. "Sometimes," she said, "you think a part of your life is over, but then someone comes along and takes you to the opera!"

"To the opera!" I said, marveling at how much younger, how might lighter she looked while telling me this story.

Eva smiled. "We saw each other at the market, in the tea aisle. It turns out we both enjoy a cup of Lady Grey in the afternoon."

"And then?" I asked.

"We got to talking," she said as we walked. "He's a widower—his wife had been quite a talented sculptor and passed a few years ago. He's also a retired judge and an opera aficionado. And quite handsome."

I laughed. "There must be something in the air," I told her. "I met a remarkable man in Italy. He's a New Yorker but working there for an NGO." Just talking about Dax made my heart beat a bit faster.

"A philanthropic doctor," she said. "Are you finally ready to entertain the idea of another man?"

I thought about how she'd phrased it, what that meant. "Entertain the idea, yes," I told her. "But I think maybe it's good that he's in Italy right now." As much as I wanted to be with Dax, as much as he kept sneaking into my thoughts, I was still scared.

She nodded. "Just remember: Time is finite."

And then I thought about you. "I know," I told her. She patted my hand. "I know you do, darling."

"There's actually something I want to ask you about," I said. "I think it's time to tell Samuel the truth. There's going to be a big gallery show and retrospective and a new edition of Gabriel's book to commemorate ten years since he died, and it just doesn't seem fair to keep this secret anymore. I want to tell the truth—I want Samuel to know about his biological father, to feel connected to him. I wanted to be honest from the beginning, but Darren disagreed. We said we'd tell him eventually, when the time was right, and I think that time is now, but Darren suddenly doesn't want to tell him ever. He thinks it'll be more harmful to tell the truth than to keep the secret. What do you think?"

"Come," Eva said, pointing me toward a bench.

We sat together on the promenade, looking over the water to Manhattan.

"The truth comes out," she said. "From what I've seen in my eighty-nine years, always, the truth comes out in the end. You know that during the war I was sent to a convent and then adopted by Christian parents—wonderful, kind people who wanted to keep me safe. Well, there were many parents like that who adopted babies even younger than I was. Little ones not even a year old, toddlers who had no memory of another life. And when the war ended and those babies' biological parents had perished, some of the Christian parents kept the secret from the children, pretended that they were their own. And mostly it was fine, but there were always questions: the way people looked, talents they had. When those children later found out the truth, many of them said similar things: that their lives finally felt like they made sense. That they had always felt like they didn't quite belong, but they couldn't quite put their finger on why. And then, it all fell into place. Their lives felt more stable, more solid. I'm not saying that's how your Samuel feels—his situation is different—but those observations, the similarity of them, has always stuck with me. Especially because it could have been me experiencing them, if I'd been some years younger."

It was an interesting connection.

"So how did they feel about their families after they found out?" I asked.

"Often there was some anger at being lied to, but also understanding about why, and then in the end, the love overcame it all. One person I spoke to said that she felt like she had gained a second family but still had the family that raised her and loved her. Like with an open adoption, your family expands. And with divorce and death, remarriage, you can have multiple fathers and mothers. There isn't just one way to define a family."

"My kids already have two mothers, essentially," I said. "They know firsthand that some family members are connected by blood, and others are connected solely by love."

"Lead with that," Eva said. "Lead with love."

I nodded. "Thank you," I said. "Now, tell me about your night at the opera!"

Eva's face glowed as she told me about her evening out—they saw *La Bohème*—and as I listened, I kept thinking: *Lead with love.*

XXXIV

LATER THAT DAY, A PACKAGE ARRIVED AT MY HOUSE
from your publisher. It was a printout of the updated version of your book, with the additional images Eric had
asked for and his captions, for my review and approval. I
spent the rest of the day looking through the pages and
thinking about your life. Your photos from Lampedusa
had been added in, together with an update from Eric
about the Syrian refugee crisis ten years later as well as
Lampedusa ten years later.

What struck me about the updates was that they were
about situations, about the general contours of a group of
people, but not about specific individuals. Not about the
little girl whose photo you had taken with her doll, for
example. After meeting Bashir, it made me wonder, how
were these particular people? The ones whose lives you'd
touched, who'd touched yours—what happened to them?
I wondered if it would be possible to track them down.
Yes, these photos represented something larger, but they

were also photos of individuals, of sons, daughters, best friends. What had happened to them?

I sat down at my computer and typed Eric a message:

Hi Eric,

I just got the book pages and had an idea. Is there any way to find the actual people in the photographs? To see how they are now? I'd love for the readers to be able to see each person as an individual instead of as a representation of something larger. Not sure if it's possible, but a thought I had. One I think Gabe would appreciate.

—Lucy

Eric must be on email at all times because I got a message back from him almost right away.

Lucy,

I love the idea, but not sure it's possible. But maybe ask Bashir? See if he knows what happened to some of the people he knew on Lampedusa? I'll be interested to hear.

—Eric

I went back over to the pages with my iPhone and snapped the images of the kids that Gabe had photographed. Then I sent a note to Bashir asking if he knew who they were and if he had any idea of how to contact them. It seemed a long shot, but you never knew what would happen unless you tried. So I tried. Honestly, I'm not sure why it was important to me. The book was lovely as it was. But meeting Bashir, knowing how you'd spent time with those kids and seen them as individuals separate and apart from the crisis they had found themselves in, it made me think you'd want this, too.

BEFORE I WENT TO BED THAT NIGHT, BASHIR HAD sent me the names of the kids. And information on three of them—one was back living on Lampedusa, working as a cultural mediator for UNHCR. Another one was picking fruit and making oil in the olive fields in southern Italy. The third one had made his way to London. And then, of course, there was Bashir.

As I was falling asleep, I had another idea: What if Bashir took over your role? What if he took photos of his friends now? Of the other places now? What if we had new visuals, not just new words? You always found images more powerful—and you were right. Now that wars are being fought on social media as well as on the ground, the images are what bring people in, make them care, make them feel.

THE NEXT MORNING, I CALLED ERIC. I TOLD HIM MY second idea. He loved it, but he knew the publisher didn't have the funds to pay for it. "Try the Joseph Landis gallery, though," he said. "If they like the idea, then they can sell the photographs. Bashir can make money, can have a New York show to his name. You'll be helping him out, too."

"What about funding any travel?" I asked.

"Tell me what you want him to cover," Eric said. "I'll see what kind of budget I have, as long as the AP gets the photos, too."

He really is such a decent guy, Gabe. You were lucky to work for someone who cared so much about you, who respected what you did. A part of me wonders if he feels slightly responsible for your death. I wonder if that's why he's been so helpful, and more than that, so eager to keep your memory alive, to keep your work alive. I never asked, but I assume he's the one that sent you to Gaza. Did you ask him not to go? Had you already told him you wanted to come home for good?

After I got off the phone with Eric, I kept thinking about you, about war, about humanity. I couldn't shake the feeling of wanting to talk to someone about it— wanting to talk to Dax about it. *Hey,* I messaged him. *You around?*

My phone rang a minute later.

"Hey yourself," he said. "I'm sneaking a sandwich for lunch on the boat, what's going on?"

"Did you make the sandwich?" I asked, sitting down on my living room couch, thinking about how good it felt to hear his voice, how warm it made me feel.

Dax laughed. "No," he said. "That's how bad my cooking skills are."

"I was trying to gauge that," I said, and could feel the smile spreading across my face.

He laughed again. I loved that he could joke about his flaws. It took confidence to do that. "What are you up to?" he asked.

"Thinking about war," I said.

"And you called me?" I could hear him swallow. "I'm not sure how I should feel about that."

"I was thinking about our conversation outside the gelato shop," I told him, "and I thought you might understand. Or . . . might be able to help me untangle my thoughts."

"I'm here," he said, his voice more serious.

"I've been talking to Gabe's editor about shifting the focus of the gallery show to the idea of then and now. Photographs capture a moment in time, you know? And if you go back to that person or that place a decade or two later, it'll be entirely different. I'm going to pitch the idea to the gallery owner."

"You can tell him our body's cells regenerate on an average of every seven to ten years," he said. "After a decade, you're essentially a completely new person on a cellular level."

"Oh!" I said. "I hadn't known that. It kind of follows what I've been thinking, though. Because our cells are new, but we're still us. As much as things are different, so much is the same. Gabe died in Gaza, and the same hate that ended his life is ending so many more."

"It makes you wonder if it will ever stop," Dax said, "Doesn't it?"

"Exactly," I said. "It makes me wonder if one day, we'll all make peace with one another, learn how to coexist. Or if one day the human race really will destroy itself, blow itself up because there are people in power who care about pride or ideology or absolute victory more than they do any human life, who don't think of people being killed as daughters, mothers, fathers, brothers, sisters, sons."

"We need to find the light, not the darkness," Dax said, his warm voice reaching through the phone to envelop me.

"Yes," I answered. It was like he was reading my mind.

"Have you ever watched *Star Trek*?" he asked.

"I'm not a Trekkie," I said, wondering where he was going with this, "but I've watched some of the movies."

He laughed. "I am a total Trekkie, and if you hang around me long enough, I promise I will convert you. But anyway, what I was going to say is that one of the things I find fascinating about the series is that while the Federation fights other beings—there's always some big bad like the Borg or the Gorn or the Dominion—humans themselves are at peace, Earth is at peace. It's like Gene Roddenberry realized that the only way to explore other worlds was for humanity to get it together first. Or maybe he created his world based on the idea that once we knew there were other species out there, we Earthlings would find our own sameness."

"I love that," I said. "Finding our sameness. You actually might make a Trekkie out of me." I imagined what it would be like to sit next to him on the couch, under a blanket, watching starship captains travel through space.

"Sometimes I think about what's going on in our world," he said, "and I wonder why we're even here."

"Gabe would say we make our own purpose," I said, remembering the conversation you and I had on the day we met, about what constituted a life well-lived.

"I like that," he said. "And I guess it's true—we do make our own purpose. And I like how in this moment, part of my purpose is to talk with you."

"I like that, too," I said, my voice soft.

And I like that part of my purpose was to talk to him.

XXXV

DARREN DIDN'T CALL ME THAT TUESDAY TO TALK
about Samuel.

And when I called him, he didn't pick up.

He didn't even send a text.

XXXVI

ONE THING I'VE LEARNED IS THAT GROWING UP
means friendships take on a different shape. Kate and
Julia are still my closest friends—Kate more so than
Julia—but if I see them once a month, I'm lucky. Usually,
it's more like once every two or three months. We text
and FaceTime and follow each other's social media to
stay connected. And we all recognize that not seeing
each other isn't because we don't want to, but because our
schedules and our kids' schedules are so insane all the
time that hardly anything ever aligns.

Which is why when all three of us get together, it's
kind of a miracle. That miracle happened two weeks after
I got back from Italy. I think Julia and Kate were worried
about my mental state given the impulsive trip to Europe,
the ten-year anniversary of your death, and that my forty-
fourth birthday was in two weeks, so they made the time
to see me. Which: fair. And also: why they're my best
friends.

Julia got married right before COVID and had a son three years ago. Kate's kids are around Vi's and Liam's ages, and she's still living in the house she and Tom bought right after Samantha, her second, was born. When Darren and I got divorced, Kate took me out one night, and, after we'd split a bottle of wine, she said to me, "I'm jealous. You get to try someone new."

I know she loves Tom, but I also know she's been bored with him for years. It's like the older she gets, the more adventurous she wants to be, and the older Tom gets, the safer he wants to be. They started out similar and now she's hoping to take a cruise to Antarctica while their kids are at camp for the summer, and he's hoping to play golf at their country club. Both valid choices, both valid desires, but just not quite the same.

We met up in Manhattan at Bad Roman, a restaurant sort of near my office, near enough to Grand Central for Kate to get home, and down the 1 line for Julia, who had moved to a two-bedroom on the Upper West Side when Owen was born. She was a freelance designer now, working part-time from home.

When I walked in, Kate was already there and handed me a present.

"Thank you," I said. "You didn't need to."

"I know," she said. "But I wanted to. How Instagrammable is this place?"

I looked around. She was right—it was beautiful and looked a bit like it was designed with social media in mind. The wait staff walked by with gorgeous plates of food and placed them on meticulously set tables in a room filled with flowers and sparkling lights.

"It's gorgeous," I answered. "And supposed to be delicious, too."

We sat at the bar and each ordered a glass of wine, waiting for Julia to arrive.

"I don't want to make you say anything twice," Kate said, "so I'm going to hold off on asking you about your trip to Italy."

"I appreciate it," I said, wondering how to spin my trip there, how to talk about Dax. "How's everything going with you?"

She smiled. "It's nice to be out for the night in the city. Nice to see you. And it's only been about a month this time!"

"Go us," I said as the bartender set our glasses of wine in front of us.

Kate laughed and then picked up her wine.

I picked up mine, and we clinked them together, looking into each other's eyes until we both took a sip.

"And how's Tom?" I asked, after I swallowed.

"Same Tom," Kate said, taking another sip of her wine. "But we decided something big, I think."

"Oh yeah?" I asked, wondering what this could be.

"We decided to take separate vacations this summer. I'm going to spend a week in Iceland, and he's going to spend a week off from work at home, golfing and gardening. Other than for friends' bachelor or bachelorette parties a hundred years ago, we've always traveled together. But when he suggested we take a week off to garden and go to the club this summer instead of traveling somewhere, I knew we had to figure out a better way. He didn't like the idea at first, but I think he's getting used to it now, maybe even looking forward to it. I told him he could take complete control of the garden and the landscaping, and I wouldn't say a word, which made him happy."

I was glad they'd figured something out that worked for both of them.

"Iceland sounds fun," I said. "Do you want a travel buddy?"

Kate looked at me, then patted my hand. "I would love to travel with you, Lu, but for this trip, my plan is to go solo. I want to make all the choices, do all the things I want to do, not have to take anyone else into consideration. I want a selfish vacation."

I laughed. "That sounds like a perfect plan," I said.

I was alone so often, a selfish vacation wouldn't be that much different from usual life, but I knew for Kate it was huge.

A moment later, I was enveloped in the scent of almonds and coconut and turned to see Julia behind me. She'd started wearing that Laura Mercier perfume just before she'd met Sebastian, and now no matter where I am when I smell that combination of almonds and coconut, I expect to see Julia turn the corner.

"Jules!" I said, giving her a hug. Her cheek was still chilled from the outside air where it pressed against mine, and she handed me a gift bag when I turned to face her.

"It's a big container of your favorite banana pudding from Magnolia," she said. "I put an ice pack in there, too, to make sure it keeps until you get home."

"Thank you," I said.

Kate slid down from her stool and grabbed both our wines. "Let's head over to the table," she said.

Kate and Julia weren't friends on their own, but since they'd both been friends with me for so long, they had their own sort of relationship.

"How are the girls?" Julia asked Kate, as we followed the hostess to our table.

"So big, it's absurd," she said. "Victoria has been researching colleges—she has her eye on Wesleyan at the moment—and Samantha's in high school now, too. She just introduced us to her first serious girlfriend—they've been together since homecoming in October. For the time being, my daughters are both happy and healthy, which is really all I can ask for."

"College," Julia said. "Wow. I can't imagine Owen in college. Even 3-K seems like a big step."

"Yeah, 3-K is huge," Kate said.

We sat down and ordered, and then Kate looked at me. "Okay," she said, "now spill. What's going on?"

So I told them about Eric Weiss's call, about the address, the trip to Rome, and meeting Bashir. I told them about traveling to Lampedusa and my time with Dax. They *oooh*ed and gasped at all the right places.

"And so?" Julia said. "Have you heard from him since?"

I laughed. "I have," I said. "I think he wants something real, but I don't know."

"It's so romantic," Julia said. "You always have the best meet-cutes. Sebastian and I were a setup. Bor-ing."

"How are you feeling about the tenth anniversary?" Kate asked quietly.

I looked at her. She knew about Samuel. I hadn't told Julia yet, but I felt like it was time. Now that Bashir knew, now that Dax knew, it didn't seem fair to keep it from one of my two closest friends.

"Jules," I said, not answering the question. "I have something I need to tell you."

Her face became serious, her dark eyes focusing on me, one eyebrow raised as if to say *Why me and not Kate?*

"Sure," she said.

"I've been keeping a secret for the last ten years. It's about Samuel," I started, then took a sip of wine.

Julia put her hand on my arm. "He's Gabe's son?" she asked softly.

I stared at her. How could she have known? I looked at Kate.

"I didn't say anything," Kate said, holding up her hands.

"Lucy," Julia said, "I know what Gabe looked like. I know what Darren looks like. How could I not know?"

I felt my cheeks get hot. "Does everyone know?" I asked her.

"Definitely not," she said. "Not everyone knew Gabe, knew what he meant to you. And some people might not want to put it together."

"I don't think Tom has any idea," Kate volunteered.

"When did you figure it out?" I asked Julia.

"I don't know," she said, "maybe around his second birthday, when his hair got long enough to curl, when his dimple started to become really pronounced, I suspected. And then as he grew, it became more and more obvious, not just from the physical side of things, but some things he says sound so much like things Gabe would say, his talent for art—I remembered when you told me Gabe's mom was an artist. It all just made sense."

"And you're not mad?" I asked, my eyes getting teary. "You're not mad I didn't tell you?"

Julia shrugged. "I was at first—or more just sad that you didn't think you could trust me. But then I realized there was a lot you were dealing with and that there were a lot of reasons you might not have wanted to say the words out loud. I forgave you a long time ago."

I wiped the tears off my cheeks and leaned over to hug Julia. "I'm sorry," I said to her. "It's not at all that I don't trust you. I do. But you were right, there was so much going on."

I felt her arms around me, but then she pulled away. "Kate knew?" she said. And now I could tell she was a little hurt.

"Right place, right time," Kate said. "I called during a breakdown, it could've just as easily been you who called."

Julia nodded.

"She's right about the timing," I said. "I spoke to her before . . . before Darren made it clear what he wanted, before I promised him I wouldn't talk about it to anyone. And then I was stuck. I wanted to tell you, but I didn't want to betray him . . . again."

Julia nodded again. "I get it," she said. "And . . . thank you for telling me now. Does anyone else know?"

And so I told her and Kate about my conversation with Bashir, about Dax, about how I wanted to tell Samuel, how I thought it was time, but Darren didn't.

"Oh, Lucy," Julia said with a small smile. "Your life will never be simple, will it?"

"Never," Kate said. "But always exciting."

I was laugh-crying, trying to keep my mascara from turning into train tracks down my cheeks, when the waiter arrived with our food.

"Let's talk about 3-K," I said, after Julia snapped a photograph of her beautiful salad. "How's Owen liking it?"

And we chatted for the rest of the evening. Things mostly seemed back to normal, but I made a mental note to call Julia again tomorrow, to explain more and make sure we were okay.

When dessert came—we shared a stunning and delicious tiramisu ice cream cake—I realized that I was going to have a lot more of these conversations if Darren agreed to tell Sammy about you. I'd have to tell my parents, my brother, all three of the kids. Would Darren tell his parents and siblings? What about the twins? If Sam knew, it would be hard for the rest of the family not to. I understood why Darren wanted to keep this quiet. We were going to set off a bomb in the middle of our family if we told the truth.

But the truth always comes out in the end.

xxxvii

I LOVE HOW CLOTHING CAN FUNCTION AS ARMOR, or as a shot of confidence, a tool to project what you want people to see. The next morning I looked at my closet and, instead of going with the jeans I typically wear these days, I put on a long patterned accordion skirt with high-heeled leather boots and a black V-neck sweater. I added gold hoops in my ears and an extra coat of mascara to my lashes. I had my appointment with Joseph Landis at the art gallery where they were going to show your work in June, when the book launched, and I wanted to look put-together, confident, like I was sure of my plan.

I HADN'T YET COME UP WITH A PLAN TO TALK TO Darren, though, who still wasn't returning my calls or my texts. I had to figure out what to do to make him understand, to see how secrets can poison lives and rela-tionships. How much I worried it would poison ours with our kids—and how much we owed Sammy the truth. As he grew, as he developed his own identity, it should be based on all the facts of his life. I thought about that the whole way to Manhattan.

When I got off the subway in Chelsea, I got a message from Dax: *Good luck talking to the gallery owner. That's today, right?*

I smiled when I saw his words. *It is*, I typed. *And I will take that luck!*

Let me know how it goes, he wrote back.

As I walked to the gallery I remembered the only other times I'd been there—twice for your show, once with Julia, and once with Darren. What a debacle that turned into.

I walked in and let the person sitting at the front reception desk know who I was and who I was there to see. He left to go get Joseph Landis and I looked around the gallery. The current show was by an artist named Luca Bartolomei; he had painted biblical figures as if they were living in today's world. Each painting had a biblical quote on the plaque next to it, along with the painting's title. I stopped at one of a woman holding a tambourine at a nightclub, lost in the music, other women onstage in soft focus around her. It was called *Miriam's Song*, and the quote said: *Exodus 15:20 Then Miriam the prophetess, the sister of Aaron, took a tambourine in her hand, and all the women went out after her with tambourines and dancing.* The woman's hair was painted so beautifully, so realistically, that I wanted to reach out and touch it.

I moved to the next painting—a man in overalls tending to a vineyard: *The Fruit of Knowledge*. The quote said:

Genesis 2:8–10 And the Lord God planted a garden in Eden, in the east, and there he put the man whom he had formed. And out of the ground the Lord God made to spring up every tree that is pleasant to the sight and good for food. The tree of life was in the midst of the garden, and the tree of the knowledge of good and evil.

"Lucy?" I heard.

I turned and saw Joseph Landis there. He was dressed in a pair of gray pinstripe pants and a button-down shirt.

"Yes," I said. "Nice to meet you. This art is stunning. And I love the concept behind it."

"Luca's a rising star," he said. "New to our gallery. We only have a few pieces left that haven't been purchased, if you're interested."

I was interested but was sure the art was way out of my price range. "I'm not surprised you only have a few left," I said.

"But you're here to talk about Gabriel, not to buy art," he supplied.

"Yes," I said, and cleared my throat. I looked over at Adam, at the fruit of knowledge that was a grape, not an apple. "As I think you know, I'm responsible for Gabriel's estate."

He nodded.

"Eric Weiss let me know you'd like to show Gabriel's photographs again here," I said, "timed with the relaunch of his book, and I'd like to suggest an addition to the show."

"I'm listening," he replied, leaning against the counter at the front of the room.

"The theme of Gabriel's new book is 'then and now,'

and I love that idea, the way Eric wrote about the world as it is now to counterbalance Gabriel's photographs, but I'd love it even more if it could be represented visually in the show. Of course, that's impossible with Gabriel's work, but he has a protégé of sorts, a young man named Bashir Hassan in Rome. I've seen his work, and I think it's beautiful. His eye for photography is very similar to Gabriel's. So I'd love to look at the photographs of Gabe's you'd like to show, and then ask Bashir to go to those places, to take similar compositions, or if it's a portrait, find the same people if he can, and truly make the show 'then' and 'now.' For example," I said, pulling out my phone, "this is a photograph Gabriel took of a child at the Lampedusa refugee center. I'd love for Bashir to find this child now and take a similar photograph. Or another option would be to have him go back to the refugee center, and take this photograph in that spot. It looks quite a bit different now."

Joseph was nodding. "I like this," he said. "But what has always drawn me to Gabriel's work is the way he can capture emotion. I need to see what this Bashir Hassan can do before I agree. His photographs have to be as good as Gabriel's, worth selling on their own, for me to say yes."

I nodded. "I understand," I said. "Art and commerce cross paths in here, you need both."

"That's right," he said with a small smile.

"I'll talk to Bashir," I told him. "I'll send you some of his work. You can see what you think."

"Perfect," he said. "Here's my email." He paused and

then said, "You're the one he photographed in the early aughts. The laptop, the shoes, the smile."

I nodded. "That was me," I said.

He looked me up and down. "Then and now," he said. "It's an honor to meet you."

I took his card and told him I'd be in touch soon.

You've pushed me, Gabe. I'm reviewing book pages, setting up art exhibits, making gallery connections. Even with you gone for so long, you're still helping me to learn and grow. And I like it, I like stretching my mind, doing more than I knew I could. I love you still. Always.

XXXViii

THE SATURDAY AFTER I MET WITH JOSEPH LANDIS at the gallery was a waiting-for-the-kids-to-come-home Saturday, and I spent a lot of it wondering what would happen when the kids came to me—would Darren be the one with them? Would I have a moment to pull him aside and talk after the kids ran into the house? Would he let me? I decided my best plan would be to ask him to go out to coffee with me, somewhere we could have some privacy away from the rest of our family.

While I thought about that, I cleaned the house, I went grocery shopping, I looked at the calendar and organized my week, and I sent an email to Bashir asking his thoughts on my idea, whether he would take up your mantle, so to speak, become your eyes from beyond the grave. He wrote back quickly, saying that he didn't think he'd be able to fill your shoes, but that he would be honored to try, and he sent a link to a folder of photos he'd taken for school assignments and for pleasure. I flicked through them on my phone, just as impressed as I was by the original images he showed me in Rome. The photographs weren't as . . . I'm not sure how to explain it, but maybe the word is *polished*? They weren't as polished as yours, but they were wonderful, and I could tell that given more time, his photography would be spectacular. I sent them over to Joseph and asked his thoughts.

Then I looked through your book's proof pages and the catalog you'd saved from your first gallery show and noted the images that I thought might work for a then-and-now, knowing that Joseph and Eric would choose just a few, with time and money as the limiting factors. I marked the Arab Spring protests in Cairo, Egypt. A celebration of the end of the Iraq War in the Green Zone. The Moscow metro station after the bombings there. A family in Myanmar looking at their flattened home after a cyclone hit it. One of the damaged coaches from the Mumbai train bombing. Ground Zero. And, of course, Bashir and the other children in Lampedusa.

I looked at the last photos you shot, the ones in Gaza, before you died.

I wouldn't ask Bashir to go there, wouldn't risk his life, but I couldn't help but think about you, about how disheartened you would be knowing that the same centuries-old hatred that took your life is taking so many more.

I sent my ideas for then and now over to Joseph, and he wrote back quickly saying he liked Bashir's work, he liked the idea, and then added: *I also want Bashir to take a photo of you. And one of Gabriel's grave site.*

Reading those words sent an involuntary shudder

through my body. Your grave was like Ground Zero to me. Something I didn't need to see. Something so painful, I wasn't sure if I could keep myself together if I did see it. Something that might break me altogether. I didn't even want to see a photograph, but I knew why Joseph did.

Sounds good, I wrote back, just glad he was interested in the idea.

I let Bashir know and put him in touch with Joseph and Eric so the three of them could work out the logistics and the creative plan.

Then I made myself a quick salad for dinner, which I ate with a glass of white wine, while I texted Dax and waited for the kids to arrive.

Wish you were here, I typed. *Darren is driving me to the brink of insanity. I've been trying so hard not to involve the kids in any argument we've had over the years, but it's getting harder as they get older.*

Wish I were there too, he wrote back. *I'm on the boat now, but maybe we can talk later?*

I hearted his message but was left still wondering how to treat Darren when he arrived. But all that wondering and worrying was for nothing.

It was Courtney who brought them over.

"Hey," I said to her, walking down the front stoop as the kids came running up. Sammy's foot was still bandaged, but he was able to put weight on it now.

"Hey," Courtney said. Her face looked tense.

"Are you okay?" I asked.

She sighed. The kids had already gone into the house. "Darren told me," she said. "About Sammy."

I was a bit surprised she hadn't known, but not entirely. "He hadn't said anything before?"

She shook her head. "Not great for marital trust," she said.

I winced. "I'm sorry. I'm causing trouble . . ."

"No," she replied, shoving her hands deeper into her coat pockets. "This isn't about you. This one is on him. Entirely on him. And for what it's worth, I agree that Sammy should know the truth. Though are you sure the time is now?"

I shrugged. It was cold enough that her words were coming out in puffs of smoke. "The older he gets, the more he's like his biological father," I said. "And I don't want him to be the last to know. I just found out that a friend of mine who knew Gabe had already suspected it."

Courtney nodded.

We were both quiet for a moment.

"It's a control thing, right?" Courtney said.

I realized she was talking about Darren. "It is," I said. "The secrets he keeps aren't a reflection of how he feels about you. They're about controlling how the world sees him. How you see him."

"He likes to control the narrative," Courtney replied, as if the thought had fully crystallized for the first time.

"Always," I said, thinking about how he chose our old dog, Annie, on his own, how he didn't tell me when he bought the beach house and renovated it, how his need to control the narrative was a part of our eventual downfall.

We were quiet again. I wondered if I should say more, offer more support or comfort. I was in a unique position to do so. But I also didn't want to get in the middle of their marriage any more than I already was.

"Well," Courtney said finally, "I should get back home."

"I'll see you next week," I told her.

I watched her walk down the street, her body hunched slightly in the cold. I know she said it wasn't my fault, and the fact that Darren kept secrets from her wasn't, but the fact that he had this secret to keep was on me. If I hadn't cheated, they wouldn't be having this particular fight. I just . . . I couldn't get over how much had come from our one night together, Gabe, how the repercussions were still being felt a decade later.

That was what I'd thought then. I'm trying not to think that way anymore, though. It's toxic, it's too much. And my new therapist—I started to see someone Julia recommended when I told her how hard it was to unravel all this on my own—has been trying to show me how we all make our own choices, and the ones Darren made, Courtney made, they're not on me. Even if the situation was on me, the choices weren't.

xxxix

THERE ARE SOME DAYS THAT FEEL LIKE A GIFT. LIKE somehow the universe has decided it's time for a day that's so spectacular, so special, that I know I will start using this day as a reference point for others. We had days like that, Gabe, you and I. Darren and I did, too, of course. When I'm feeling sad or alone, I try to remember ours, though, like when we went out for your friend Adam's twenty-fourth birthday. We were at that long table with so many of your friends at the beer garden in Astoria. The day was warmer than we'd thought it would be, so you'd taken off your Henley and just had on a white Hanes T-shirt and jeans, and I had stripped off my sweater and was in a tight black tank top with my denim skirt. We both had our sunglasses on and were drinking beer and eating those sausages and big pretzels they have there. People were talking and laughing, and the sun was shining, and it was one of those absolutely beautiful fall days that makes it feel like the sky is smiling down on you. I felt so loved that day, so deserving of love, and it was so easy to give my love to you. You snaked your arm around my waist and pulled me so close to you that I was practically sitting on your lap. And then you kissed my neck with lips cold from beer and whispered, "Mmm, salty." I turned toward you and you caught my bottom lip with your teeth, and then you kissed me, hard, in front of your friends. Jason whooped, and you kissed me harder, your mouth turning up in a slow grin during the kiss.

You pulled away for a moment and then said, "I need another beer. Let's go take a walk, Luce."

I knew you didn't need another beer—the one in your hand was still cold and mostly full—but I got up and took your hand, and you led me not to the bar, but to the restrooms. We got there just as someone was walking out, and you smiled at them and held open the door, then said to me, "Let's go."

I was a little embarrassed that people had seen us walk into the restroom together, but then not, because I didn't care if the whole beer garden knew what we were going to do in there.

Ignoring our surroundings, you bent down to kiss me and then lifted me up, pinning me against the wall. I wrapped my legs around your waist and leaned back against the tile, balancing there without your arms holding me. You kept kissing me and managed to unzip your pants. I felt you hard against my inner thigh, and then your arms came back around me and slid me down so my legs were around your hips. I held on to you with one hand and pulled my underwear to the side with the other.

With your mouth still on mine, you managed to lower my body onto yours, and I moaned into your mouth as you filled me.

I opened my eyes for a brief moment and saw you, your eyes closed, blissed out. You rocked against me, and I held on tight to your shoulders, feeling the wall against my spine. I pulled my legs tighter around your waist, moving away from the wall.

You felt amazing, but I knew there was no chance I'd orgasm like this, in this bathroom, my back against a wall. But you did, and then said, "I'm sorry I couldn't wait."

"It's okay," I said, still in your arms, still wrapped tightly around you. "I like watching you."

You kissed me again and I loosened my legs and you slowly pulled out and lowered me to the ground.

I felt so empty without you inside me.

I rose up on my tiptoes to kiss you.

"How is it that I want you so much?" you whispered to me.

"How is it that I always want you back?" I answered.

I looked at us in the mirror, our lips swollen from kissing, my hair slipping out of its ponytail, and laughed.

"We look like we just had sex," I said, fixing my hair.

"Perception matches reality," you answered.

And then we left the bathroom, grabbed two more beers, and went back to the party. As we stepped into the sun, its warmth kissing my cheeks and haloing your curls, I kept thinking how grateful I was that we had found each other, that we were together. And I knew, in my heart, that if we were together forever, our lives would be beautiful. Breathtaking. Full of so much light. We sat back down with your friends, and it felt so good to be there. With you, with them, in the sunshine. I was so full of love then, love for you and for the whole world.

That's one of the days I live inside sometimes, when I'm feeling lonely. I have a feeling that—some time in the future, when my kids are grown—I'll probably live in my memories with them the same way. And that Sunday, the day I took them to the Museum of Math near Gramercy Park, will probably be one of those days.

In the morning, Sammy asked if we could go to Mo-Math. Liam agreed, as long as we could go to the nearby fried chicken place afterward. And Violet agreed, as long as Ji-ho could come. So we met Ji-ho at the subway station and all headed into Manhattan. Ji-ho wants to be a structural engineer, so the math museum is his jam, and he and Violet sat down to build three-dimensional shapes out of sticks and joints as they chatted. Liam found a section talking about the math of music, and Sammy found another one that let you draw with a digital pen on a screen and turned your art into patterns. As usual, his art attracted other people, and he made a few friends. They made fractal trees together in another part of the museum, and then became the three points of a triangle on a magical floor that connected them together with lines of light that followed them where they walked. Liam joined them, and then Violet and Ji-ho, and the kids all tried to outsmart the floor by jumping, first up in the air, and then the little kids jumped into the bigger ones' arms.

We closed down the museum and then all chowed

down on fried chicken at Sweet Chick. After that, we searched for the perfect dessert and ended up at Jacques Torres for hot chocolate. When we took the subway back to Brooklyn, Liam and Ji-ho were deep in conversation, Sammy was falling asleep on my shoulder, and Violet looked at me and said, "I love seeing you happy, Mom."

I wasn't sure what to say. Did this mean I wasn't usually happy? That it was so rare she needed to remark on it? I hoped that wasn't the case, but I didn't push it. Instead, I said, "Thanks, sweetheart."

But it made me wonder: What was it exactly that made me happy? That was the dream I had for my kids— I wanted them to grow up to be happy and healthy. But what did that mean for them? And what would it mean for me? If I really thought about it, I'd been content these past years, but not quite happy.

As we came up from the subway tunnel, my phone buzzed. It was a message from Dax: *Only a dozen days until I'm back in NYC. Looking forward to it. Hoping I'll get to see you.*

"Who's that from?" Violet asked, reading over my shoulder.

I blushed. "No one special," I said.

She looked at me seriously. "He seems kind of special to me." She paused and then said, "Mom, I hope he is."

I found myself hoping so, too. And wondering if there would come a time when I'd be telling my kids about him, telling Violet about my relationship. But not yet. There was another conversation that had to happen first, and that one was more important.

xl

THE NEXT NIGHT, SAMMY WAS HELPING ME DO LAUN-
dry. He was done with his homework, he'd already used
up his hour of screen time, his room was relatively neat,
and he was frustrated by the drawing of a sandwich he
was working on (why a sandwich? I have no idea), so
when I suggested he be the laundry delivery man, he re-
luctantly agreed.

I've told my kids that I wash, dry, fold, and deliver, but
I don't put away, that's their job. And mostly they do, because they've all learned the hard way that it's much more
difficult to find your clothes when they are in unsorted
piles on your dresser than when they are sorted and in
drawers.

So Sammy had delivered Violet's clothing to her room
and Liam's to his. Then he took my stack of clothes to
deliver to my room. He came back to the living room,
slowly, looking at a framed picture.

"What have you got there?" I asked him. Sometimes

the kids find photos of me and Darren together and are fascinated by them—amazed, I guess, that we were happy once, married, in love.

"It was on your dresser, Mom," he said.

And then he handed me the photo.

My stomach flipped. He'd found the photo of you and your mom, the one I'd taken out of the box a couple of weeks before.

"Is that . . . me?" he asked, confused. "It looks like me. But I don't remember that picture. Or the person I'm with."

I thought I might—I don't know what—faint or vomit or just spontaneously combust. After I didn't say anything, he asked again.

"Is that me, Mom?"

His eyebrows were furrowed, clearly trying to make sense of this.

"It's . . . it's someone named Gabriel," I told him.

"Do I . . . have . . . a twin?" he asked, still trying to puzzle it out. "Was my twin adopted? Was *I* adopted?" His face was still telegraphing curiosity, but I could hear a note of panic in his voice.

"No, no," I said. "You were not adopted. I grew you right here," I said, patting my stomach. "Right inside me, for thirty-nine weeks and two days."

He smiled for a brief moment, but then his face went serious again. "But was I a twin?"

I shook my head.

"That's not you, and it's not your twin," I said. "It's a boy named Gabriel, who looks a lot like you, but that picture was from a long time ago. Probably the mid-1980s."

I could see his brain trying to process but clearly still not having enough information.

"So why do you have the picture in your room? And why . . . why does he look like me?"

I swallowed. I stalled. "He died," I said. "This boy became a man. And when he died, he left me this picture."

"Because it looked like me?" Sammy asked.

I closed my eyes. *Should I say yes*, I thought, *and leave it at that?* But I knew I couldn't. My son—our son—was asking me a direct question. The least I could do, as his mother, was answer it honestly.

"No," I said. "He didn't know what you looked like. He didn't even know you existed before he died."

"So why does he look like me?"

I took a deep breath. I was going to do this. I was going to set off this bomb—in his life, in my life, in Darren's life, in his siblings' lives. But it was time. The photograph made it time. My carelessness in leaving it out made it time. But also, Sammy's curiosity made it time.

"Come sit down," I said. "And I'll tell you why."

I thought about Eva, about what she had said about leading with love, about the familiar idea of having multiple parents.

Sammy sat down next to me on the couch. He was still clutching your photo.

"Okay," he said.

"Okay," I echoed. I paused, and he waited. "So let me tell you about the man in the photo," I said. "The one who looks like you."

He nodded.

"His name is Gabriel Samson, and he was a very, very good friend of mine."

I looked into Sammy's eyes, which are the same shape as yours, but the same color as mine.

"We met in college, in New York City, and then he decided to become a photographer. His dream in life was to travel around the globe to find stories, and find beauty, and share those stories and that beauty with the world."

"So he was kind of an artist?" Sammy asked.

"Yes," I said. "I think a lot of people would call him an artist. And see his mom, the woman in the photo with him?"

Sammy nodded.

"She was a painter. And his dad was a sculptor."

"That's really cool," Sammy said.

"Yeah." I nodded. I was starting to think maybe just telling him about you might be enough for now. Maybe it would distract him. Maybe I shouldn't tell him the whole truth, just a little piece of it. But how could I do that? I wished Darren had called me back, had actually spoken to me—and that he saw my perspective. Even Courtney agreed with me, for Chrissake. As I was sitting there, I made a new deal with myself. If Sammy asked again directly, I'd answer honestly. If he didn't, I'd leave it be.

"Do you know what medium she used? The artist mom?"

I tried to remember what you had told me. I think at

one point you'd told me she made images of desert sunsets, but that her real work was huge canvas abstracts with oil paint. Was that right? Did I remember correctly?

"Oils," I told him, giving the word the weight of a certainty I didn't feel. "She painted the desert in Arizona."

He nodded seriously, taking that in. "Oil paints are hard," he said. "You have to layer them just the right way, thin to thick is what Ms. Hammer says, otherwise your painting could crack."

I nodded this time.

"Is she alive?" Sammy asked. "The mom?"

I shook my head. "She died, too," I told him. "But maybe we can find some of her art online." I'd never looked for it before, but you can pretty much find anything on the internet.

"Ooh! Can we?" he asked. "Do you have your phone?"

I pulled it out of my sweatshirt pocket and keyed in your mother's name. I knew she had painted under her name from before she met your dad: Vivienne Gabriel. I typed *Vivienne Gabriel artist* into my phone and for the first time I saw your mom's work. There were tons and tons of her desert sunsets. And then a few of her larger-scale abstracts.

"Look at that one!" Sammy said, excited.

He was pointing to an abstract in shades of green and purple that looked sort of ocean-inspired to me.

"I love how the color wheel opposites are there, but also the shades of the same colors, too." Sammy jumped up. "I have an idea for a picture!"

He ran off to his room. And I sat in the living room, alone with the laundry and your picture, feeling relieved, but also slightly disappointed that I didn't get to tell Samuel who you really were to him.

But I knew that one day soon I would. Because he'd come back to me again with that question, and this time I'd have to be ready with an answer.

xli

THAT NIGHT, I TEXTED DARREN A PICTURE OF THE photograph Sammy had found. *Sam saw this. He thought it was a photo of him, and when I told him it wasn't, he wanted to know why this person looked like him. When I started telling him about Gabe and his mother, he forgot about his question. But we have to talk. He's going to ask again, and I want to be able to answer him.*

My phone rang immediately.

"Are you fucking kidding me?" Darren's voice was somewhere between a hiss and a shout. "Why was that picture displayed in your house? When did you put it up?"

"It wasn't displayed," I said. "It was lying on my dresser in my bedroom. I took it out when I was going through Gabe's boxes for the book and the gallery show a few weeks ago. And honestly, I forgot I'd put it there."

"You sure you didn't leave it out on purpose? To force my hand?" he asked.

"Oh my god, no," I said. "I can't believe you'd even

suggest that, Darren. Do you really think that little of me? There has been so much on my mind recently, I didn't even think about the photo. I'm sorry," I added. "I didn't mean to force anything. But also, why have you ignored my calls and texts? Why haven't you called me back?"

"I told you I didn't want to tell him." His voice was steely.

"I told you I did," I said, angry and exhausted. "And now I think we have to be prepared. If he asks me again, I won't try to distract him, I won't lie. And I think we should get ahead of it now, before he asks."

I heard Darren breathe.

I waited.

"You're manipulating me," he said.

I could feel the fury roiling inside me. "This is not about you," I said. "Not everything is about you and me. This is about lying to our son about who he is, where he comes from. The only way in which it's about you is that you're the one forcing me to lie. And I'm letting you. Maybe I shouldn't anymore."

"You wouldn't dare," he said.

I took a breath. Tears of frustration were filling my eyes, hot and salty.

"We need to figure this out," I said.

"You are fucking up our lives again, Lucy."

"No," I said. "I'm fixing them."

I could hear Darren breathing hard on the phone. Then I heard Courtney in the background, her voice tinny, saying, "Darren, who are you shouting at? Is that Lucy?"

Then sounds were muffled, as if Darren had put his hand over his phone's mic. I waited.

Darren came back to say. "I'll call you later. I have to go talk to Courtney."

And then he hung up, and I was left staring at the phone, unsure about what I'd do if Sammy asked me about you again.

It was too early in Italy to call Dax, but all I wanted to do was talk to him, share with him, tell him what had happened.

WHEN MY PHONE RANG AN HOUR LATER, IT WAS Courtney.

"Lucy?" she said. "Hi."

"Hi," I answered, a little unsure of what was going on. Even though we'd been coparenting for years, I could probably count on one hand the number of times we'd spoken on the phone. Darren was always the one who called.

"Darren told me what happened, with Sammy and the photograph, and I agree with you. You can't lie to him when he asks you a question like that. You both are going to have to rebuild your trust with the kids, and the last thing you should be doing now is digging yourself a bigger hole."

I wanted to weep. I took a shaky breath. "Thank you," I said.

"Anyway," she said. "I'm putting Darren on. The two of you can work out the details, but he understands."

In that moment I thanked God and the universe and fate for making Courtney the person that Darren married.

"Hi," Darren said, sounding resigned. "So let's say we do tell him. What would you say?"

I walked into the bathroom attached to my bedroom and closed the door. That way I'd have even more warning if one of the kids came looking for me.

"I'd say that you and I have been talking about how best to answer his question," I started slowly, leaning against the tile wall next to the door. "And I'd tell him that you will always be his dad, the man who is raising him and loves him and would do anything for him, but that the reason that Gabe looks just like him is that Gabe is also his dad, his biological dad. And that Gabe died before he was born, which is why he's so lucky to have you as a dad now. How about that?"

"Does he?" Darren said quietly.

"Does he what?" I asked.

"Look just like him."

I sat down on the lip of the bathtub.

"Yes," I said. "Other than the color of his eyes, they could be twins."

Darren was quiet again.

"And looking at Gabe's mom's art inspired Sammy to go start a new painting," I added.

Darren sighed. "It doesn't sound so bad the way you just phrased it," he said. "And Courtney said I can't let how competitive I've always felt with Gabe cloud my judgment."

"Courtney's smart," I said, and left it at that. It was so sad, so absurd that he still felt that he had to compete with you, Gabe. I wanted to strangle him.

"I'm doing this for Courtney," he said. "She's incredibly

pissed at me for not telling her. I'm doing this to help fix that relationship."

I wanted to strangle him a second time. I had to close my eyes and take a deep breath before I could respond.

"I'm sure you'll work through it," I told him.

"I hope so," he said.

I picked up a sock that had fallen out of my laundry hamper onto the floor. "So when do you think? Do you want to be here?"

"How about next Saturday?" he said. "It's the day after his birthday, the day of his birthday scavenger hunt. Maybe I could come over when you four finish dinner and we could tell them all together then."

I took a deep breath. This was what I wanted to happen, this was what I knew needed to happen, but that didn't mean I wasn't afraid—afraid of how Sammy would react, afraid of the fallout. All of a sudden, everything felt very real. "Okay," I said. "If Sammy asks before then—"

"Just put him off," Darren said. "Please."

"Okay," I said. "Okay. And . . . please thank Courtney for me."

"See you Saturday" was his response.

And we both hung up the phone.

I knew I would barely be able to think about anything else until Saturday.

xlii

I HADN'T SEEN ERIC WEISS IN PERSON FOR YEARS, not since the one time he'd invited me out for a drink right after Darren and I split. This time, he asked if we could get together to go over the plan for the book and the gallery, and for the promotion of both. He'd taken point on the logistics and said it would be easier if we met in person.

"Sure," I told him. "How about over coffee?"

It turned out he'd moved to Brooklyn, in Park Slope, so we met at Clever Blend on Fifth and Park Place. I recognized him immediately. He had a full head of dark brown hair that I wondered if he colored. Darren's going gray at the temples, and I'm always suspicious when I see men older than he is without any gray hair.

"Hey," I said, shaking his hand.

His smile was filled with warmth.

"Lucy!" he said as he sat back down. "It's so nice to see you."

"Same," I answered. There were two coffees on the table.

"Now that we're seeing each other in person, I feel like I should apologize for trying so hard to flirt with you the last time we saw each other. My wife and I were going through a rough time with our daughter, and . . ." He trailed off.

I can't even imagine how my face looked when he said that—a mixture of confusion and surprise—and then I started laughing.

"What?" Eric said.

"Apology accepted, but honestly, I had no idea."

"You had no idea?" he repeated.

"No idea you were flirting with me seven years ago," I said. "My head just wasn't there. It hasn't been for a long time."

Then it was his turn to laugh. "Okay, then. I guess I can stop feeling bad about that. It's been eating at me for years."

I smiled kindly at him. "I wish we'd had this conversation sooner, then, so you could've stopped feeling so bad years ago."

He cleared his throat. "Well, now that that's over . . ." He gestured toward a cup of coffee. "I took a risk and ordered for you," he said. "But I'm happy to drink both and get you something else if I guessed wrong."

"Oh!" I said. "Thank you. What did you order?"

"Medium roast, cold brew, black."

I laughed again. "Well," I said, reaching for the cup on my side of the table, "pretty much what I would have ordered myself."

He smiled. "I remembered Gabe saying that you'd gotten into coffee at some point. Figured that was the safest bet."

I picked up the cup. "To Gabe," I said.

He clinked his plastic cup with mine. "To Gabe," he echoed.

Then he laid out prints of your photographs.

"Okay," he said. "So here's what Joseph is planning for the gallery. Bashir has reached out to the other kids from the Lampedusa photos and has plans to photograph the two in Italy this week. He asked each of them to write their own story to post beside it. What they've done from then to now. Bashir also wants to share his payment for these particular photos with each person who's in them. I was hoping you might be open to doing the same with Gabe's photographs of them?"

"Of course!" I said. "Actually, they should have all of it. I don't need it. I was planning to donate any proceeds from the show or the book to Tuesday's Children, a charity I know Gabe felt strongly about. But I'm sure he'd be happy for them to have it."

"I agree," Eric said. "We'd also like to use this photograph." He slid the one Bashir had taken of Gabe at the refugee center toward me. "This would be the then. The now would be—"

"His grave," I said, remembering Joseph's words.

"Or his son," Eric said. "Bashir told me what you'd told him. About Samuel."

I winced. I hadn't thought that Bashir might share that with Eric, but why wouldn't he. I hadn't told him it was a secret.

"You know my wife was pregnant when he died, too. My daughter is only a few months older than your Samuel and her middle name is Gabrielle, after him. Hannah Gabrielle."

That was the first I'd heard his daughter's name, and it just about broke my heart open.

"That's beautiful," I said to him, tears in my eyes. "In Judaism, it's a way to honor people who have died, to name a baby after them, to keep their memory alive."

"Does your daughter know about Gabriel?" I asked.

He nodded. "There's a photograph of him in her bedroom; there has been since she was born. And another one of my wife's aunt Hannah."

I thought about the irony that Eric's daughter grew up learning about you her entire life, while our son had only learned about your existence a few days before.

"That's amazing," I said. Then I paused. "I'd rather keep Samuel out of the show, though." I took a deep breath. "Most people don't know he's Gabriel's son. Actually, he doesn't know yet."

Eric's eyebrows rose, almost as if the motion was involuntary, but then he nodded. "I understand. Maybe I'll see if Bashir can take a photograph of an empty seat in our newsroom, an abandoned camera. We'll figure something out. The photograph of his grave seemed too— depressing. Who would buy that image anyway?"

"That sounds better," I said. "Did Joseph give you a date for the show?"

"We want to do it when the book releases," he answered. "Which is timed for the month Gabe died. Right now, the publication date is scheduled for the first Tuesday in July. I think the show will likely open the following Friday night. So that would be July fifth."

"A little more than two and a half months," I said. "Sounds good."

So much can happen in eleven weeks.

xliii

THAT NIGHT DAX WHATSAPP'D ME AGAIN AFTER
the kids had gone into their rooms for bedtime. I doubt
any of them were asleep, but at my house, at eight thirty,
everyone went into their room in pajamas for quiet time
until they were ready for bed. I went in at nine to make
sure Sam's lights were out, at nine thirty for Liam, and at
ten for Violet. Usually they all were tired enough to turn
their lights off and go to bed themselves. But I always
checked. If they were already asleep, sometimes I tiptoed
into their rooms to adjust their blankets and kiss their
cheeks. Remember how we used to say we were a binary
star, orbiting around each other? Now I'm a moon, somehow orbiting around three planets. They are how I orient
my life these days, so much of how I define who I am.

The nightly check-ins that week made me feel emotional. I was dreading what would happen that weekend
when we told the kids, when it was possible that all of
their feelings about me would change.

A little bit after I'd made sure Violet's lights were out, a WhatsApp came through from Dax.

You were in my dream just now, he wrote, *and you were in trouble. I wanted to say hi, make sure you're okay.*

Just seeing Dax's name made me smile. It was a little after four A.M. his time. I wondered if he was one of those people who didn't need much sleep.

I'm okay, I typed back, *but on Saturday Darren and I are going to tell the kids the truth about Sammy, and I'm kind of terrified. So I guess not really okay.*

My phone rang immediately. "Do you want to talk about it?" Dax asked, his deep voice traveling through the phone and enveloping me, just like last time.

I sat down on my bed. "I do and I don't," I told him.

"We could talk about something else," he said. "To take your mind off things. There's so much we don't know about each other. Like, what's your favorite color? Your favorite food? Your middle name?"

I laughed. "Blue," I said. "Chocolate. And Bea."

"Like the letter?" he asked.

"Like short for Beatrice," I said, "my grandmother, except it's just Bea."

I could hear the smile in his voice when he said, "I like that."

"How about you," I asked.

"Green," he said. "Pizza. And Jameson. My father's name was James. So I'm Jameson."

"Cute," I said. "Was Zachariah's middle name Daxson?"

He laughed. "You know, I tried to convince Aviva, but she wouldn't do it. Instead we went with Amadeus. It means love."

"That's cool," I said. "All my kids have family names from one side or another."

"That's special, too," he said.

We kept talking about nothing of importance until he said, "So, how *are* you doing?"

"Scared out of my mind," I said. "Scared that my kids will hate me. That they'll judge me. That they'll never trust me or Darren again. That this will put them all in therapy for the rest of their lives."

"I don't think it'll be as bad as all that," he said. "I could tell from your phone calls with them how much they love you. And love lets you forgive a lot. But . . . lining up a therapist might not be bad. Let them have someone professional to process this all with."

I nodded, then said, "You couldn't see me nod, but you're right. Any recommendations?"

"I'll send you some later today," he said. "Let me just reach out to see who is taking new patients and who might have availability next week."

"Thank you," I said. "I so appreciate it."

"My pleasure," he said.

I looked at the clock. It was nearly eleven thirty P.M. I needed to get to bed if I was going to be up before the kids in the morning.

"This was so nice," I said. "But I think I've got to go to sleep now."

"That's a lovely thought to have with me today," he answered. "Before you go, will you tell me what your room looks like?"

I smiled, touched that he cared. "Let's see," I said, trying to figure out how to build my room in his mind. "The floors are wood, stained a dark mahogany color. There's a gray-and-white chevron rug with white fringes along the edges. I have a brass-and-iron headboard with white, gray, and light blue bedding."

"Tons of pillows?" he asked.

I laughed. "Tons," I answered. "Nine, to be precise."

"I love it," he said. "Tell me more."

"The walls are painted a light blue with white trim. There are gray-and-white chevron curtains, white blackout shades underneath. And a gray-stained wooden dresser that matches the night tables."

"Lamps?"

"One on each side of the bed."

"And what's on your night table?"

I glanced over: "A clock radio, ChapStick, my phone charger, a glass of water, and a copy of the Jim Henson biography, which my brother, Jay, got me for Christmas this year."

"I like that I can picture your house now, your bedroom." His tone turned flirtatious. "Maybe I'll be able to see it in person when I come back."

"Maybe," I said.

Dax was quiet for a moment and then said, "Good night, Lucy," his voice a soft rumble that I felt in my core.

"Good morning, Dax," I replied softly.

As much as I'd told him I was horrible at relationships, and as scared as I was of what it all could lead to, I couldn't deny the thrill I felt in knowing he'd be back in New York soon, in knowing that I'd be able to feel his arms around me again.

xliv

SOMETIMES, YOU KNOW WHEN SOMETHING WILL BE a life-changing, life-defining moment. There are moments that change the world, like the day we met—the day the Twin Towers fell—and then there are days that change the world for only a few people—the day I got married, the days Violet, Liam, and Sammy were born, the day I told the doctors to let you die, the day Darren and I decided to divorce. And now, the day we decided to tell our children the truth.

The night before, Violet, Liam, Sammy, and I went out for his birthday with my parents, who drove down from Connecticut. He wanted pizza and ice cream, so we complied, stuffing ourselves with pepperoni pizza and sharing one massive ice cream sundae among the six of us. It was called the "preposterous sundae" on the menu, and Sammy had been dying to try it: twelve scoops of ice cream, chocolate sauce, caramel, whipped cream, both rainbow and chocolate sprinkles, a whole banana, and a maraschino cherry on top. We did our best, but after all that pizza, we couldn't finish it. Liam said we should come back and try again for his birthday.

"I'm in," my dad said right away.

Liam gave him a high five.

I wished we'd had more moments like this through the years. Once we told Sammy, I knew I'd have to tell my parents—and Jay. I wasn't sure if it would make things between us better or worse.

THE NEXT MORNING, SATURDAY, THE NIGHT DAR-ren and I were going to tell the kids about you, Sammy and I picked up Abe at his house and headed into Manhattan for the Met Scavenger Hunt the two of them were so excited about. Remarkably, they came in third place in a competition against mostly adult museumgoers.

It was a rainy day, and, after a celebratory frozen hot chocolate at Serendipity 3, Abe came home with us, and the boys spent the afternoon creating an elaborate game in which the basement couch was some sort of boat and a metronome relocated from the living room was a croc-odile that had eaten a bomb. They each had to run across the pillows they'd put on the floor, jump into the boat, find the hidden metronome, and then perform surgery on the crocodile and defuse the bomb all within six minutes.

I witnessed this from the laundry room, then listened to it from the kitchen, where I decided to make the kids' favorite meal for dinner—spaghetti and meatballs with crispy (or as Liam named it when he was little, "burned up") broccoli and garlic bread.

Tasting the pasta sauce turned my stomach, I was so anxious about the conversation to come.

At around four thirty, Sammy and I donned our raincoats to walk Abe home. When we got back, Violet had just gotten home from Keisha's, and a few minutes later, Liam had been dropped off by his friend Clyde's dad. We sat down around the table at five thirty, and I asked the kids their best, worst, and wished.

"Easy for me," Sammy said. "Best: Playing with Abe all day, coming in third in the scavenger hunt at the Met, and the frozen hot chocolate. Worst: Um, I think we broke the metronome, Mom. Sorry. But maybe you could fix it? And Wished: It wasn't raining when we walked Abe home." He looked at me sheepishly.

"I'll look at the metronome later, and maybe next time tell me when it happens?"

"Sorry," he said, staring down at his plate.

"It's okay," I said, not wanting to go into the conversation after dinner with him already upset. "Not a big deal. I'm sure I'll be able to fix it."

"I can go next," Liam said. "Best: I think Clyde and I found two more people to start a real band! There's this new girl in our class who plays the bass guitar and she's really cool and her twin sister is a good singer, and they live on Clyde's block and that's my best."

It made me wonder if this bass-playing cool girl is the reason Liam blushed on Valentine's Day, but no way would I ask.

"What about worst and wished?" Violet asked.

"Worst is that Clyde's mom's in the hospital again,

and wished . . . well, I wished she wasn't because it makes Clyde mad and also makes me worry about you, Mom."

I got up and walked around the table to give him a hug. "I'm fine," I said. "I promise."

"Then why aren't you eating your dinner?" he asked.

"I ate too much while I was cooking it," I lied and kissed the top of his head before I sat down again.

"Vi?" I asked.

"Best: Ji-ho came to the movies with his friends today to meet me and Keisha so everyone could hang out together. Worst: The movie was actually kind of boring. Wished: I had gotten M&M's instead of popcorn."

"Why was it boring?" I asked.

"It was one of those car-chase explosion movies. I guess boring isn't the right thing to say. Maybe just not for me."

I nodded. "Those aren't for me, either," I said. Working in an industry where the creative work I put out was judged all the time, we talked a lot in our house about things being created that some people liked and other people didn't, and that it usually just meant you weren't the right audience for that film, the right reader for that book, the right eater for that snack, et cetera. I told the kids that *not for me* was a kinder, more respectful way to frame it. I would so much rather people post *not for me* than *This is the dumbest show I've ever watched. Why is it about a tiger and a bunny? I hate anthropomorphic animals. Whoever created it must be a moron.* I try to teach my kids that a post like that is really more about the person who posts it than my show. But it does still sting.

"What about you, Mom?" Liam asked.

The kids had finished their dinner, and the clock was ticking closer to the time Darren would come, the time our secrets wouldn't be secrets any longer.

"Best: I got to celebrate Sammy's birthday again. Oh, and I got the laundry done."

"Yay, Mom!" Sammy cheered.

We all laughed again.

"Worst: I'm too full to eat more of this delicious dinner. And wished . . . wished . . ."

"Wished what, Mom?" Violet said, looking at me expectantly.

"Wished all three of you could still fit on my lap together."

"Let's try!" Sammy said.

I smiled at him. "Okay, let's try. But I think we need to move to the couch for this."

I sat down and Violet looked at me.

"Okay," she said. "How about if I sit mostly on the couch next to you with one leg over yours. Does that count as on your lap?"

"Sure," I said. "We can make our own rules."

She sat that way. Liam mimicked her on the other side, and Sammy, who still actually did fit on my lap, sat in the middle. I wrapped my arms around all of them and pulled them together for a huddle of a hug.

"We fit!" Sammy said.

And that was how Darren found us.

I had left our door unlocked, and he walked in, dripping wet from the outside.

"Um, hello?" he said.

"Dad!" Sammy jumped off my lap to take his umbrella.

"Is it seven already?" Violet asked. "Did Dad come because we're late?"

I shook my head. "Your dad is here early because there's something we have to tell you three."

"Is Dad sick?" Liam asked.

"No one's sick," I said. "But this is important. How about you three sit on the couch, and Daddy and I will sit over here on the love seat together."

I looked at Darren. He had taken off his raincoat, and between the raincoat and umbrella he had remarkably managed not to get wet.

"Hi," I said to him.

He nodded and sat down next to me.

I had no idea how this would go but was glad he'd come around enough to do this with me. Glad, for our kids' sake, that we would be telling them together.

xlv

OUR KIDS SAT FACING US IN A ROW. VIOLET ON THE left, Liam on the right, and Sammy in the middle. Their faces were upturned, expectant, and a little scared. I couldn't remember the last time we'd gotten them together like this, with both me and Darren there. I wasn't sure if it had ever happened. When we'd gotten divorced, we told them one by one. We'd explained it to Sammy, even though he was only sixteen months old. Who knows what he understood, but we figured we owed him an explanation, just like we owed one to him now.

"So," I started, glancing at Darren. He had said he would be there, but he wanted me to be the one to talk. "So, there are a lot of families that have secrets," I started again. I had practiced this a ton of different ways, and this seemed the least threatening. "And when people in the family are old enough, that secret can be shared. And sometimes, it doesn't have to be a secret anymore."

Their eyes were all on me.

"In our family, Daddy and I have kept a secret, and we decided, now that Sammy's nine, you're all old enough to know the secret—and that it doesn't have to be a secret anymore. Once we tell you, you can tell other people, if you'd like."

I looked at Darren again, and he gave me a nearly imperceptible nod.

"And our secret is a story I'm going to tell you now."

Our kids were silent, staring at me.

"Earlier this week, Sammy found a photograph in my room. It was a picture of a boy and his mom."

Violet and Liam looked at Sam.

"His name was Gabriel Samson," Sammy said quietly. "And his mom was an artist. They're both dead now."

"That's right," I said. I had taken the photograph out of the frame and put it in my pocket. I pulled it out now and handed it back to Sammy, who showed Liam, who passed it to Violet. "When Sammy found the photograph, he asked me why the boy in it looks like him."

"He really does," Violet said softly, the photograph in her hands.

"You never ended up telling me," Sammy said.

"That's right," I told him. "And now I will. So, you all know that your dad and I loved each other so much when we were married, and we still love each other now."

They all nodded, like little birds.

"Well, Gabriel and I loved each other very much right after we graduated from college, and we still loved each other after that. And after Daddy and I got married, and after Violet and Liam were born, I got pregnant again, with Sammy. Daddy is Sammy's dad, of course, but

Sammy actually has two fathers. The one who is raising him and loves him—"

"That's me," Darren said, his voice a little gravelly.

"And the one who made him biologically," I finished. "And his biological dad is Gabriel. That's why they look alike."

Sammy reached for the photograph and Violet gave it back to him.

"So, was that because you and Daddy were having trouble getting pregnant again, and Gabriel helped instead of doing IVF like with the twins?" Violet said.

I shook my head. "No," I said, glancing at Darren again. His face was stony. "It's because I was feeling really sad one day, and Gabriel made me feel better, and we ended up making Sammy that day."

There was silence in the room while the kids processed that. I waited, giving them space.

"So you cheated on Dad?" Liam asked, finally.

I knew I had to walk a fine line here of telling the truth, but not making Sammy feel like a mistake. "I did," I said. "But the important thing I want all of you to know is that each one of you was created with love."

There was silence again. Sammy looked down at the photo in his hands.

"Dad, did you adopt Sammy?" Violet asked.

Darren cleared his throat. "Because your mom and I were married when he was born, my name is on Sammy's birth certificate, so I didn't have to adopt him. I've always been his dad. And Sam—" He turned to face him directly. "I will always be your dad. Biology doesn't change that. I was the first person who held you in the hospital, and in that moment, you became my son forever."

"I have two dads," Sammy said quietly, gripping the photograph of you, Gabe.

"That's right," I said. "You all have two moms, me and Courtney, and now Sammy has two dads. Families come in all different shapes and configurations, and ours is a little complicated, but knowing this information doesn't change our family. This is what we've been all along."

Sammy looked up from the photograph. "Do you have a grown-up picture of Gabriel Samson?"

"I do," I said. "Would you like to see it?"

He nodded.

I pulled out my phone and scrolled to the picture of you that Bashir had taken, the one that was hanging in the library in Lampedusa. "Here," I said, handing him my phone. "This is Gabriel when he was at a refugee center in Italy, a few months before he died. He was a photojournalist and was taking pictures there for an article about the Syrian refugee crisis and a boat that had capsized off the coast of a small island called Lampedusa. I can show you the photos he took, too. I have a book of them upstairs in my room."

"This is so unfair," Liam said, kicking the bottom of the couch with his heel. "Sammy gets everything. Even a cool second dad."

That wasn't a reaction I was expecting. Darren and I stared at him. Violet stared at him.

"Liam," she said quietly. "His second dad died. In reality, he only has one dad. Like us." Then she turned to me and Darren. "May I be excused?" she said. "And can Sammy come with me, if he wants?"

Sam still had my phone and was looking at you, tapping the screen each time it started to go dark.

"You can be excused," Darren said to Violet. "But I want to talk to Sam for a minute more."

"You're not really his real dad," Liam said.

Sam looked up at Darren, his eyes instantly filling with tears.

"I am absolutely his real dad," Darren said. "Sam, did you hear me? I am your real dad. I don't want to hear that again, from any of you. Ever. Do you understand?"

All three nodded mutely, and then Violet headed to her room.

"Liam," I said, "do you want to help me clear the dinner dishes? So Dad and Sammy can talk?"

"No chance," Liam said, and walked off to his room, too.

I got up to clear the table, giving Darren and Sam their time together. I don't know what Darren said or how Sammy responded, but they ended up hugging each other. Sammy went to his room to get his backpack to bring to Darren's, but when he came back out, the other two kids were still in their rooms.

I knew this would be hard on the big kids, too, but I hadn't expected them to be angrier than Sammy.

"Hey, Sam," I said, sitting down next to him on the couch. "How are you feeling about all of this?"

He shrugged. "I guess it's like Dad said, he's always been my dad, and I've always been me. Nothing about me has changed, and nothing about us has changed . . . But . . . now . . . now I get to see someone who looks like me. I never had that before. I always looked at Liam and Dad and Violet and you and could see the connection, you know? You and I have the same color eyes, but with Gabriel, I see myself in him the way I see Violet in you. And . . . I don't know, but maybe I see my art in him, too, you know? In his pictures? And in his mom? And that's cool, because that wasn't ever like anyone in our family either. So now it feels, I don't know, like, there's someone like me. And it feels . . . it feels nice to have that. But . . . it's weird that . . . that it's a part of me I'm learning about for the first time."

I let out a deep breath. Other feelings would surface later, but in that moment, I knew we'd done the right thing. We'd given Sammy a way to feel connected.

"How did you get so wise, Sammy?" I asked.

He shrugged again. "Was Gabriel wise? Maybe it's in my blood."

I laughed and gave him a hug and then kissed the top of his head. "You're wiser than Gabriel ever was," I said. "I love you so much, kid."

"I love you too, Mom," he answered.

Then I stood and turned to Darren. "Do you want Violet or Liam?" I asked.

"I think you need to talk to Violet," he said.

He was right.

"Be right back," I said to Sammy.

He nodded and took out his sketchbook. I wondered whether his art would help him process this, the way your photographs helped you process the world. I've always seen so much of you in him, Gabe, and what's amazing is now he does, too.

xlvi

I KNOCKED ON VIOLET'S DOOR.

"Who is it?" she called out.

"It's me," I said. "Can I come in? Can we talk a little more, just us?"

Wordlessly, Violet opened the door. I could see that her eyes were puffy from crying. She stepped aside to let me in and then shut the door behind me.

I wasn't sure what to say.

"Vi—" I started. But then she interrupted.

"Is Sammy why you and Dad got divorced?" she said, sitting down on her bed, the lavender bedspread crumpled around her. "When I was a kid, when you and Dad sat me down to tell me you were getting divorced, you said that you both still loved each other and loved us, but that you argued too much living in the same house and that it would be better for our family if you lived in two separate houses. And I know . . . I know some of the way you explained it was because I was only seven, but I'd always thought you got divorced because you're so different. I mean, you are so different. But now I feel like there was a lot more to it, and my whole world is kind of wobbly and weird and can I even trust you guys? If my brother is biologically my half brother and you didn't tell me, how can I believe anything anyone says ever? You're my parents. You're supposed to be the people I can trust most, and if I can't, then where does that leave me? What do I do?"

My heart was breaking. I understood exactly how she felt, I understood why, and I wished I could take her pain away, wished we had made different choices. I sat down next to her and reached out. She let me wrap my arms around her and I hugged Violet to me. In that moment, I realized that she had finally gotten taller than I was. Only about half an inch, but she had to lean her chin down to rest it on my shoulder.

"Oh, Vi, I'm so sorry. To answer your question: Sammy wasn't the reason we got divorced, it was the fact that I'd broken your dad's trust that really did us in. I'm not proud of the way I acted, and I've apologized to your father for it more times than I can count. But I'm not sorry Sam was born. It feels to me like this is how our family was meant to be. And Gabriel died while I was still pregnant with Sam, so in a way, it's a comfort to know that some of his DNA is living on in Sam."

Violet nodded and wiped her eyes.

"As far as trust . . . I hadn't wanted to keep Sammy's biological father a secret from him or you or Liam, but your dad thought it was important that all three of you feel the same, that you all grew up feeling like you were equally his. I understood his perspective, and agreed, as long as he agreed that you'd all know the truth one day. I'm sorry it's made you feel like you can't trust us—or anyone. And I promise, now that the day has arrived, I'm an open book. Ask me anything you'd like. I'll answer you honestly for the rest of your life."

She looked at me critically, and I could tell her next question would be a test.

"Did you love Gabriel more than Dad?" she asked.

I shook my head. "Not more," I told her, "but differently."

"Is Sammy more important to you than me or Liam?"

I shook my head again. "Absolutely not. I love all of you—for who you are, for the choices you've made, for the way you exist in the world. And I'm so, so proud of all three of you. None more than the other."

She leaned over and hugged me again.

"Okay, one last question," she said. "Do you actually like those mayonnaise cookies that Grandma makes, or do you pretend like Liam and Sam and I do?"

I started to laugh. My mother makes these cookies that her mother used to make, where she swaps mayonnaise in for the eggs and oil. She has always thought they were incredible. Jay and I did not, but I had no idea my kids didn't like them either.

"Hate 'em," I said. "Well, maybe that's too strong a word, but definitely not in my top twenty desserts."

Violet looked at me. "I thought so." she said. "I'm glad you didn't lie about that."

I hugged her to me again and caught sight of the digital clock behind her on her night table. It was almost seven thirty.

"I think it's time to grab your stuff for Dad's," I said.

She nodded.

"But if you or either of your brothers need me, or need anything this week, I'm only a few blocks away. I can come whenever. You can call whenever."

"We know, Mom," she said.

"And I promise you, Violet, I will do everything I can to make sure you know you can trust me."

She nodded, and then she grabbed her backpack and the two of us headed back into the living room, where we found the rest of the family waiting.

I hugged Liam and then Sammy and whispered to both of them how much I loved them and to call me if they needed me.

They both hugged me back and said, "You too, Mom."

And those three words let me know that we'd all eventually be okay. It would take more conversations, more breakdowns, more proof that they could trust me and Darren, but I knew that as long as we had love, we'd be okay.

xlvii

WHEN THEY'D ALL LEFT FOR DARREN'S, I LAY DOWN on the couch, exhausted. It went both better and worse than I'd expected. And I still had to tell my parents and Jay. Darren and I had decided that we'd tell our immediate families and closest friends, the people the kids might go to if they wanted to talk. If word spread, so be it. And if not, not. It was no one else's business, and if people thought about us differently because of what they'd heard, that was on them.

After about an hour of staring at the ceiling, I got up and made myself a whiskey on the rocks in honor of you, the cocktail you were drinking when we reconnected at Faces & Names.

As I sat back down on the couch, my phone pinged. I grabbed at it to see if it was Darren or the kids, but it was Dax.

Just wanted to check in, he said. *How did it go? How are you?*

I stared at my phone for a while. I felt like a wrung-out washcloth. I was drained and lonely, and I wished he were there. I wished I could lay my head against his shoulder, that I could feel his arms, strong and warm, holding me tight.

I miss you, I wrote.

The phone rang. It was him. I picked it up. His voice sounded tired. It was close to three A.M. over there, but maybe he'd been out on the ship, or triaging people whom they'd found and brought to shore.

"You're not okay," he said.

"I'm not okay," I whispered and started to cry. The strength I'd used to hold myself together through all the conversations dissolved, and I felt everything: the stress, the emotion, the fear, the guilt, the pain.

"I wish I were there with you," Dax said. "I'm so sorry you're hurting."

"I wish you were here with me, too," I said. "When are you coming home?"

"As soon as I can," he answered. "Next week."

"I'll teach you to make marshmallow pies," I said, my voice still thick with tears.

"I can't wait," he said.

We stayed on the phone a bit longer while I told him what had happened.

"I'm not sure what to do next," I said.

"I don't know your kids, of course," he said, "but I wonder if a one-on-one day with each of them might be helpful? Give them a chance to ask you questions, share how they're feeling with just you. I did that with Zac when we found out he was sick, and Aviva did, too. He ended up talking about different fears he had with each of us."

"It sounds like Zac was lucky to have you as a dad," I said.

Dax was quiet for a moment. "I did the best I could," he said. "And that's one of the things I noticed about you, Lucy, when you were talking to Sammy and Violet on the phone from Lampedusa. You do the best you can with your kids, too."

His words brought tears to my eyes. I *did* do the best I could. But that wasn't always good enough. I swallowed a sob. "Lucy," Dax said, his voice wrapping around my heart, "is there someone you can be with tonight? Or tomorrow? I hate the idea of you being alone right now. I'm sorry I'm so far away." I don't know if it's all doctors, or if it's just Dax, but he is so thoughtful, so insightful, and— like our Sammy—so wise.

I took a shuddering breath. "I'm okay," I said. "I have plans with Eva tomorrow."

"And tonight?" he said, his voice so warm.

"It's just me tonight," I told him.

"Well, then imagine me there with you," he said. "Imagine my arms around you, my lips in your hair. Imagine me holding you close until you fall asleep. Imagine me being there for you."

"I will," I told him, already closing my eyes, already feeling his arms wrapped around my shoulders.

That night, in bed, I imagined everything he told me to. And I also imagined much more.

xlviii

I DON'T KNOW HOW YOU FELT WHEN OUR RELATION-
ship first started, but I had all these moments of: Should
I call him? Text him? Would he write back? Would he
ignore me? Would it feel worse if I reached out and he
didn't respond, or would it feel worse if I didn't reach out
at all and instead sat wondering how he was doing? That
next week, I had the same feelings about the kids. Should
I call them? Text them? Would they write back? Would
they ignore me? Et cetera, et cetera, et cetera.

I gave them Sunday. I spent the morning with Eva,
the afternoon reading through the scripts for the next
batch of episodes of *Tiger & Bunny*, and the evening or-
ganizing the house and eating carrots with hummus for
dinner, with a spoonful of Nutella for dessert. Sometimes
it felt good not to cook.

Monday afternoon I sent a message to Violet. *Thinking about you and your brothers, like I always do. Hope you
all had a good start to your week.*

I heard back from her after dinner. *We're dealing,* she wrote. *The boys haven't said much about it. Dad hasn't mentioned it at all. At least not to me. I still can't believe you cheated on him.*

I closed my eyes, took a breath. Maybe I should have insisted we tell them when they had another few nights at my house. But I thought Darren would want to be with them, would want to be with Sam, and that I owed it to Darren to give him those days, but . . . I don't know. Maybe it was the wrong choice.

I'm so sorry, Vi. You can ask me whatever you want, I wrote back. *See you all on Thursday for Sammy's art show. Love you.*

I held my breath, waiting to see what she'd say, the way I used to with you.

You too finally came through, and I let out a breath.

Eva said to lead with love. That it would all be okay if I led with love. I took her words to heart. I didn't only lead with it, I followed with it, too. I wanted them to feel my love everywhere.

xlix

I USED TO MAKE MY BIRTHDAY A BIG DEAL, BACK IN my twenties and thirties. It was a chance to do something special, invite people out or to my place. Darren had made an even bigger deal of my birthday than I did, with trips and extravagant gifts. My fortieth birthday happened a week after the COVID pandemic hit, which meant the dinner I'd planned got canceled, and I celebrated on Zoom with Kate and Julia, my parents and Jay, and friends from work all toasting me from their living rooms. The pandemic made the next couple of birthdays tricky, too, and I decided that maybe it was better that way—less pressure, lower expectations. So I hadn't planned anything at all for this birthday. I'd figured, when I first thought about it back in February, that I might do something with Darren and Courtney and all the kids, since my birthday fell on one of their weeks. But Darren hadn't really been speaking to me the week leading up to my birthday, so I knew that wouldn't happen.

Instead, I left work a little early and treated myself to a pedicure, and then ordered some tacos and a margarita to go from Rosa Mexicano. I was replying to Kate's and Julia's happy birthday memes when Courtney texted to ask if I was home yet. I told her I would be in about forty-five minutes, and she said she'd call with the kids then. I noted that it was Courtney, not Darren, who had sent that message. At least it sounded like the kids were still talking to me. I closed my eyes and let myself get lost in the audiobook I was listening to on the subway ride home. I don't think you and I ever talked about audiobooks, but I'm so into them now that Julia calls me the audiobook proselytizer. They bring me back to the days of having parents and teachers read books to you, where all you have to focus on is the lilt of someone's voice and the story they're telling you.

When I got home, I was still listening to Gabrielle de Cuir's wonderful narration, so I didn't notice at first that the kids and Courtney were standing inside my living room. There was a chocolate cake on the dining table and a banner hanging across the living room wall that said *Happy Birthday!*

I can't tell you how hard I cried when I saw them all there.

Sammy saw me crying, and he ran over and put his arms around me. "Did we scare you?" he said. "It's just us. Don't worry, Mom."

At that, I wiped my eyes. "You didn't scare me, sweet boy," I said. "These are happy tears. I'm really glad to see you. Thank you for coming over to wish me a happy birthday."

Liam and Violet both hugged me, too, and wished me a happy birthday, but there was something slightly forced about it. They were there, though, which I really appreciated.

After we all finished eating cake, Courtney helped me clear the table. "I'm sorry it's me here," she said.

I turned to look at her after I put the plates in the sink. "I'm not," I said. "With the way he's feeling about me right now, I'd rather spend my birthday with you."

She squeezed my shoulder.

"How are things between the two of you?" I asked her.

"We're working on it," she said.

I nodded. "I truly am sorry that this secret hurt you, too."

"I appreciate that," Courtney said, "but it's not your fault."

"And I appreciate you saying *that*," I answered, starting to fill the dishwasher.

"I said it because it's true," she said. "This has really been like a crack in a dam, though. It's brought up a lot for both of us. I hope we'll be stronger for it."

"I hope that for you, too," I said. My love for Gabe had already hurt Darren so deeply. I sent a prayer up to the universe to please not let his marriage, his wife, be part of the collateral damage.

Courtney looked at her watch. "We should head back. I hope you have a nice rest of your birthday, and that this coming year is a great one for you."

I gave her a hug and wondered if maybe, after all these years, this was what it might take for us to become actual friends.

She rounded the kids up and they went back to her

place. I sat down in the quiet kitchen with my margarita and tacos.

A WhatsApp message came through. And I felt a small thrill at the sound of it. *Dax*, my heart said.

I opened the message and it said: *A little birdie told me today was your birthday. Wanted to wish you a happy day and a happy year ahead.*

I looked at the message.

A birdie? I asked.

Okay, fine, I'll embarrass myself: I Googled you after we first met. I found your Wikipedia page, and it had your birthday on it.

I laughed out loud, remembering how I'd once Googled you, Gabe, and been so jealous of your Wikipedia page.

Well, thank you, I texted back.

It's been a long day and I'm exhausted, he wrote, *so I'm going to bed, but wanted to make sure I got you before I passed out.*

Sleep well, I wrote back.

You too, he said.

I finished my tacos and my margarita, ate another small sliver of cake, and then went upstairs. As I got into bed, I thought about my birthday more than two decades ago, when I saw you at Faces & Names, when I was there with Julia and Alexis and Kate and you sent us a round of drinks. It's so incredible to me how much has happened between then and now. It makes me wonder what's in store for the next two decades. You never know what the universe has planned.

1

ON THURSDAY I RACED BACK TO BROOKLYN FROM
the office to make it to Sammy's school in time for the art
show, which was in honor of March being Youth Art
Month. I swear it wasn't until the kids were in school
that I learned there is a month or a day for pretty much
everything. Did you know there's a National Journalism
Day? May 3. There's even an International Children's Day
of Broadcasting. The first Sunday in March. I don't know
anyone who celebrates it, though, including me. After
Liam's kindergarten class celebrated International Talk
Like a Pirate Day, Darren and I joked about it for years.

I got to the auditorium before Darren and the kids.
It always feels odd being at a school function without
them, like, who am I? What right do I have to be there
alone?

But it was still too cold to stay outside, so I hovered by
the door, waiting for them to arrive. When they did, I
saw Liam, Sammy, Darren, and Courtney.

I waved and Sam came over to give me a hug. "Violet's babysitting Ivy and Sage because Angie couldn't stay," he said. "But I promised her I'd take pictures."

I looked over at Darren to confirm that it was a babysitting thing, not that Violet was upset with me. He was looking at Courtney, though, who was talking to Liam. There are so many personalities in our family. So many relationships and so many feelings always happening at once.

"Oh, we'll definitely take pictures," I told him. "Let's go find your painting."

He took my hand, and we walked toward the wall where the art was hung. About a quarter of the way down, Sammy stopped and pointed.

"That's mine," he said.

I took a step closer. I saw a woman with dark hair walking down an autumn street in Brooklyn. The artist's vantage point was from behind her, and she was slightly slouched, her hands tucked into the sleeves of a big sweater. She was wearing black leggings and had black boots on her feet. The boots looked familiar, the hair, too. But I wasn't sure. I looked at the small piece of paper taped to the wall next to it, and it read: *Left Behind by Samuel Maxwell*. I didn't know how he was relating the title to the image.

"Will you tell me about it?" I asked him. It's what I've been saying ever since he started showing me his artwork scribbles when he was two. That way I wouldn't say *Ooh, beautiful kitty!* when he'd drawn something else altogether.

"That's you," he said, pointing to the woman with her

head down. "And you're walking away from Dad's house on a Saturday night. See, that's his street. That's the house that's being redone next door, but I left the construction work out. I just imagined what it'll look like when it's finished. And that's Dad and Courtney's car, parked right there."

"I thought that might be me," I said. "It looks like my hair."

"And your leggings and slouchy boots, with your big thick sweater, the one you wore, like, the whole fall."

I laughed. I had worn a thick gray sweater a lot this past fall.

"Is the title because you feel like I leave you behind on Saturday nights?"

Sam shrugged. "I guess sort of," he said, looking down at his sneakers. "But more because I feel like we leave you behind sometimes. Like, you're in the house all alone, and we're all together somewhere else. And it always makes me wonder if you're lonely without us."

I pulled Sammy to me and laid my cheek against his hair, so he couldn't see the tears in my eyes. "You really do have an artist's soul," I whispered.

He pulled away and then looked up at me.

"Mom," he said softly. "Do you think Gabriel would think so? And his mom? Do you think they would be proud if they saw this drawing?"

I looked at his picture and then looked at our boy. "I do," I said. "I think they'd be really, really proud, just like I am. Not just because of your talent but because of how hard you work on your art, how much you love it, and how thoughtful you are when you draw and paint."

Courtney, Darren, and Liam joined us soon after, and Sam explained his drawing to them, too. Then his art teacher, Kathy Hammer, came by to talk to us and we migrated over to the cookies-and-juice table near where Ms. Hammer walked up onto the stage to make a speech about the importance of art in schools and nurturing our children's talent and love of creation. She announced that the pieces included in this show were going to be relocated to a gallery wall in the school's media center for the remainder of the year.

The parents all clapped, and then Ms. Hammer walked off the stage.

Liam looked at Darren hopefully. "Time for a celebratory ice cream?" he asked.

"We should get back to Violet and the girls," Darren said, looking at the time on his iPhone.

Sammy's face fell.

"I can take the boys and drop them off at your house," I said.

Darren turned to Courtney, a pained look on his face. "I told the girls I'd be home to read them three Elephant & Piggie books before bed."

"I'll take the boys," Courtney said, looking at me. "Lucy and I will."

Darren nodded. "Okay," he said. I could hear the relief in his voice. I wasn't sure if he was relieved not to have to disappoint the twins, or if he was relieved that he wouldn't have to spend more time with me. He'd barely said a word to me at the show.

It was rare that Courtney and I were with the kids together without Darren, and this was the second time that week.

"Ready to go, Mr. Artiste?" she said to Sammy.

Sam laughed. "Yes, but maybe hot chocolate instead of ice cream?" he said, looking at Liam. "What do you think, Li?"

"Good plan, dude," Liam said. "It's cold out there."

So the four of us walked to the diner down the block and sat down, with Courtney and Sam on one side and Liam and me on the other. I wondered how the waiter saw us. Two single moms out with their sons? A married couple with the boys they're raising together? A mom, her two sons, and an aunt? There were so many ways someone could perceive us. But perception and reality can be so different.

We started sipping our hot chocolates—the boys through whipped cream.

"Did Gabriel's mom ever have an art show in a gallery—a show that was all her own?" Sammy asked me.

I nodded. "I'm pretty sure she did," I said. "She sold a lot of her paintings at galleries in Arizona, where she lived."

Courtney cleared her throat. "Actually," she said, "your dad told me that Gabriel had a gallery show of his photographs once."

Sammy's face lit up. "Did you go, Mom?"

"I did," I told him. "And you know what? There's going to be another gallery show of his work in July, to honor the tenth anniversary of his death."

"Can I go?" Sammy asked, just as Liam said, "That's

kind of sad. His art is getting this cool recognition, but he's not there to see it."

"It is sad," Sammy agreed, "but also it's kind of cool that his photographs live on without him, you know? Like, he's gone, but the stuff he did isn't. It's like the painters from long-ago times who have their art in a museum; they're dead, but they're kind of still alive because of their paintings."

"I like that idea, Sammy," Courtney said.

Liam wiped whipped cream off his lip. "I bet you could have a painting in a museum one day, Sam," he said.

"And I bet you could play drums on a song that people sing over and over," Sam said. "We'd both kind of live forever."

Liam smiled. I could tell he liked that idea.

"Your mom, too," Courtney said. "She'll live on for a long time—as long as people are watching her shows." She picked up her diner mug for another sip of hot chocolate.

"What about you, Courtney?" Sam asked.

"Courtney will live on in the minds and hearts and history of every single kid she's helped," I said.

I thought about how so many seemingly small things can have such a huge impact. I wondered if tonight was one of those things for Sammy or Liam. Or for Courtney.

"You never answered Sam's question, Mom," Liam said. "Can we go to the art thing?"

I loved how Liam expanded Sammy's request to include him, too. "If you want to go, then you absolutely can."

Liam nodded, and Sammy smiled.

"Thanks for coming tonight," I said to Courtney, as the boys got into a conversation about how many ounces of hot chocolate they could fit in their mouths.

"It's a little hard to breathe in that house right now," she said. "I'm happy to be here."

"I know the feeling," I said.

She smiled sadly at me as I flagged down the waiter for the check.

51

I KNOW WE'VE TALKED BEFORE ABOUT HOW DAYS that at first seem ordinary can become extraordinary in the most unexpected ways. The next day, just as I was getting ready to figure out dinner, I got a WhatsApp message from Dax.

Hey, are you around? he wrote.

Mm-hmm, everything okay? I answered.

All good, he said. *I'm actually at JFK. Just landed. I was thinking about what I wanted to do first, now that I'm home, and all I could think of was seeing you. Any chance you're available?*

I stared at the phone. He was home. I'd thought his plane wasn't landing until tomorrow. And we hadn't made any real plans to see each other. Hadn't said much about what might happen once he got home, other than that at some point we'd make marshmallow pies together. I imagined him in my kitchen, his eyes smiling at me across the counter, then him kissing me as we stirred and mixed melted marshmallows. My heart yearned for that, for him. My body did, too. I knew what I should do to keep my heart safe, to keep his heart safe, but I also knew what I wanted to do. And desire won out over duty. Over fear.

I opened up my cabinets and my freezer, quickly cataloging the contents.

Want a home-cooked meal? I typed.

Marshmallow pie? he said.

We can make it, I wrote back, *but it'll need to set, so we can't eat it for a few hours at least.*

Baking before dinner.

Sounds like a deal. You're what, 45 minutes away?

I have to get my luggage and go through customs, so maybe an hour and a half?

Perfect.

But as I typed that, I realized it was not quite perfect. I'd have the exact right amount of time to get dinner started, run to the corner store for graham crackers, marshmallows, and whipping cream, and come back to finish dinner and set the table. But not quite enough time to reapply makeup or fix my hair, which was now thrown into a bun on the top of my head, with a few of the shorter strands falling down around my face. Somehow, though, I didn't think Dax would mind. I don't know if it was because I was so much older than I was the last time I'd been dating people, or because I knew I could thrive on my own, but I was okay with letting Dax see me as I usually looked at the end of the day—slightly disheveled, makeup all worn off. Though the bun was maybe pushing it.

I quickly put together a salad and the ingredients for a Boursin orzo recipe, preheating the oven at the same time. The recipe, which was essentially orzo, Boursin cheese, sun-dried tomatoes, and spinach, is one of those set-it-and-forget-it sorts of recipes that I found on Instagram and love.

While the oven was preheating, I ran to the corner market to get the ingredients for a marshmallow pie and then came back to set the table and open a bottle of wine so it could breathe.

Be there in five, Dax texted.

Luckily, since the kids weren't around that week, the house was neat. I ducked into the half bathroom off the kitchen and took down my hair, finger-combing it enough that it didn't look like I'd been running around in a wind tunnel all day. I always felt more confident with my hair down.

Then the doorbell rang, and all of a sudden, my heart was in my throat. With all that racing around, I hadn't had time to feel anxious. But in that moment, my palms got sweaty, my knees went weak.

I closed my eyes and took a deep breath, then walked to the door.

I couldn't believe I was really going to have a man in my house after all this time. I took another deep breath, then opened the door. All my anxiety faded away. Dax's smile was warm and when he stepped in to hug me hello, my body fit into his like we had been carved that way. I closed my eyes and rested my cheek against his chest, feeling his muscles shift as he wrapped his arms around me tighter.

"My goodness, this feels good," Dax said softly. The relief in his voice made me melt.

"It does," I answered. I realized the door was open behind him. "Come in, come in," I added, pulling away for a moment.

He dragged a massive suitcase and duffel bag in and pulled them to the side of the entryway. "Sorry about the enormous luggage," he said.

"No apologies necessary," I answered. "I'm honored you wanted to see me before even going home."

"Well," he said, "I'm honored you wanted to welcome me home." Dax looked around the main floor of the house. "This place is huge," he said. "And beautiful."

"Thank you," I said. "One day, when we have time, I'll tell you how I got it. It's a very random New York kind of story."

He laughed. "We have time now," he said, following me into the kitchen and then weaving his fingers through mine when we got there. "Can I just look at you?"

I looked up at him, slightly embarrassed at first, but when I saw the hunger in his eyes, the pleasure he got from looking at me, I stood a little straighter. I could feel my smile grow a little wider as I looked back at him.

It had been five weeks since I'd last seen him, and I could already see that his eyes were a little more golden than I remembered, his hair a slightly bronzer shade of brown. I didn't think it was possible, but he was even more ruggedly handsome than in my memory.

"Look at you," I said. "How can you be so stunning after traveling for like a dozen hours."

He laughed, a deep throaty chuckle. "Me?" he said.

"I'm nothing compared to you. You are even more beautiful than I remembered."

"You too," I said.

He squeezed my hand, and I leaned in to kiss him, melting again into the warmth of his body.

"I've wanted to kiss you so many times these last weeks," he said against my mouth. "Every time we spoke on the phone," he said, kissing me again. "I want to make up for all of them."

"One more," I said against his mouth, "or maybe two"—our breath mingled—"but then we have to get baking or we won't have any marshmallow pie to eat."

"How about three?" he said, kissing me once more.

"Three's good," I said, my body going liquid as he grazed his teeth along my bottom lip.

When he finally pulled away, my heart was racing. I took his hand and walked toward the stack of ingredients I'd left out for marshmallow pie.

"What can I do?" he asked, rolling up his sleeves and washing his hands in my sink. He washed them like a doctor, slowly and thoroughly.

"Here," I said, handing him the box of graham crackers. "You can start by opening these."

He complied. "So what's the story with this house?" he asked as we crushed the graham crackers.

"Well," I said, "a few years after Darren and I split, I was in a two-bedroom apartment with the three kids, when my friend Julia called me and said, 'Are you ready for the New York City real estate deal of a lifetime?' Of course, I said yes, and then she told me that she worked with this children's book illustrator who'd never been married and never had children, but had this massive brownstone in Brooklyn Heights. It needed a lot of work, and the illustrator, Eva, wanted to sell it to someone who would let her live in her studio there for the rest of her life."

Dax's eyes were wide as he looked around my kitchen. "Was she sick?"

I shook my head. "She's still living up on the third floor," I told him. "And she's eighty-nine."

"Wow," he said.

I started melting the butter and marshmallows and said, "As odd as the arrangement seemed, the idea of more space, of Liam and Sammy and Violet each getting their own rooms, of storage in the basement and a small yard . . . it was all really appealing."

"Of course it was!" Dax said. I handed him the spoon and he started stirring.

"So," I said, "I went over to meet Eva, and we really hit it off. I asked her what she was asking for the house, and her answer was: 'What can you afford?' And so here we are. I did a lot of work on it over the past six years, and it feels like home now."

"What a lovely story," he said. "Julia sounds like a great friend."

"She is," I said, thinking about how wonderful she was to me, even when she suspected I was keeping a secret from her. I poured the melted mixture into the crust and then put our pie in the refrigerator. "We've been friends for a long time now. About half our lives."

I walked over to the oven to take out the Boursin orzo, which had been warming. When I turned, he had already started wiping down my kitchen counter.

"Thanks," I said.

He shrugged. "Want to be a good guest, make sure I get invited back."

I smiled. "Dinner's ready," I said. "Can you grab the salad in the refrigerator, please?"

"Anything else I should get?" he asked. "Plates? Forks?"

"The table's already set," I said. "Just follow me."

We walked into the dining area—when I bought the house from Eva, it had been a formal dining room, but I knocked out the walls, so the dining area was now set off by pillars that used to be the corners of the room, and the view was open to the living room. I had the moldings along the ceiling restored on the wall that remained, the one that backed the kitchen, and added a built-in sideboard along with a long wooden table and chairs.

"This house really is amazing," Dax said.

"It was fun getting to reimagine the space," I told him. "So how was it leaving Lampedusa after six months?" We put the food down on the table and sat opposite each other. "Please, help yourself," I added, handing him the serving tongs for the salad.

As he served himself, he said, "Before I met Aviva, I worked with Doctors Without Borders in Nairobi, Bangladesh, and Lampedusa. Then once we got married, I stayed in New York, working in the ER at Columbia Presbyterian. This was my first time back in the field in fifteen years. After Zac died, after being on the front lines during the COVID pandemic, after getting divorced, I needed a change. And working back on Lampedusa was that change. It reconnected me with who I am when the chaos of my own life doesn't get in the way—and why working in emergency medicine is so important to me. But an assignment like that always feels a bit like running away. And it was time to come back."

"That makes sense," I said. "I can't even imagine the last few years you've had—personally and professionally." I refilled our wineglasses. "Were you running from something when you first went to Nairobi?"

He took a sip of the wine and then said, "The future, I guess. After medical school, I wasn't ready to do all the things everyone is expected to do. And I wanted to heal people, I wanted to use my degree where it was needed most, so I signed up. I'm glad I did. But I'm also glad I came back home."

I finished swallowing the orzo. "If you had a crystal ball, is there anything you would change?" I asked. I realized after I said it that it was the kind of weird question I usually asked my kids, but he rolled with it. In fact, I'd meant it kind of flippantly, but he took it seriously.

"In my personal world," he said, "knowing then what I know now, I would have put Zac in isolation once he started chemo. It wasn't really an option, but if I had known the pandemic was coming, I would have pulled any strings I could to make it happen. Professionally . . . let's see . . . I would have started a committee of ER doctors to really ramp up pandemic response protocols at Columbia, but also across the whole country and the whole world. Increased the production of PPE, the stockpile of ventilators, the vaccine distribution capability—and I would have set up a mental health network for the frontline workers at the hospitals."

"You would change the world," I said.

He looked down at his place and gave a self-conscious laugh. "I would try," he said.

When he looked up, my eyes were on his. "That's . . . so . . . wonderful," I said. "That's not quite the right word. But I love where you took my silly question. I love what it says about you."

He smiled and it felt like we were magnetized toward each other. We both leaned across the table and kissed softly. When our kiss ended, I looked quickly at my watch.

"It's late for you," I said. "You must be tired."

He looked at his watch, too. "A bit," he said. "But we haven't had our marshmallow pie yet. How much longer until it sets?"

"Another couple hours," I told him.

He yawned. "I'm not sure if I'll make it," he admitted. "I guess I should probably head home. And maybe . . . you could save some for when we hopefully see each other again?"

It's so funny—there were points in my life when friends of mine were in tears because the men they were dating wouldn't acknowledge the future in any way. But with Dax, I really wanted to live in the present. I was lonely, yes, I loved being with him and talking to him, but I still didn't know what I wanted my future to look like. I didn't know if I could handle a real relationship again, how a boyfriend would fit into the puzzle of my life.

I took a deep breath. "How about if we have it tomorrow morning, for breakfast?" I asked, taking a leap I wasn't quite ready to take, but knowing that I'd miss him desperately if I let him walk out the door right then.

He looked at me for a beat, cocking his head slightly. I could see that he was tired, there were shadows under his eyes, but he was still so handsome, so incredibly sexy.

"I guess my apartment can wait one more night for me," he said. "And I don't start work at NYU for another two weeks—figured I'd give myself a reentry period—so I don't have anywhere else to be." He stood, taking his dishes with him. "Are you the kind of person who is very serious about dishwasher loading?" he asked.

"I let my kids load the dishwasher," I told him, standing up and taking my dishes, too. "So, no."

"This is getting better and better," he said, walking to the kitchen. "You can cook, and you'll let me load the dishwasher any way I like."

I could tell there was some baggage there from Aviva, but I wasn't going to probe. It was too late, and honestly, it didn't really matter. I was just so happy he was there with me, in that moment, sharing the evening.

After clearing the table, Dax went to his bag for a toothbrush, then said, "Is it time for a tour of the house?"

I gave him a quick one of the first floor, pointed down the stairs to tell him where the rec room and laundry room were, and then led him up the second set of stairs to the bedroom level, pointing down the hallway to the left for the kids' bedrooms and bathroom, and to the right for mine.

We walked into my room, and he paused just in front of the doorframe. "Your bed is just how I pictured it," he said, "with all the pillows. It looks really comfortable."

"It is," I said, realizing just as the words left my lips how flirtatious it sounded.

Before long, we were in the bed together, under the covers.

He reached his fingers across to me from his side of the bed, so we were holding hands beneath the blanket, like we did on Lampedusa. I thought about that night together. How many times we'd both orgasmed.

"How tired are you?" I whispered.

I heard him laugh slightly. "If you're thinking what I'm thinking, I'm not too tired for that."

I rolled close to him and he put his fingers to my mouth and then slid them inside. Then he pulled them out, and I felt them appear lower down, warm and slick, sliding inside me. I moaned and then reached down to where I felt him throbbing against my thigh.

"You are so wet," he said, his voice a gasp.

"You are so hard," I answered.

"I know," he moaned.

"I've been dreaming about you inside me," I said, and felt him stiffen even more against my hand.

"I've been thinking about you, too," he said. "Whenever I close my eyes."

He reached to the night table next to him, where he'd left his glasses and phone and a few other things I hadn't seen. One of those things, apparently, was a condom. He slid it on, and I climbed on top of him.

"My god," I said when I felt him fill me.

I heard his breath catch as his thrusts became faster. And then my breathing matched his, my body did too, until we both came hard and hot, the power of it moving me to tears.

He was the first man I ever slept with in that bed—in my bed—the one I bought after Darren and I divorced. But it didn't feel strange, it felt wonderful.

We separated and lay back on our pillows, catching our breath.

"You're crying," Dax said, touching the tears that had overflowed onto my cheeks. "Did I hurt you?"

"No," I said, reaching my hand out to catch his fingers. "I think you're healing me."

lii

YOU KNOW WHEN YOU WAKE UP AND YOU FEEL FINE, well-rested, maybe even happy, and then a feeling of dread hits you in the stomach? That's how I felt when I got out of bed the next morning, not because Dax was there—he was why I'd felt so well-rested and happy—but because I remembered I had lunch plans with my parents and brother to tell them about you, to tell them that you were Sammy's biological father.

"You okay?" Dax asked, after I cut myself a small sliver of marshmallow pie. His piece was about four times the size.

I sighed. "I'm going to tell my parents the truth about Samuel today. That Darren's not his biological father. And I'm just . . . dreading it."

He nodded and took a sip of the coffee I'd made, his knee pressed against mine. "Dreading their response?" he asked.

"I guess," I said, then thought about it. "Actually no," I amended, leaning my head on his shoulder, "I think I'm dreading having to admit that I cheated, that I lied."

Dax wrapped his arm around my shoulder and gave it a squeeze. "I think you'll feel so much better afterward."

I nodded. "I hope you're right," I told him.

He licked a bit of marshmallow off his fork. "By the way, we make a mean marshmallow pie. This is delicious."

"You can take some home," I said, "if you'd like."

He shook his head. "Your kids should have it. They're coming tonight, right?"

I took a tiny bite of pie. "They are—and they'll love it," I said.

We were both quiet for a moment, and then Dax said, "Will I get to see you this week?"

I shook my head. "Not when I have the kids."

He smiled at me a little sadly. "That's what I figured," he said. "Can I invite you over next weekend, then? Saturday night, after they've gone, or Sunday? Dinner at my place? Don't worry, I won't cook."

I felt a tiny butterfly of fear fluttering in my heart, but then I remembered how wonderful last night was, how sleeping with another person in the same bed had felt good, not scary. I thought of how Dax was so comforting. "Sounds good," I said. "How about Sunday?"

"Deal," Dax said, after eating the last of his pie and taking the final sip of his coffee. He looked at his watch and then at me. "I guess I should get going. It was really, really nice being here."

We both stood up and wrapped our arms around each other. "I had fun, too," I said. "More than fun."

He zipped his toothbrush back in his suitcase, then brought his luggage outside to flag down a taxi. I waved from the door, then turned back into the house to get ready. Being with Dax stirred up such a mix of feelings, the kind I'd kept at bay for years: desire, hope, fear, and a yearning for something more—for connection, for love. The more I saw him, the more I wanted to see him, but an undercurrent of panic was starting to thrum through me, too. Outside, I'm sure I looked fine, but inside I was a mess, Gabe. As usual, I was a mess.

THE LUNCH WITH MY PARENTS AND JAY WENT OKAY. Better than I'd thought it would. I told them the truth right after we ordered. Jay was the first one who spoke. He looked thoughtful and then said that he'd always wondered how two average-sized people with straight, dark hair made such a tall kid with blond curls. My dad said it was a shame you weren't around to see Sammy grow up. My mom said she wished I'd told her sooner— that I'd trusted her with this—but when I explained that Darren had wanted to keep the secret from everyone, she said she understood, even if she didn't like it. Darren and my mom have remained in touch, even after our divorce. Not that they talk all the time or anything, but Darren sends her pictures of the kids, and she sends his twins holiday presents and birthday presents. She really liked having him as a son-in-law, and

I understand why. He can be charming, when he wants to be.

It turned out Dax was right, I did feel better afterward. Lighter. Like this heavy weight I'd been carrying for so long had been lifted from my shoulders. I felt the wall I'd put up nearly a decade ago between my parents and my brother and me start to crumble.

"I'm sorry," I said to them as we walked out of the restaurant. "I think I let this secret get in the way of us, of our relationships. With this big boulder I had to talk around, it was hard to really engage about other things, you know?"

My mom wrapped her arms around me. "Well," she said, "we can only move forward, right?"

"Right," I said, feeling tears prick my eyes. The fact that she was so understanding made me even sadder that I hadn't shared this with them from the beginning. That I hadn't given them the chance to help.

"I understand so much more now," Jay said to me when he walked me to the train. "I understand what happened between us and why. It makes me sad that we lost each other for so long, but I hope we can find our way back to each other again."

He gave me a hug, and I knew my tears would leave a wet spot on his sweater.

"Hey," I said. "I'm really sorry I never called you after I got back from Italy. I've been meaning to, but it's been so hard to have to keep so much back from you."

"I know," he said, and sighed. "Now we'll do better."

"We will," I said, and I hugged him again.

Here's what I have to say, Gabe: Even if they don't seem to be a big deal while you're keeping them, secrets are insidious. They work their way into relationships like moths chewing holes in fabric, until you realize that your favorite coat has been destroyed. Luckily for me, things didn't get that bad—with my kids or my parents or my brother. But they could have.

liii

THAT NEXT WEEK WAS A ROUGH ONE. WHEN I ASKED
the kids on Sunday night to tell me their best, worst, and
wished, Violet said no thank you. Actually, what she said
was, "Mom, I don't want to do this anymore." And then
Liam said, "If she doesn't have to, I'm not doing it either."
And then Sammy looked at all three of us and burst into
tears, running off into his room.

I followed and knocked on his door. "Sam?" I said.
"Do you want to talk?"

"You can come in," he said, still sniffling. I pushed
open the door and noticed he'd taped a new drawing he'd
made to the wall next to his bed. It was a drawing of you
as a kid next to a drawing of him now. He did an amazing job of cataloging your similarities and differences.

"What's wrong?" I asked.

He looked up at me, anguish in his eyes. "It's just that
everything is changing," he said. "First you told me about
Gabriel, and now Violet and Liam don't want to do best,

worst, wished. And Violet's annoyed all the time, and Dad and Courtney are weird and mad, and nothing is the same as it used to be."

He threw his arms around me, and I held him close. "I'm so sorry things are changing," I said. I was thinking about Dax. About whether I could really spring that change on my kids, too. What Sammy would say.

"Sometimes things can't change back," he said, his voice muffled against my shirt. "Even if you want them to. Once you know things, you can't not know them."

"That's right," I said. "But I still think it's better to know. Even if it means you can't go back to who you were before."

"Everything is just so hard," he wailed.

"For me too, sometimes," I told him, pulling him even closer to me, leaning my cheek against his forehead, feeling his soft curls against my skin, his warm little body against mine.

We stayed like that for a moment.

"I saw you hung up a new drawing," I said. "Do you want to tell me about it?"

He looked up at the one next to his bed. "I just wanted to see how the same we were," he said. "Our hair is the same." He pointed to the hair in both the images. "And the shape of our noses and eyes. But our eye color is different. And I think my chin is shaped a little more like yours. My lips, too. See how my top lip is a little thicker than his?"

I nodded. "I do," I said. "I guess there's more of me in you than I realized."

He smiled. "It's nice to find you in my face."

"It's nice to be in your face!" I said. Then after a beat I added, "Do you want to go back to dinner now?"

He nodded. "But first I want to do best, worst, and wished."

"Go for it," I said.

Sammy cleared his throat. "Best," he said, "was our conversation just now because it made me feel a little better. Worst is Liam and Violet not wanting to do best, worst, wished. And wished is . . . wished is that . . ." He looked at me. "You won't be mad?"

I shook my head. "I'm never mad about best, worst, wished."

"Wished is that I always knew the truth."

"I wish that, too, Sammy," I said.

He nodded, then stood up and took my hand. We went back to the kitchen to salvage dinner.

The rest of the week was rocky, too. Violet was clearly furious with me, more than when we first told the kids, and she was acting out in predictably teenage ways—not doing the things around the house she was supposed to do, not calling when she was supposed to call, not turning out the lights when she was supposed to go to sleep. Essentially, trying to push my buttons, an attempt—conscious or subconscious—to make me as mad as she was. And Liam seemed extra quiet, barely speaking to me or his siblings at all. I called Darren and told him I wanted to get them all into therapy. I was waiting for pushback, but he agreed, and I called one of the providers Dax had recommended to set up appointments. That was when I called Julia for the name of her therapist so I could set up my own appointment, too—that's who I've been seeing now, for a while, but it took more than a month to get that initial appointment, a month during which things spiraled even more.

The only thing that kept me together was the idea of seeing Dax again. We texted a few times the week my kids started melting down, but not nearly enough—which was my doing, not his. And when I finally fell into his arms that Sunday, it felt like such a relief.

"I made it," I said to him.

"You made it," he echoed, giving me a sweet kiss. "What do you think?" he asked, indicating the apartment behind him.

I stepped in.

The apartment was a one-bedroom, prewar, with high ceilings. It was sparsely decorated mostly in simple, neutral furniture. There were maps and a few photographs of Dax and Zac hanging on the walls. But the most marvelous part of the apartment was the huge wall of windows overlooking Central Park.

"What a view!" I said as Dax bent to hug me.

"It's why I bought the place," he said.

It was interesting to me that he'd bought a one-bedroom. A real statement that he wasn't planning for a future with many more people in his life, wasn't looking for visitors. If he could afford this building with this view, he clearly could have bought a bigger place without such a spectacular view, if space had been important to him.

"I ordered us some Italian food from my favorite local restaurant," he said. "It's in honor of where we met."

I laughed. "I'm so glad we met, and even gladder I'm

here with you right now," I said. "I adore my kids and would do anything for them, but it's been a hard week."

"Here," he said, handing me a glass of wine. "Do you want to talk about it?"

We sat down on the couch, and I leaned into him while we talked. I felt the stress leave my body, felt myself relax against him.

"I just . . . I'm worried that they'll never feel the same way about me again," I said.

"They probably won't," Dax said, his hands massaging the knots out of my shoulders.

"What?" I interrupted, turning my head to look at him. I thought he was on my side.

"And that's not a bad thing," he finished.

"It's not?" I asked, closing my eyes as his massage got deeper.

"As they grow, their view of you will always shift and change," he said. "I'm sure the way Violet felt about you two weeks ago was very different from when she was five or ten. At some point, our parents become real people, separate from us. And once that realization happens, kids see their moms or their dads in a more three-dimensional way. And out of that comes real respect, admiration, and a deeper appreciation for the people who raise them."

"And you think that's what will happen here?" I asked.

"I imagine so," he said. "And once your kids see what I see—what a strong, brave, kind woman you are, they will respect and admire you, just like I do."

My heart squeezed and I couldn't come up with the right words to convey my thanks, so instead I put my gratitude into a kiss. He kissed me back, then traced my jawline with his fingers.

"You feeling a bit better?" he asked. "Ready for dinner?"

"I am," I told him. "Thanks to you."

He smiled, then stood up and led me to the dinner table. He'd set it so we'd be sitting next to each other, overlooking the park.

"I keep thinking about something Darren said when he was telling me why he didn't want to tell Sammy the truth," I said to Dax, as we sat down.

"What's that?" he asked, passing me a serving dish of tortellini with basil and parmesan.

"He said that he was worried Sammy would compare him to Gabe, like he always felt I did, and that he would lose that competition, too." I served myself some tortellini.

Dax turned to give me his full attention. "Listen," he said. "You will compare me to Darren, you will compare me to Gabriel. Even if you don't say it, you will. It's natural. I'll compare you to Aviva. But comparison doesn't mean competition." He picked up tortellini with his fork. "You will compare these tortellini to other tortellini you've eaten in your life, but it's not a tortellini competition. You can appreciate them all. You can enjoy them all. For a long time, my marriage to Aviva was great. And then it wasn't. But there's space in my heart to acknowledge what was great about being with her, and also what's great about being with you."

"I like that," I said. "I know you loved Aviva. I'm glad you had that love in your life. I'm not competing with that love."

He took a sip of wine. "I imagine it's like having more than one child—you probably compare what they like, how they act, what they did at the same age—but they're not competing. You can love them all. There's always more room in your heart."

The particularly lovely thing about sitting next to each other was that it was easy for him to lean over and kiss me. Which he did, and I felt my heart expand. I kissed him back, hard.

"You know," I whispered flirtatiously. "There's room for you in more than just my heart."

"Oh yeah?" he said softly.

"Oh yeah," I replied, my lips close to his ear.

"Mmm," he said, pulling me onto his lap. "Should we take a brief intermission, then? Finish our dinner later?"

I kissed his neck, then his lips. "I like how you think, Dr. Armstrong."

I climbed off his lap, and he led me to his bedroom. There was a big king-sized bed inside, with a blue-and-gray-striped comforter on it. Far fewer pillows than mine had. "Looks comfortable," I said, echoing his response to my bed.

"It is," he answered, planting kisses on my neck and my wrists and my fingertips. I imagined each of those kisses would bloom inside me, expanding my heart even more. He tugged me onto his bed, and I could feel how luxuriously soft it was.

We shimmied out of our jeans and sweaters, our socks and underwear, and he planted more kisses on my breasts before making his way down to where I was soft and wet and wanting him.

"Ohhh," I said when he touched me with his tongue, shivering at the sensations he was already causing in my body.

"I love how you taste," he said.

I smiled, my eyes closed. It was like he was a wizard with the power to make my worries, my anxieties melt away with a single touch.

"Let me taste," I said.

And he kissed me.

"I want you inside me," I whispered into his mouth.

He leaned over to his nightstand and rolled a condom down onto his erection.

"I love knowing what you want," he said.

I looked down at him. "I know what you want, too." I kissed him again and then guided him inside me. "You feel so good," I whispered as he entered.

"You too," he said, his voice made of breath and air more than sound.

We rocked into each other, the city lights twinkled outside his window, and I had this overwhelming feeling that I was just where I was supposed to be, in that moment, at that time, in that place.

I kissed him harder, he thrust faster, and we both came, looking into each other's eyes.

It felt like exploding into stars.

liv

I STAYED OVER AT DAX'S PLACE THAT NIGHT, AND AS I was leaving for the office the next morning, he handed me a travel coffee mug filled with the Guatemalan coffee he'd made in his French press and said, "Is it too much to ask what you're doing tonight? I waited so long to see you again in person, and now that we're both in the same city . . ."

I took the coffee mug and then stepped toward him to show my gratitude with a kiss. I ignored the little voice of fear inside me that said: *Not too fast! Someone will get hurt!* Instead, I said, "Seeing you, I hope."

He smiled and ran his fingers through his bed head. "Come back here? After work? I'll even try to make dinner."

I smiled at his earnestness. "Sounds good. I usually leave work around six. See you a little after that? And I can definitely help with dinner."

He shook his head. "I'm not working this week. The least I can do is figure out dinner."

I spent that whole day at work half paying attention and half daydreaming of Dax, reveling in the beautiful feeling of going home to someone special, of knowing that he was waiting all day to see me, too.

"You okay?" Versha asked me when it took me a moment longer to answer one of her questions.

"Yeah," I said. "I'm good."

She looked at me skeptically but kept pushing through the conversation. And I kept listening with half my mind while daydreaming about Dax with the other.

THAT NIGHT, I WAVED TO DAX'S DOORMAN AND headed up to his apartment, a thrill of excitement already fluttering in my stomach.

I knew he left his door unlocked, so I turned the knob, feeling equal parts brave and happy as I did it. "Hey," I called out. "It's me, I'm home."

"I'm in the living room," he called back.

I slipped off my shoes and lined them up at the front door next to his, then dropped my bag on the entryway table and slipped off my jacket.

"Coming!" I said, wondering why he hadn't come to meet me. "Dax?" I said as I walked through the hallway to the living room.

"Hey, my girl with kaleidoscope eyes," he said, looking up at me. He was sitting on the couch and was surrounded by paper and photographs and markers and glue.

"Hey," I said, making some room next to him and sitting down. "What are you up to?" I picked up one of the photographs. It was Dax and a little boy I assumed was Zac on the rowboats in Central Park.

"I'm trying to make a book of memories," he said. "I had put all the photos and ticket stubs and whatever else I'd saved of Zac's into that shoebox, and all of a sudden it felt awful keeping him in a box. So I wanted to make a book so I could keep the memories easily accessible."

I leaned my head against his shoulder. "You want some help?" I asked.

Dax kissed my temple. "I'd love some help," he said. "And, by the way, I ordered us Moroccan food. I decided it was too early to subject you to my horrible cooking, but I wanted to honor my word. It should be here soon."

"Moroccan sounds delicious," I said as I picked up the pile of photos on the table. "Want me to sort these into age, or activity?"

"Age, please," Dax said.

I nodded and started going through them. It was amazing to see Zac, but even more amazing to me to see Dax as a younger, much more carefree man. I wondered whether the two of us would have connected so deeply then, or if we both needed to experience sorrow first.

"Is there anything specific that precipitated this project?" I asked.

"It's April," he said. "Zac died on April nineteenth."

"Oh, Dax," I said, putting the photographs down and wrapping my arms around him. "I'm so, so sorry."

He rested his chin on my head, and we stayed that way for a while, not speaking, just breathing, just feeling the warmth of each other's bodies.

The kids' spring break was from April 22 to April 30 this year. Darren had the kids the week before.

"I don't know if you want to be alone that day," I said, quietly, "or if it's easier with company, but . . . I can take the day off and—"

"Yes," Dax said. "Please."

I nodded. "Of course."

His arms tightened around me, and mine tightened around him.

"Do you disappear again next week?" he asked, as if maybe by holding me tighter, he could keep me there.

I cringed. "I hate to," I said. "But I think so."

He nodded slowly. "I hope you'll tell your kids about me when you're ready, Lucy. I want this to be real, I want to be a part of your life. And I want you to be part of mine."

That flutter of anxiety kicked up again, but I ignored it. "I'd like that, too," I said.

lv

DAX ASKED IF WE COULD SPEND APRIL 19 EATING
Zac's favorite foods and doing things Zac loved. So I
made us sheet pan chocolate chip pancakes for breakfast,
following the *New York Times* recipe Aviva used to make
for Zac, and then we went to the Museum of Natural
History and the planetarium, ate Shake Shack for lunch,
and headed up to Yankee Stadium to watch the Yankees
play the Tampa Bay Rays. Dax gave me an extra baseball
cap he had, because Zac had always insisted on wearing
one when they went to a game.

He spent the whole day telling me stories about the
things they'd done, the memories they'd made together.
I could see it was draining him emotionally, but I could
also see that it felt good to him to remember, too.

As we rode the subway to the Bronx, Dax said to me,
"On one of these train rides to Yankee Stadium, I told Zac
how hip-hop started in the Bronx in the seventies, and
since then people have been calling it the Boogie Down.

From then on, that's the only way he referred to the Bronx."

I laughed. "I like it. Glad we're going to the Boogie Down in his honor."

Dax took my hand. "I was thinking," he said, "about Nathan's hot dogs for dinner. With cheese fries."

"Was that Zac's favorite at the ball field?" I asked.

Dax nodded. "And Cracker Jacks."

"Then we should get those, too," I said as the subway stopped and everyone planning to see the ball game got off.

We walked into the stadium and found our seats. Everyone stood for "The Star Spangled Banner," and I saw Dax wipe a tear from his eye. He started crying a little harder when the announcer introduced the players, and I put my arms around him. In my embrace, he really began to sob.

"It's okay," I murmured. "I've got you."

His sobs didn't seem to be letting up.

"Do you want to go home?" I said. "Maybe today was a little too much."

He shook his head no, but then he nodded. He took a few deep breaths, and we left the stadium and hailed a cab.

"I wasn't expecting to have that reaction," he said once we got in the cab, his breath still shuddering.

"Emotions hit like that sometimes," I said, twining my fingers in his, thinking about all the times my grief for you hit me like a tsunami, with little advance warning.

When we got to his place, I made us some tea, and we sat down on the couch. He laid his head in my lap, and I stroked his hair. I couldn't believe how important he had become to me in such a short time. How much my heart felt for his.

We were sitting there quietly, his cheek still resting on my lap, when the doorbell rang.

"Are you expecting anyone?" I asked.

"No," he said. "Maybe it's the super?"

"I'll get it," I told him, thinking he might push back, but he just said, "Okay," and sat up on the couch, reaching over and taking the tea I'd made him off the table.

When I opened the door, it wasn't the super at all. Instead, it was a petite woman with long, strawberry blond hair that tumbled in a mass of waves to the middle of her back. Her eyes were light brown and set in a way that reminded me of Disney princesses. She was holding a box of cookies in one hand and a bottle of vodka in the other. She had a surprised look on her face.

"Um, hi?" I said, wondering if maybe she'd knocked on the wrong door. "Can I help you with something?"

She looked at me and blinked those wide eyes the color of gingerbread. "Who are you?" she asked.

"Me?" I replied. "Who are *you*?"

"Aviva," she said. "Landsman."

Dax's ex-wife. My heart stuttered for a moment. "I'm Lucy," I said.

"A subletter?" she asked. "I thought Dax was going to be back by now."

I heard Dax's footsteps behind me.

"Not a subletter," he said, putting his arm around me.

"Your girlfriend?" Aviva said, a touch of breathy surprise to her voice.

Dax looked at me, as if to ask if he could use that word. I nodded slightly. "My girlfriend," he said.

"Oh." I could see Aviva swallow hard. I imagined she felt that same punch-in-the-stomach feeling I had the first time Darren told me about Courtney.

"Do you want to come in?" I asked her.

She looked back and forth between Dax and me. "I brought Zac's favorite cookies," she said to Dax. "And our favorite drink. I thought maybe . . . I'm sorry, I should go."

I looked at them. "Maybe I should go?" I said to Dax.

He looked paralyzed by the situation.

"How about I take a walk?" I said. "I think you need some milk anyway."

"Okay," Dax said, "but just to get some milk. Don't stay away too long."

I grabbed my phone and wallet and headed out the door.

In the elevator, I texted Julia: *Dax's ex-wife just came to his apartment with cookies and vodka while I was there.*

My phone rang almost instantaneously.

"I need more information," Julia said.

So I told her how it was the anniversary of the day their son died, and that I was now going to buy Dax some milk. And also that he'd introduced me as his girl-friend for the first time.

"Well, that's exciting," Julia said. "Should we focus on that? How did that make you feel?"

I laughed as I walked down the street to the nearby bodega. "That part felt really nice," I said, cradling the phone against my cheek. "The other day Dax said that comparison isn't competition, and he meant it with previous partners. That, you know, I may compare him to Darren or Gabe, but he's not competing with them. Every relationship is unique. But I have to say, Jules, his wife looks like a Disney princess."

"Ex-wife," Julia reminded me.

"Right," I said. "Do you think she's rethinking the ex part?"

I could almost hear Julia shrug over the phone. "It doesn't really matter unless he is, too."

I sighed. "You're right."

"Do you think he is?" Julia asked.

I thought about him telling me not to stay away too long. "I don't think he was," I said. "But I don't know what it's like to lose a child. He was in such pain today; if she can be there for him in a way I can't, I could see how he might."

"Well," Julia said. "Get the milk and go back. And then ask. He seems like the kind of guy who would tell you the truth."

"He is," I said. "Thanks, Jules."

We hung up, and I headed back to his place. I thought about how speculation about Darren's thoughts and actions was what led me to cheating on him. I wasn't going to speculate again.

lvi

WHEN I GOT BACK TO DAX'S APARTMENT THAT
night, Aviva was gone, along with her cookies and her
bottle of vodka. Dax looked entirely wrung out. As soon
as I walked in the door with the milk, he wrapped his
arms around me.

"Can we please go to sleep?" he said. "I'm three steps
past exhausted."

"Of course," I said, kissing his shoulder, which was
level with my lips.

We quickly got ready for bed and climbed underneath
the covers. Dax laid his head on my chest, and I wrapped
my arms around him.

"Was it good to see Aviva today?" I asked him, keeping my promise to myself that I wouldn't speculate.

He was quiet for a moment. "Better to be with you,"
he said. "I loved her for a long time, and I love her for
being Zac's mother, but there is still so much pain between us. So much guilt. So much that went wrong. It's

hard for that not to sneak into every conversation we have."

"I know what you mean," I said softly, thinking of Darren eight years ago, thinking of Darren now.

"Will you hold me until I fall asleep?" Dax asked.

"I will," I said.

I held him the whole night long.

lvii

I WAS HOME THE NEXT WEEK WITH THE KIDS. IT was their spring break, and, in an attempt to make things better, I took the week off from work and told the kids we could do a series of adventure days for the days school was closed. That Sunday night, I asked all three kids to come up with two adventures the family could do together that were either in the city or within two hours of our house, preferably by train. We'd plan each adventure the night before.

"Do we have to?" Violet asked. "Can't I just hang out with my friends?"

"You'll still have hang-out time," I said.

Violet rolled her eyes at me but took the pen and paper I offered her.

As they were writing, I pulled one of Liam's baseball caps from the entry hall closet and told them to fold their papers in half and put them inside. I shook the hat, then picked a paper.

"For our first adventure, we will . . ." I said, then opened up the paper and read: "Go on one of those red bus tours that come with butterbeer."

It was in Liam's handwriting. "I'm going to need some help with this one," I said to him.

He shrugged. "Clyde's cousins came to visit from Ohio, and they went on one of those, and he said the butterbeer was really good. And the tour guide was kind of funny."

"Got it," I said, and googled *red bus tour butterbeer.* Amazingly, one came up right away, and I bought us tickets for the next day. "We'll plan to leave at ten A.M.," I said, "so you'll all have time to sleep in. And everyone can stay up half an hour later tonight before lights out."

"Cool," Sammy said, then headed upstairs to get ready. "Li, will you tell me about the tour? Should I bring my sketchbook?"

Liam followed, giving him info, and Violet slumped up after that.

I wished I had another adult with me. Dax, actually. I wished I had Dax with me, to help figure out these kids, to be my support. To go with me on adventures.

Miss you, I texted.

Miss you too, he texted back. *You in bed yet?*

Soon, I wrote back.

I'll save Connections for you, he answered.

When I was at his place, we'd started doing the *New York Times* games together: Wordle, Spelling Bee, and—my personal favorite—Connections.

I went upstairs and saw that all the kids' doors were closed. I could hear the murmur of one side of a conversation behind Violet's door, sticks on a drum pad behind

Liam's, and nothing behind Sam's. He was either drawing or reading. Or he had fallen asleep. I checked my
phone for the time—still an hour before I had to tell him
lights out.

I got into my own pajamas, brushed my teeth and
washed my face, then shut my door and took out my
phone. I pulled up Connections and then called Dax.

"Hey," I said, "it's me. What've you got?"

"Hey, me," he said, and I laughed. "Okay, so cabbage,
lettuce, pin, and state all have heads."

I looked at the words. "Wait," I said. "Pimple has a
head, too. How about state, country, city, town. And put
pimple in the other category."

"Okay, I'm giving it a try," he said.

I heard the ping over the phone that meant we'd gotten it right. "Yes!" I said, before relaxing farther back into
my pillows, the stress of the day and the kids and the
week ahead disappearing now that I was on the phone
with Dax.

"How's work been?" I asked.

"It's been good," he said, "Nice to get to know new
colleagues. And to be at a new hospital that isn't all tied
up with memories of the pandemic—and of Zac. It was
the right decision to start over somewhere new. What do
you think about line, hive, sting—all have to do with
bees. But what's the fourth?"

I looked at the words. "Knees!" I said. "Bee's knees!"

"No way," he replied. "That's not a thing."

"Totally a thing," I said. "When something is the bee's
knees, it's the best." I took a breath. "Like you. You're the
bee's knees."

"I'm googling," he replied.

I waited. I knew I was right.

"Huh," he said. "Well, I guess you're the bee's knees, too."

I laughed. And then heard his Connections ping.

"We solved it," he said. "Just putting jaws, dune, alien, and frozen in this last category. What in the world do those have in common?"

I thought for a moment. "One-word movie titles!"

"Ooh, you really are the bee's knees, Lucy," he said. "Gold star for you."

"I'd rather collect a different prize," I said, thinking about his hands on my body, his lips on my mouth.

"This week is going to feel so long without you," he said.

"I know." I was falling for him—fast, hard, and deep—and it seemed like he was doing the same. "Let's make a really good plan for next Tuesday night," I said. Spring break meant I had extra time with the kids before our handoff.

"Deal," he said. "I'll come up with some ideas. But for now, I should probably go to sleep. My shift starts at six A.M. tomorrow."

"Good night," I said, "and sweet dreams."

"Thank you," he said. "You too."

We were both quiet, and then he added, "I miss you, Lucy. I really, really miss you."

"I miss you too," I said.

We both hung up and I felt the emptiness of my bed more acutely than I ever had.

lviii

I SPENT THE REST OF THAT WEEK WITH THE KIDS— we hiked Bear Mountain, went to Coney Island, visited the Museum of Ice Cream, and took a helicopter ride around Manhattan. Then for the weekend, I took the kids out to Montauk—my adventure choice, which I packed full of ice cream and hiking and boating and pizza—and on Tuesday we were back in the city for our one last adventure activity: a pasta-making class, surprisingly put in the hat by Violet. By the end of all our family togetherness, I thought everyone seemed a little better. A little less angry, a little more connected. Their smiles came more easily and their harsh words came less frequently. Spring break didn't heal us, but it definitely helped.

And it left me twelve steps past exhausted.

I think I have the perfect idea for tonight, Dax texted me on Tuesday afternoon.

We'd been going back and forth all week and nothing seemed quite right.

What? I wrote surreptitiously, making sure the kids didn't see.

Movie night at your place. Or as one of the nurses called it today: Netflix and chill.

You're right, I wrote back, *perfect. Also, how did you not know about the concept of Netflix and chill?*

Been on a boat for six months? he replied with a shrug emoji.

I couldn't believe how endearing I found every single thing about this man. But I couldn't say that, of course. Instead I wrote: *See you soon. Can't wait.*

HANDING THE KIDS OFF TO COURTNEY THAT TUES-day night was emotionally complicated. I was sorry to see the kids go, especially when it felt like we'd made real progress that week, but also I was so excited to see Dax. The two emotions were all twisted up and it left me feel-ing a bit like a yo-yo.

When I got home, I poured myself a glass of wine and sat on the couch, staring into space, waiting for Dax to ring my doorbell. Then, all of a sudden, an idea for a TV show started forming in my mind: a duck—no—a rabbit on a hot air balloon who travels the world saving animals who are endangered. *Rescue Rabbit.* He has a crew with him on the hot air balloon. I started envisioning it. Were they all rabbits? Different varieties of rabbit? *Rescue Rab-bits* maybe?

I took another sip of wine, fully realizing that Dax was the inspiration for this idea. He had made his way from my heart to my mind. I was smitten. I got up and headed into the first-floor bathroom and opened up the cabinet under the sink. I had stashed some extra tooth-brushes there when I bought a bunch on sale a while back. I picked out a green one just as the doorbell rang. I stuck the toothbrush in the back pocket of my jeans and went to answer it.

"Lucy!" Dax said, holding a pizza box in one hand and a bag from a local liquor store in the other.

"Dax!" I said, feeling my whole self smile at the sight of him. I took the pizza box, but before I could even turn to bring it inside, he reached out for my arm and then leaned in for a kiss.

"I missed you," he said, kissing me again.

"Hold that thought," I murmured as I walked a few steps to put the pizza box on the table in the entry hall. "Now," I said. "What were you saying?"

Dax enveloped my body with his and kissed me with such passion it left me breathless.

"Mmm," he said. "You taste like wine."

"You want some?" I asked.

"That would be great," he answered. "I brought a bot-tle, but I see you've already got one open."

He walked in and shut the door behind him as I turned to get him a glass of wine.

"Is that a toothbrush in your pocket?" he asked.

I stopped. "It is," I said. "It's a gift. For you."

"For me?" he said.

We'd moved from the doorway to the living room area at this point. I pulled the toothbrush out of my pocket. "I thought maybe you'd want to keep it here," I said. "So, you know, you'd feel a little more at home."

Dax bent forward and kissed me again. "From the first night I met you, you felt like home," he said. "Toothbrush or not."

My laughter turned into another kiss, and we found ourselves on the couch, groping each other like teenagers. Before I knew it, I was shirtless, we were both pantsless, and Dax's tongue was circling my nipple while his fingers were stroking deep inside me. I wrapped my hand around the base of him and stroked upward, matching his rhythm.

We were both breathing hard, and he whispered, "I'm so close," just as I orgasmed with his fingers inside me. Then he came, too, and I grabbed my T-shirt to keep the couch clean.

"Sorry," he said, a bit chagrined. "I didn't mean to ruin your T-shirt."

"Not ruined," I said. "And even if it was, so worth it."

We laughed and put our underwear back on. He gave me his T-shirt. It came down past my midthigh. "Looks better on you," he said.

"I refute that statement," I told him, opening up the pizza box. "Ready for some Netflix and chill?"

We turned out the lights, wrapped ourselves in the big fleece blanket on my couch, and turned on *Casablanca* while we ate pizza and cuddled.

"I want to tell everyone about you," I said to him as my fingers wove into his under the blanket.

"I want you to," he said, giving my hand a squeeze. "I want us to be real, no hiding, no secrets."

"Would you be willing to meet my ex-husband?" I asked. "Because I want you to meet my kids, and a million years ago we made a deal . . ."

"If it means you're asking me to meet your kids . . . well . . . I would like nothing more than to meet your ex-husband," he said. "Because I would like nothing more than to meet your kids."

Sitting there, half-naked, my body pressed against Dax's, I sent Darren a text: *Do you have a minute to talk?*

Is it about the kids? came back.

No, I wrote, *but I have something I want to tell you.*

There was a long, thirty-five-minute pause, then a text came back: *I'm really busy now, Lucy. Sorry. Can't really talk.*

I stared at the screen and then showed it to Dax. I thought about the toothbrush I gave him. The idea of hiding it before the kids came back, of editing him out of what I shared with them about my week. And I hated it. I hated that I'd be lying to them, again, when I'd just told them I was an open book.

"How about just meeting my kids?" I asked. "And forgetting about Darren?"

"Even better," he answered, lifting my fingers to his lips for a kiss.

The spot Dax occupied in my heart was growing bigger and bigger, and even though it still scared me a little, it made me feel truly alive for the first time in years. I had fallen in love with Dax Armstrong.

lix

THE NEXT WEEK, I TOLD MY KIDS I WAS DATING someone. I wouldn't lie to them, not even a lie of omission. After Darren's response to my text, I honestly didn't care that I hadn't told him first. Courtney kept doing the handoff. He clearly wasn't speaking to me, and I wouldn't want him to meet Dax like this anyway.

"I promised no more secrets," I said to the kids over dinner, "so I'm telling you about a man I've been dating, who is starting to mean a lot to me. His name is Dax Armstrong."

I told them how we met, that he was a doctor, that we liked spending time together a lot, and I told them about Zac, too. And that Dax wanted to meet them—and I wanted them to meet him. I told them that he wanted to show them some spots he loved in Central Park that Saturday, right near where he lived, and that the meeting would mean a lot to me.

Violet, who had wanted me to find love for so long, just shrugged.

Liam said, "With the way Courtney and Dad have been snapping at each other, you might want to reconsider dating someone."

Sammy asked if Dax looked more like him or more like Liam.

"Like neither one of you," I said. "He's got brown, wavy hair and hazel eyes."

Sam nodded seriously, as if that were a very important bit of information.

But from those reactions, I thought our meeting had a chance of going well.

I was wrong.

Things started out that Saturday with a subway that got stuck in between stations because of one of those vague messages like "train traffic ahead," so all four of us were a little off balance—and hungry—by the time we met Dax for lunch. He had ordered us a picnic from Zabar's with bagels, fruit, and lemonade. I introduced him to each of the kids. Liam shook his hand, Sam waved shyly, and Violet just raised her eyebrows and said, "Hi."

Then we sat down on the blanket Dax had set up for us.

"I asked your mom which bagels you all liked . . . so . . . Samuel, I think this plain bagel with butter is for you; Liam, yours is the sesame with cream cheese; and Violet, here's your whole wheat with egg salad."

He passed them out, handing me a scooped-out bagel with veggie cream cheese and a sliced tomato on it.

"I actually don't like egg salad anymore," Violet said, handing him back the bagel.

He took it back, clearly unsure of what to say.

I handed Violet my bagel. "Here, we can trade," I said. "Veggie cream cheese and a tomato."

Violet shrugged. "I'm not really into that either."

I wanted to strangle her. She knew what she was doing, and it was completely purposeful.

"You can share mine, Vi," Sammy said, splitting his bagel apart.

"Thanks," Violet said, sitting down next to him, as far from me as she could. I started to worry that all the progress we'd made over their spring break was backsliding.

We ate our bagels while Dax and Liam talked about the Yankees' game against the Tampa Bay Rays the night before. I was amazed that my least talkative child was the only one talking here.

After we finished, Dax said, "I know your mom told you about my son, Zac. He really loved going on the rowboats near the Boathouse here. I thought maybe we could do that together."

None of the kids said anything, so I responded with "Sounds good, let's go."

Dax and I cleaned up the post-lunch mess, putting all the trash into a plastic bag to throw away, and folded up the picnic blanket while Violet texted and Liam and Samuel watched.

We started walking, and I started talking to fill the space, telling Dax how Liam took his first steps at Central

Park and Violet had done a park cleanup project there in middle school. I was babbling, really, the bagel a rock in my stomach.

We got to the street in the park with bicycles and horses and runners on it. I reached out for Sam's hand and he took mine. It was instinct, which is why I wasn't surprised that Dax reached out for Liam's hand.

Liam looked down at it. "I don't mean to be rude," he said, "but I'm not your son, and I don't need to hold anyone's hand when I cross the street. I'm thirteen."

I saw Dax's face blanch, but all he said was "Noted."

We went on an awkward boat ride, where Dax rowed us around the lake, pointing out the different landmarks we could see.

When we got out, I whispered to him. "I'm sorry, maybe this wasn't the right time to meet them. Or the right way . . . maybe we should just go home."

"Let's get some ice cream first," he said.

I nodded. "Okay," I said, but even as I said it, I knew it was a mistake. We should have just left.

"Time for ice cream," I said out loud to the kids, "and then we'll head home."

"I see the ice cream cart!" Sammy said, and started running toward it pell-mell, with Liam jogging behind him.

Sam was running so fast that he tripped over something—a rock, his own feet, I have no idea what—and went flying. Before I could even react, Dax was racing toward him and had scooped him up in his arms. Sam was wailing and there was blood dripping from a cut in his forehead. But then his wailing changed to shrieking.

"PUT ME DOWN!" he was shouting. "YOU'RE NOT MY DAD! I WANT MY DAD! LET GO OF ME!"

People in the park turned to look, and a few started heading toward them. I ran faster to where they were.

"Let me have him," I said. Dax handed Sammy over to me, all sixty-eight pounds and nine years of him. "I got you, Sam. You're going to be fine." I turned to Liam. "Take my wallet," I said. "It's in my bag. Get a bottle of water and some napkins."

Liam went off running.

I sat down on the side of the road with Sammy in my lap.

"You're fine," I said to him. "You're fine. You're going to be fine."

When Liam came back, I wiped away the blood that was already there and held a napkin to the cut to stop the bleeding. Sam's wails turned to whimpers and then to nothing.

Dax was standing a few feet away, blood on his shirt. I could tell he wanted to help but was afraid to make things worse.

Violet had picked up my bag and hers. "Can we go now?" she asked.

I closed my eyes. "Yes," I said. "We can go now."

"I'm sorry," I said to Dax.

He nodded. "I'm sorry too," he said, his eyes forlorn.

I felt so bad. So bad that the day was such a flop, that my kids were miserable, that Dax was miserable, that I was miserable. As I sat on the subway on the way back to Brooklyn, the anxiety that had been growing all day thrummed through my body. I realized I'd been right from the beginning. Nothing good would come of me dating. I'd just end up hurting everyone I cared about, including myself.

THE NEXT MORNING, BEFORE I WAS SUPPOSED TO meet up with Eva for coffee, while I was still in bed, I called Dax, unsuccessfully trying to hold back tears.

"I think we have to put the brakes on this," I said, steeling myself against the effect his voice, his presence— even on the telephone—had on me. "What's happening between you and me, we have to stop." It was killing me to say it, but I knew it was true.

"Lucy," he started.

I cut him off, my voice cracking. "I love spending time with you. I love being with you. I actually . . ." *I love you,* I thought. But I couldn't say it, not now when there was nothing we could do about it. "I don't want to hurt you or my kids. If something is going to happen between us, now is not the time. My kids aren't ready. And they come first." I wiped my nose with a tissue from the pile that had steadily built next to me. How could the universe have done this to me? Brought me to Dax, shown me how to love again, at the exact same time it compelled me to tell Sammy the truth, to throw my family into chaos. It didn't seem fair. But fate wasn't always fair. It just . . . was.

Dax was quiet on the other side of the line.

I waited, sniffling again, swallowing a sob.

"I understand," he said; his voice sounded thick. "But

please don't make this the end. Promise me you'll call when you're ready—when they're ready. Please promise we can try again." I heard the gravel in his voice that told me he was holding back tears, too.

"I promise," I said, but even as I said it, I wasn't sure I was telling the truth.

"Maybe we can be friends in the meantime," he said. "Just be there for each other?"

I loved the idea of not losing him completely, but I knew that being in touch with him at all would make things too hard. "Let's not torture each other," I said. "It's too much."

I heard a shuddering sigh on the other side of the phone. "Okay," he said. "It sounds like no matter what I say, you're set on this."

I thought of my children's faces when they looked at Dax. I thought about the progress we'd made and how yesterday had destroyed that, too. "I just . . . I can't now, Dax. I'm sorry. I'm so, so sorry."

"Me too," he said.

We sat there in silence, neither one of us wanting to hang up. Until finally I got the courage to say, "Bye, Dax."

"Bye, Lucy," he answered.

And I hung up the phone.

Then I sat in my bed and sobbed. I knew I was doing the right thing, but it still hurt so damn much.

lx

FOR THE FIRST TIME IN SIX YEARS, I CALLED UP-stairs and canceled on Eva fifteen minutes before we were supposed to meet. I told her I had just ended things with my "gentleman" and didn't think I'd make it out of bed.

"Oh, my darling," Eva said. "I'll be right down."

I tried to protest, but Eva would have none of it. Using the key she had to my part of the house, she let herself in. I heard her slow footsteps on the stairs, and then she was in my bedroom.

She sat down on the edge of my bed and held her arms out. "Come here, darling."

In Eva's arms, I let myself sob while she patted my back and I choked out the story. "There, there," she murmured.

"I was greedy," I said to Eva between sobs. "I thought I could have a third love in my life. Some people don't even get one. What made me think I could have three?"

"You were not greedy," she said, stroking my hair.

"Everyone deserves love, no matter how many times you've loved before. You remember that. You deserve love. You deserve to be loved. And not just by me."

I looked up at her through my tears. "I love you too, Eva," I said, my breath shuddering. "I'm so lucky to have you in my life."

She waved her hand as if shooing away words that embarrassed her.

"Listen, my darling," she said. "You shout. You cry. You scream at the universe. You do whatever you need to do. And then you keep going, do you hear me?"

I nodded.

"I cry, and I keep going," I repeated, almost an affirmation.

"Good," she said, standing up from my bed. "And call me if you need me. I'm just upstairs."

"Thank you," I said, my voice a little steadier.

AND I LISTENED. FOR THE NEXT WEEK I FOCUSED ON the "keep going" part of Eva's affirmation. I went to work, I came back home, and I tried not to feel the emptiness of my house. I called Kate, Julia, Jay, my parents. I read books and watched movies. And I looked forward to Saturday when the kids would come back and my life would feel full once more. I knew it would be a time for healing for all of us.

lxi

THE KIDS WERE ALL SEEING THERAPISTS AT THE OF-
fice Dax recommended, and even with our setback, they
seemed a bit more even-keeled when they returned—the
boys at least. I started seeing Julia's therapist that week,
and talking through my fears and hopes, my guilt, helped
me feel more balanced, too. Though I still missed Dax
desperately. All day long there were things I wanted to
tell him, thoughts I wanted his opinion on. I started
working on a pilot episode for the *Rescue Rabbits* show,
which made me think about him even more. But I kept
going.

While I was cooking dinner that week, I asked Alexa
to play some mellow music for me. That song "Turn!
Turn! Turn!" by the Byrds came on, the one based on that
line from Ecclesiastes: *To everything there is a season, and
a time to every purpose under the heaven.* It made me think
about the seasonality of things. In the larger sense, for
me there was a time for school, a time for romance, a

time for mothering. In the smaller sense, month by month, week by week, or day by day, there's a time for work, for play, for creation, for relaxation. The next few weeks really felt like a time to concentrate on healing.

Bashir was coming to New York. The gallery show was about two months away, and Joseph Landis had gotten even more into the idea of then and now, pulled more of your photos from the flash drives. There was a lot to be done, but it all seemed to be coming together. At least that was one thing in my life that didn't feel like an utter disaster.

Bashir was going to take a photo of the Freedom Tower, of the building where you'd once snapped the haunting image of a little girl, of the bridge in Central Park you'd photographed while we were still living together, just as the flowers were starting to bloom. And of me. Joseph had pulled the photos of me that were in the original show: me laughing with a drink in my hand, me in the kitchen with waffles, me putting on high heels, me asleep on the couch. He asked Bashir to see if he could re-create photos like those, or at least like one of them, to include in the show. So we had a date set. I'd taken off from work and, after I walked the kids to school, I'd blown out my hair and put on a little more makeup than usual.

And then, about an hour later, I got a call from Sammy's school nurse.

"Ms. Carter Maxwell?" she said. "Samuel's in my office complaining of a sore throat. His temperature is 101.2. And we've had a number of cases of strep recently. I'd suggest you make an appointment with his pediatrician for after you pick him up."

Of course, right?

I texted Bashir about the emergency key taped to the bottom of the flowerpot on our front stoop and told him to let himself in if he got there before I returned. And I went to pick up Sammy, making an appointment with Dr. Sweeney as I did.

The poor kid looked miserable when I got there, and when Dr. Sweeney's receptionist saw him and pointed us toward the sick waiting room, she promised she'd have us in and out as quickly as possible.

It was strep, of course, and he was prescribed antibiotics, which we jumped in a cab to pick up at Duane Reade before heading home.

Bashir still wasn't there, so I sat down with Sam on the couch.

"Can you be my pillow, Mom?" he asked.

"Of course," I said.

"The long way," he added.

So I lay down on the couch with my head on the armrest, and Sammy lay down, too, his head on my chest and his body resting alongside mine.

"I'm not going to die, right?" he mumbled as he was falling asleep. "Like Gabriel or like Dax's son?"

"Eventually we'll all die," I said, stroking his head. "But no, right now you're just sick with strep throat. The antibiotics will kick in soon, and you'll feel better before you know it."

I kept stroking his hair, and he fell asleep on me.

Which is how Bashir found us.

When he walked in the door, I held my finger to my

lips, and he nodded. But then he took out his camera and started shooting.

The photo of me on the couch with Sammy was a perfect corollary to the one you took of me and my computer. You can't see Sam's face in the photo—he was turned toward the back of the couch—but you see me, my arms around him protectively, a look on my face that's a mix of exhaustion, relief, and love.

When he saw it later, Sammy said he was okay with it being in the show. And since he was, Darren eventually was, too. It was, perhaps not surprisingly, one of the most written-about pieces in the collection.

After Bashir took the shot, I pulled a throw pillow from behind my neck and then maneuvered myself off the couch slowly and carefully, so as not to wake Sammy. I motioned Bashir into the kitchen.

"It's so good to see you," I said to him, trying hard not to think about the last time I saw him, because Italy made me think of Dax. And thinking of Dax made me cry.

"Your house is beautiful," he said.

I thanked him and offered to make some coffee, which he accepted and then photographed me making it.

"I have to do my job," he said, and I laughed.

"Thank you," he said. "For this job. I can't believe I'm going to be part of a gallery show in New York City. That it's given me the chance to travel, to come to America."

We sat at the counter with our cups of coffee.

"I'm so glad this all worked out," I said. "It was your photographs that got you the job, I just suggested it."

Bashir smiled and as I smiled back, he snapped another photograph. I remembered living with you, Gabe, how you would capture my smiles, my tears. How you turned my emotions into art.

"So how's it been going?" I asked.

Bashir looked thoughtful and put his camera down. "I'm just concentrating on the work. Because if I think about the larger picture, it becomes overwhelming. What if my photographs aren't good enough? What if I disappoint Joseph? You? What if I mess up this opportunity? So I go frame by frame, image by image, and I do my best."

"You are so like Gabe," I told him. "In your spirit, in your heart. There is nothing I wish more than that he were here to see you now. To see Samuel. To just . . ."

I got choked up then, felt my eyes filling with tears. It was all so much to keep inside. Ten years without you, Darren's silent treatment, these weeks without Dax—the fear that all my chances at love were doomed.

Bashir snapped my photo.

That one was in the show, too.

lxii

THE FOLLOWING SUNDAY, EVA AND I WERE SUP-
posed to go shopping together.

"To take your mind off things," she said. "Plus it's
good luck to buy a new dress for the opening night of a
gallery show."

I didn't really believe that shopping would take my
mind off Dax, or the heaviness that settled on my heart
when I thought about a future without a partner, without
that kind of love. Still, it was nice to have something to
look forward to. But for the second time in a row, we had
to change our plans. This time she was sick—not strep
like Sammy'd had, luckily, but a head cold—so instead of
shopping, I went up to her studio with some tea.

"How are you feeling?" I asked when I walked in the
door, glad I could take care of her for a bit, the way she
took care of me.

"Like my brain is full of cotton wool," she said.

"Can I get you decongestants? Something else?" I asked.

She shook her head. "I have what I need. Come, sit." She indicated a chair set near her couch.

Eva's studio was beautiful. Being there felt like living inside a museum. She had one wall that was covered floor-to-ceiling with her framed artwork, and another that held a huge tapestry she'd made. She'd embroidered pillows, which were placed artfully on her bed. The sun was streaming in her window.

"So," I said, wanting to hear about something happy, something hopeful. "How have things been with your paramour?"

Eva laughed. "We had to cancel our plans for dinner last night, but we're having fun together. Enjoying each other's company."

I loved that Eva was having a romance at eighty-nine. I wanted that, too.

"I've never asked," I said, "but at one point you intimated that there was someone in your past . . ."

Eva looked down at a ring she wore on her right-hand ring finger. "He gave me this," she said, showing me a delicate gold ring with a small ruby in it. I knew she always wore it, but I hadn't known there was a meaning to it. "It was a promise ring, right before he left to serve in the Korean War. He said that when he came back, he would trade it in for a diamond, and we would get married."

I looked at the ring again. "He never came back?" I said softly.

"He never came back," she repeated, turning my question into a statement.

Then she looked up at me. "But that was a long time ago. A very long time ago."

I nodded.

"Speaking of lovers," she said. "Any new developments with your doctor? A change of heart?"

I shook my head. "It's over," I told her, blinking back tears. "It's just . . . it's not the time. I don't know if it will ever be."

"That's what I kept thinking," she said, handing me a tissue for my tears, "that it wasn't the time. And then the time passed me right by. Don't let it do the same to you."

I took the tissue and wiped my eyes. "I won't," I said. "Promise."

But I wasn't sure if it was a promise I could keep.

"Even though we're not going shopping today, please make sure you get a new dress," she said, seemingly out of nowhere. "For the show. For luck."

"I will," I said.

And that I knew I would do.

lxiii

I SPENT THAT NEXT WEEK WORKING LATE IN THE office getting a solid pitch done for *Rescue Rabbits*, along with a draft of the pilot, to share with Phil. I was channeling my feelings for Dax into something productive, something creative, and as much as I still missed him and wanted to share it with him, it felt good to be so immersed in creativity again.

By the time Friday rolled around, I was beat. I was having a cheese-and-crackers dinner with a glass of wine on my couch, reading an article analyzing the success of *Bluey*, when my phone buzzed. I looked down. It was a message from Darren. The first I'd gotten in about two months.

Since Violet is staying with you tonight, I expect to trade a night next week.

I looked at the message and read it again. "Violet's not here," I said out loud to no one. "But if she's not with me and she's not with him . . ."

I picked up the phone and called Darren.

"What are you talking about?" I said to him. "Violet's not staying with me tonight. I haven't spoken to her since Wednesday."

"She said she wanted to sleep at your house," Darren said, "so I told her fine. I didn't think I needed to call you. I trusted her."

I closed my eyes for a moment and took a deep breath, panic fluttering in my heart. Where was my child? Why did she lie to Darren? Who was she with?

"I'm trying Find My Friends," I said, navigating to the app on my phone. Her dot was gone. "She's not there," I said.

"What the fuck?" asked Darren. He paused a moment. "She's not on mine either. Did she turn it off, or is she out of service? I swear, if she turned it off . . ." His voice trailed off.

We'd never bothered to lock her phone settings—she hadn't ever given us a reason to.

The panic was taking over my heart, but I needed to think straight.

After I heard Violet telling her best friend, Keisha, earlier this year that she and Ji-ho had found a stairway at school where she could go down on him, I'd taken her out for hot chocolate, a long walk, and a serious talk about sex and pregnancy. It felt like an out-of-body experience, having that conversation with my daughter, and I'm sure she was cringing her way through most of it, but I knew it was important. Was that what she was doing now? Having sex with Ji-ho?

"Let me call Keisha," I said. "I'll call you back."

I got Violet's best friend on the phone, and after clearly not wanting to tell me anything, she finally admitted that Violet was with Ji-ho and that they'd heard about an underground party in a retired subway station. Ji-ho's cousin, who went to NYU, wanted to check it out and invited them along. But Keisha swore she didn't know where it was. I believed her. Keisha has always been a great kid—really responsible—and I could tell she didn't like that Violet was at that party either.

I asked her to see if she could reach Violet or find out from some other kids where this was. She said she'd try, but that if Vi really was underground, there would be no reception. Which might explain the missing dot on Find My Friends.

I called Darren and reported back.

"So what do we do?" he asked.

"I don't know," I answered.

"Can we call some other parents? Some other kids? See who else knows about this?" I could hear him pacing on the other side of the phone. "Maybe find out who this cousin is?"

"And do what?" I asked.

"Go get her!" he said. "Do you have Ji-ho's parents' number?"

"I don't," I said, cringing as I said it. Why didn't I? I hadn't met his parents. I should've done that, too.

"Shit," Darren said. "I don't either. Should we call the police? Or a hospital? What if she's hurt?"

At the word *hospital* my heart stuttered. What if she *was* hurt? And alone? And needed her parents?

Dax's face appeared in my mind. "I know someone who works in the ER at NYU," I said, and hung up.

Fingers shaking, I dialed Dax's number, wondering if he would even pick up.

"Lucy?" he said, after one ring.

"Dax! Thank goodness," I replied. "Violet's missing and apparently went to a party with her boyfriend and his cousin in an abandoned subway station and we don't know where she is . . . and Darren and I, we were worried she might be in an ER hurt or something . . . and I just . . . you were the first person I thought of."

"I . . . okay," he said. "Okay. I'm just ending my shift, and Violet's not in this ER. But . . . I think I might be able to help. We did have an NYU kid in the ER last weekend who had taken ayahuasca at a party he told me was underground, at the end of the line. He was hallucinating, but that part of his story seemed real. I'm assuming 'underground, at the end of the line,' is an abandoned subway station."

"Can you . . . call him? Can you find out where exactly the party is?"

"No," he said, "I can't do that. But I have some police officer friends who might be able to help. Let me give them a call. If this is a weekly thing, I bet they'll know where to find it. I'll text you where to meet me. We can go get her."

"Thank you," I said, tears of relief falling from my eyes. "Thank you so much. And . . . um . . . you're going to meet my ex-husband. Darren will want to come get her, too."

I called Darren and told him that she wasn't at the NYU ER, but that a friend who had connections with the police was going to help us.

He picked me up in his car, and we drove to meet Dax at City Hall in Manhattan. His police officer friends told him there's an old subway station there where college kids go to party often.

Dax gave me a quick hug when we got out of the car, which made me want to melt into his arms, and then put out his hand to Darren. "I'm Dax Armstrong," he said.

"Darren Maxwell," Darren answered, shaking Dax's hand. "Thanks for the help."

We spoke to the police and showed them photos of the kids. They said it would be safer if we waited, but Dax convinced them they should have an ER doc on hand if necessary. So he went down with them into the old subway tunnel. Darren and I waited. Neither of us talked for a few minutes.

Then Darren said, "You dating him?"

"I was," I answered. "I'm not now."

He nodded. And it made me realize the kids had never told him about the park. I wondered why.

A few minutes later, two ambulances came whirring down the street.

"Could that be for Violet?" Darren asked me.

"No," I said, my heart plummeting. "Please, no."

Soon one of the police officers emerged with Violet, who looked pale. I ran over to hug her. "Are you okay?" I asked. "Where's Ji-ho?"

She started to cry. "They gave him something and he took it. We went here with his cousin Dae, who's at

NYU, and I guess Ji-ho wanted to . . . I don't know what, but he started acting wild, like some of the other people down there, swinging at imaginary enemies and cowering on the ground. Ji-ho kept saying the dragons were out to get him. Dax said the EMTs will take care of him, but it was so scary."

I held her closer.

Then Darren came over and started telling her she was grounded from now until he decided otherwise.

"Let's talk about this," I said, looking at Violet's pale, scared face.

"Grounded," Darren said. "No discussion."

I sighed.

Soon Dax and the EMTs who had gone down into the station came up with about six kids, including Ji-ho, whose cousin was following him, talking on the phone in Korean, I assumed to Ji-ho's parents.

"The EMTs gave them all diazepam," Dax said, "which should counteract the hallucinations. Ji-ho should go to the hospital for observation, though. Dae is talking to his parents."

Violet looked up at Dax and gave him a small, grateful smile. "Thank you for helping him," she said.

"Time to head back home," Darren told her, shaking his car keys.

"We should wait for Ji-ho's parents," I said.

"I don't want you seeing him anymore," Darren said to Violet.

"Dad!" she said at the same time I said, "Darren!"

Four kids had already gone to the hospital in the first two ambulances, and one more was on the way. Dax was waiting with Ji-ho and Dae on a bench not far from where Darren, Violet, and I sat.

While we waited there, the semidarkness settling around us like a cloak, the sound of the ambulance's siren getting closer, Violet said softly, "I'm sorry."

"We know, Vi," I said, squeezing her shoulder.

"And sometimes sorry isn't enough," Darren said. "Especially when you lied with the intent to deceive me and Courtney. We've been cutting you slack, but this is not okay behavior. At all."

Violet hung her head.

Ji-ho's parents arrived just as the ambulances did, and we watched as Dax handed the last two patients off to the EMTs. After the ambulances blared away, Dax came over toward our bench. I stood up and met him halfway.

"Thank you," I said as I grabbed his hand. "A million times, thank you."

"I was wondering," he said, squeezing my fingers, "maybe hoping—does your phone call tonight mean you're ready to try again? I've missed you so much."

"Me too," I whispered, knowing my voice would break if I spoke any louder, "but I still don't think the time is right. I mean, look at Violet."

What I wanted to say was: *Please come home with me. Hold me. Love me. Let me love you.* What I wanted to do was wrap my arms around him and never let go. But instead, I squeezed his hand again and said, "I'm so grateful for you, Dax. More than I can say."

He nodded and turned to walk, alone, to the subway. It felt like a piece of my heart went with him.

lxiv

I HAD THE KIDS AGAIN THE FOLLOWING WEEK, AND
knew I had to work even harder to mend fences with Violet, to figure out what was going on with her, to try to
help. We couldn't keep going on the way things were. I
remembered Dax's earlier suggestion about spending
one-on-one time with each of them.

"Hey," I said when I checked on her before bed that
Saturday night, "any chance you want to go shopping
with me tomorrow? I can set up plans for the boys."

She was quiet for a moment.

"I'd really love to spend some time alone with you," I
added.

"Okay," she said. Then, "Would you mind closing my
door? I promised Ji-ho I'd call to say good night." I guess
Darren's demand that Violet end things with Ji-ho hadn't
amounted to anything.

"Sure," I said, slipping out of her room. "Glad Ji-ho's

doing better. Maybe we could have him and his parents over for dinner soon."

"Maybe," Violet said.

I wasn't sure what I would say to her the next day, if anything I could come up with would help her heal, but I had some time to figure it out.

THE NEXT AFTERNOON, AFTER DROPPING SAM AND Liam off with friends, Violet and I took the subway to Soho and started window shopping.

"Did you want to go shopping with me to tell me that I'm in big trouble?" Violet asked. "Because Dad already did that. Like, a lot."

I turned to look at her as we kept walking. "Do you think you should be in really big trouble?" I asked her.

She shrugged. "I've kind of been a jerk recently. Especially when you took us to meet Dax. And then I lied to Dad. And went somewhere I wasn't supposed to, without telling you. So probably yeah."

"I won't argue with that," I said, and she laughed a little. "Do you want to talk about why you've been acting that way?"

She shrugged again. "I guess . . . the more I thought about stuff with you and Dad and Sammy, the angrier I got that you kept this secret from us for so long."

We were walking in front of a coffee shop that had a bench out front. I stopped in front of it and said, "Let's sit for a minute."

Violet sat next to me.

"I understand why you're angry," I said. "I'd be angry,

too, if I were you. I also know, though, that being a jerk, as you put it, isn't helping you get past that. Neither is lying. Or running away. It seems like maybe you're trying to punish me? Or punish our whole family?"

Violet shook her head slowly, scuffed her shoe against the sidewalk. "I don't think that's it," she said. "I just . . ." She trailed off and looked down at her hands in her lap. I waited, but she didn't say anything more.

"You didn't know how else to show me and Dad how hurt you were?" I tried.

Violet was stretching the hair elastic she had on her wrist and letting it snap back against her skin. "Maybe," she said. "I know you said I don't have to tell anyone what I talk about with the therapist, but one thing she said is that it sounded like I usually think other people's feelings are more important than mine, and my feelings were so big this time, I wasn't able to squash them down. So it's all really uncomfortable."

I was so thankful in that moment that Dax sent us those therapist recommendations for the kids, that Darren agreed they should go, that the kids were actually talking in their sessions.

"I could definitely see that being the case," I said. "Do you want to talk more about how angry you are?"

Violet shook her head but then said, "I just . . . feel . . . betrayed. Like our family is built on a lie."

"I'm really sorry, Violet," I said. "And if it matters at all, if I had to do it over again, I would do it differently. I wouldn't keep any secrets. But when I told Grandma, she said something really smart—she said we can only move forward. So that's our choice now, right? How to move forward. I want us to try to fix things between us. But you have to want that, too, for it to happen."

Violet nodded. "I want that too," she said softly. And then she added, "And I'm sorry I was a jerk to Dax at Central Park. He was amazing the other night, helping Ji-ho and all the other kids. I'll be nicer next time, okay?"

I let out a small laugh. "Dax and I aren't dating anymore," I said. "But I appreciate the apology."

Violet looked at me. "Is it because of us?" she asked.

I shrugged. "It wasn't the right time," I said.

"'That's a nice way of saying it was us," she said.

I didn't say anything more; I didn't want to lie to my daughter. And besides, she was too smart not to see through it.

We sat on the bench in silence together for a moment. "I have a question," I said. "Dad didn't seem to know anything about Dax. You and the boys didn't tell him about our day in Central Park?"

Violet shook her head. "We made a deal not to say anything. We didn't want to make things between you and Dad worse. Or Dad and Courtney."

I sat there for a moment, taking that in. "Vi, I'm really really sorry you felt you had to lie for me. Even if it was for a good reason. Please promise me that in the future, if I've put you in a position that makes you or the boys feel like you have to lie to your dad, you'll tell me. I don't want you to have to keep secrets for me. Ever. I don't want our family to keep secrets anymore."

Violet nodded.

"I'm not mad," I said, just to clarify. "I'm just . . . I'm just sorry I did that to you without even realizing it."

Violet slid her hand quietly into mine. I couldn't remember the last time we'd held hands. "It's okay, Mom," she said. We sat for a moment longer, and then she got up. "Let's go find us both some new clothes."

I bought a red maxi dress for the opening. It reminded me a little of the dress you'd chosen for me when *It Takes a Galaxy* won a Daytime Emmy. It fluttered a bit when I walked, showed off my collarbones, and made me feel pretty.

Violet got an off-the-shoulder denim dress for the opening, along with a new pair of jeans, two T-shirts, and a pair of sneakers that she promised me were cool, even though I couldn't for the life of me figure out why.

WHEN WE ALL SAT DOWN FOR DINNER THAT NIGHT, the air didn't feel quite as tense, and Violet said, "So, who wants to go first with their best, worst, and wished?"

I swear, I almost cried.

lxv

THE NEXT FEW WEEKS BEFORE YOUR BOOK LAUN-
ched were so packed with the end of school and beginning of camp and working on the pilot for my new show
that I'd fall into bed each night exhausted, but not exhausted enough not to think about Dax . . . Would the
time ever be right? Would he take me back? Would I
miss my chance? I would fall asleep thinking about him,
thinking about you, thinking about Darren . . . and then
all of a sudden it was July 2 and your book launched with
a beautiful review in *The New York Times*. And then it
was July 5 and I got a call from Joseph asking if I wanted
to come see the show the morning before the opening.
But I demurred—I wanted the excitement of the opening
night, the drama of the filled room, hearing the chatter,
listening in on the comments.

I didn't have the kids the night of the opening, but
I picked them up from Darren's so we could all go to-

gether. Liam had on jeans and a button-down, but Sammy had dressed up in a suit.

"He's a little excited about being in the show," Liam said, putting a hand on his brother's shoulder, not teasing him or rolling his eyes. It was amazing how much Liam had grown up these past months. I was so proud of him, so proud of the man he was becoming. I made a mental note to make sure I told him that.

Just as we were about to head out, Darren opened his front door. "Lucy?" he said. I turned. "Just wanted to wish you luck tonight."

"Thank you," I said, touched by the gesture. I could feel some tension leaving my kids' bodies, too.

When we got to the gallery, Eva was already there with what Violet referred to as her "manfriend."

"You can't call anyone Eva is with a boy," she whispered, making me laugh.

Bashir was there, too, and Eric and his wife and daughter, and Kate and her family, and Julia and hers. My mom and dad were en route, along with Jay and Vanessa and their triplets. I was so touched that everyone was coming to support me, to honor you.

The then-and-now photographs were hung in pairs, with the titles of both images and the stories behind them running underneath them, tying them together.

It was amazing to see how the places you'd photographed changed. How the people you'd photographed had grown in the past decade-plus.

Violet and Liam went to talk to Kate's girls, and Sammy and I walked around the corner to the space where the photographs of me had been in the original show. And there I was again. Me, asleep on my couch with a computer at twenty-four, and then me, with my son sleeping on me on a couch at forty-four. Joseph had said I could write the caption, and I had asked Sam if he wanted to. He'd said yes, so underneath both photos it said:

In Dreams, Inspiration—Gabriel Samson, 2004
In Dreams, Healing—Bashir Hassan, 2024

Every night, my mom wishes me "sweet dreams." My dreams aren't always sweet, but they are always magical. They let me create worlds that I can paint later. And I know her dreams let her create worlds that she puts on TV. If you're reading this, I have a question for you: What do your dreams let you do?
—Samuel Maxwell, age 9

"We look good," Sammy said, clearly giddy.

"We do," I said, ruffling his blond curls.

I heard someone clear their throat behind us, and I turned.

"Dax!" I gasped. I'd never seen him in a suit before and couldn't believe how distinguished it made him look. I wanted to reach out and touch him, to follow the contours of his suit jacket from his broad shoulders to where his body narrowed at his waist.

"Can I have apple juice?" Sammy said, pointing toward a makeshift bar. "It's over there."

"Sure," I told him, "go ahead."

He walked away and Dax said, "I hope it's okay that I'm here."

I felt myself soften in his presence. I was so happy to see him, to be near him.

"How did you know when it was happening?" I asked. He and I hadn't talked much about your show once I was home from Lampedusa. It had felt private, somehow.

He laughed. "I actually got two invitations," he said.

"Two?" I asked. "From whom?"

I couldn't imagine who would have sent them to him.

"One from your neighbor Eva," he said, "who called the NYU ER looking for me."

I smiled. "Sounds like Eva. Who was the second from?"

"Violet," he said. "She sent me the loveliest email. Thanking me for coming to help her and Ji-ho, apologizing for how she acted when we met, and telling me that she really hoped I would come tonight and convince you to take me back. She said you'd been waiting for love for a long time, and she thought you could find it with me— and that she and her brothers didn't want to be the reason it didn't happen."

I could feel my eyes overflowing with tears and used my sleeve to blot them away so my mascara wouldn't run.

"Do you think she's right?" he asked, his voice low and rough. "That you and I can find love together?"

I took a step closer and wrapped my arms around him, savoring the warmth of his body, how solid he felt in my arms. "I do," I said. "I already have."

The look of joy on his face is one I'll always remember. "Me too," he whispered, his voice overcome with emotion. "Me too." He kissed me on the forehead, then looked up at a photograph across the room. I followed his eyes and saw that he was looking at an image of you, Gabe, from a decade before. And then at a camera lying, abandoned, on a grassy field.

"What would your Gabriel think?" Dax said, clearing his throat. "Of you and me, together."

I contemplated it for a moment and then said, "He always looked for beauty and light and love in the world. I think he'd be happy that I found all of that with you."

And you would, right, Gabe?

I'm pretty sure you would.

lxvi

SO HERE WE ARE, GABE. TEN YEARS LATER. THE AN-
niversary of your death. And I finally made it to your
grave in Arizona. I told Dax I was coming, told the kids.
I'm not keeping secrets anymore. And there didn't seem
to be any other way to spend today, any other person I
wanted to spend it with.

It's not lost on me that sitting here like this, sitting
here talking and talking while you can't, wondering if the
words I'm saying are making their way to you, is how
things ended for us the last time. Ended for you. A decade ago—time is so elastic. Sometimes I look in the
mirror and feel ancient. Like I've experienced a whole
lifetime in my forty-four years—love, loss, birth, death,
marriage, divorce, success, failure. I feel like I've earned
every wrinkle, every stretch mark, the stripe of white hair
I keep covering with hair dye. But sometimes I run down
the promenade in Brooklyn Heights, my sneakers pound-
ing on the pavement, my breath strong and steady, and I

don't feel any different than I did when we met at twenty-one. Sometimes my time with you feels like it was just yesterday.

Is there time where you are? And if there is, does it feel elastic, too?

I'VE BROUGHT YOU A COPY OF YOUR BOOK—THE NEW version. I wish it had the photos from the gallery show in it, but I still think it's beautiful.

Your headstone is beautiful, too. When the undertaker asked me what you would like ten years ago, I was in such a fog. I didn't want to decide. I couldn't decide. Instead, I said he should match the one you chose for your mom. I hadn't known what you'd chosen; I figured it didn't matter, really. But now that I see it, it does feel like it matters. Can you see it from where you are? I love that it's a sunrise carved in white on black marble—and that your mom's is the same image, but opposite, black on white. Hers looks like a sunset. And since you're next to each other, together, your headstones show a story, a story of hope, of the sun rising again after darkness.

When I got here, in the desert heat, I sat down next to your stone. It's under a tree—you're under a tree, a big, old tree—and I laid my head against the marble. It's the closest we've been physically in a decade. Just as I sat down, I felt a breeze blow. I could swear it was you, reassuring me, telling me you're still here, that you see me, that you understand I need to move on, to be free, to go forward.

I can only hope that my words reach you. I can only

hope that you knew then and still know now how much I loved you and will always love you. And I can only hope you know how much I love our son. He is the best of us, Gabe.

He is light, he is beauty.

He is our love.

acknowledgments

This book never would have existed if *The Light We Lost* hadn't been so embraced by so many readers around the world. Thank you to every single person who read *The Light We Lost*—and everyone who told their friends about it, posted it on social media, and suggested it for a book club read. I am so grateful for each and every one of you. To Reese Witherspoon, who blew my mind by choosing *The Light We Lost* as her February 2018 book club pick, to Emma Roberts and Karah Preiss, who featured it on Belletrist, and to the women at The Skimm who chose it as a Skimm Read: by sharing my novel so passionately and so widely, you changed my life. Thank you a million times over. To every bookseller who displayed and hand-sold my book, who hosted me in your store and shared my novels on social media: Thank you so, so much for championing my work. And for everyone who sent me a note saying that *The Light We Lost* touched your heart, for everyone who invited me to visit or Zoom into your book club meetings—thank you, thank you, thank you. My hope in writing *The Light We Lost* was that it would make readers who experienced something similar feel seen and less alone. And knowing that has been the case is such a gift. Thank you to everyone who reached out to tell me how the book touched you. I also want to thank all the writers who blurbed *The Light We Lost* and shared my book with their own fans. In this profession, where we all sit and type quietly on our computers, it means so much to have such a supportive community.

Tara Singh Carlson, my editor and captain of Team Darren, thank you for championing *The Light We Lost* from the start, for your insightful notes and suggestions, for always pushing me to make things better, and for suggesting I write this sequel to Lucy's story in the first place! And Miriam Altshuler, my agent and captain of Team Gabe, thank you for being the OG supporter of my writing, for always having my back, and for being the "tears test"—if a book makes you cry, I know I've nailed it. I feel so incredibly lucky to have worked with both of you for so many years.

And to the rest of the team at PRH, Putnam, and DeFiore, both past and present: Ivan Held, Sally Kim, Helen Richard, Ashley Di Dio, Aranya Jain, Molly Donovan, Reiko Davis, Tamara Kawar, Ashley McClay, Brennin Cummings, Nishtha Patel, Alexis Welby, Stephanie Hargadon, Maddie Schmitz, Ashley Hewlett, Katie McKee, Ellie Schaffer, Jazmin Miller, Amy Schneider, Andrea Peabbles, Kylie Byrd, Claire Sullivan, Samantha Bryant, Ben Lee, Kelly Gildea, Emily Mileham, Maija Baldauf, Erin Byrne, Tiffany Estreicher, Katie Punia,

Anthony Ramondo, Vi-An Nguyen, Leigh Butler, Tom Dussel, Ritsuko Okumura, and everyone else behind the scenes in the printing, binding, recording, shipping, and selling of my book—thank you so, so much for your support across the years, from *The Light We Lost* to now. Also a huge thank-you to the team at PYR and Philomel for their excitement and understanding, and to the writers and artists I edit for their inspiration.

None of my books would be what they are without the thoughtful notes from my trusted writing group and early readers. Thank you to Mariana Baer, Daphne Benedis-Grab, Marie Rutkoski, Eliot Schrefer, Talia Benamy, Sarah Fogelman, Kim Grant, Alison May, and Nick Schifrin for being willing to look at my early pages and giving me encouragement along with your feedback. Thank you, too, to Carolina Proenca, who took such good care of Miss Lollipop while I wrote this book. And to Courtney Sheinmel, who so loved Darren in *The Light We Lost* that I promised her years ago I'd name Darren's second wife after her if I ever wrote a sequel.

I also owe a huge debt of gratitude to the people in Rome and Lampedusa who helped me research this book. To Paola and Antonio—thank you for helping me visit all the places in Rome where I wanted to set my story. To Michele Preseter (and your little Rachele)— thank you for showing us around Lampedusa and sharing so much history and information with us. To Paola Pizzicori—thank you so, so much for working out the Lampedusa plot with me, figuring out what would be possible, sharing so much about the beautiful children's library, and reading over the manuscript to make sure I didn't mess it up! Your input truly changed Dax and his story for the better, and I really appreciate it. Thank you also to Deb Soria of Ottomomassimo bookstore in Rome for sharing more information about the founding of the Lampedusa library and the island with me. And thank you to my dear friend Cristina Prasso for once again making sure my Italian and depictions of Italy were on target.

Family is so important to Lucy, and it's important to me, too. I am so grateful for the support, encouragement, and love that keep me afloat. Andrew and Laura, you are my heart, my team, and my wildest dreams. Mom and David, Ali and Suzie, Grammy, Flavia, Becky, and all the wonderful spouses you married and children you brought into the world—I love every one of you and the time we all spend together. And Dad and Dan, I imagine the two of you together, keeping an eye on us all down here, now along with Papa ZB. You will always be missed.